Dear Reader,

Chance is an amazing t[...] are the pivot for this sto[...] my realizing it when I came across pictures of a set of Viking gaming dice discovered beneath the northern English city of York. I had no intention of writing a story involving *dice*. But the next thing I knew, I was reading about Vikings who tried to "improve" their gambling luck using the assistance of runes. Then the chance came to travel to Europe a couple of years before I meant to. The trip included a visit to York— to the place where the dice were found.

I wrote the story.

Rosamund and Boda would have called that accidental weaving of events fate, *wyrd—the way things turn out.*

In the dangerous world of the ninth century, fate was never far from the minds of Saxons (and dice-playing Vikings). The way they saw things, fate was not unchangeable. It was something still in the weaving— a web. And if you used courage, you might win your way through.

This story is about a courageous woman. Rosamund risks everything and wins the only man on earth who can help her. What she truly finds is a chance, the chance to overcome past hurts and build a future— the kind of chance we all want.

Helen Kirkman

Learn more about the Warriors of the Dragon banner at www.helenkirkman.com.

PRAISE FOR HELEN KIRKMAN

Untamed

"*Untamed* is a powerful story with its contrasts
of healing and war. A great read."
—*Love Romances and More*

"*Untamed* is an emotional and memorable story with
attention to ninth-century historical detail that brings the
past to life in a way only Helen Kirkman can."
—*Historical Romance Writers*

Fearless

"This compelling story contains
a heartrending romance.... I wanted to pick it up
and start all over again."
—*All About Romance,* Desert Isle Keeper

"Readers who enjoy tales of ancient warriors, and tender
love born in a time of turmoil, will enjoy *Fearless.*"
—*LoveRomances.com*

Destiny

"*Destiny* is a beautiful tale of the transforming power of
love and not to be missed by historical romance lovers."
—*RomanceJunkies.com*

"Writing of early British history,
a time oft forgotten, is Kirkman's passion.
She creates a brilliant portrait of the era."
—*Romantic Times BOOKreviews*

A Fragile Trust

"Kirkman's lyrically descriptive prose
sustains an unusual emotional intensity. This one
generates that rare urge to read it straight through."
—*Romantic Times BOOKreviews,*
Reviewer's Choice Award winner

"[A]bsolutely awe-inspiring and sure to be
one of the best historicals of 2005!"
—*Cataromance.com*

helen
kirkman

captured

HQN™

ISBN-13: 978-0-373-77237-7
ISBN-10:   0-373-77237-8

CAPTURED

www.HQNBooks.com

Printed in U.S.A.

To Michelle, Stuart, Rosie, Jackie and the team—
for all your support and encouragement.
Sincerest thanks.

Also by Helen Kirkman

Untamed
Fearless
Destiny
A Fragile Trust
A Moment's Madness
Forbidden
Embers

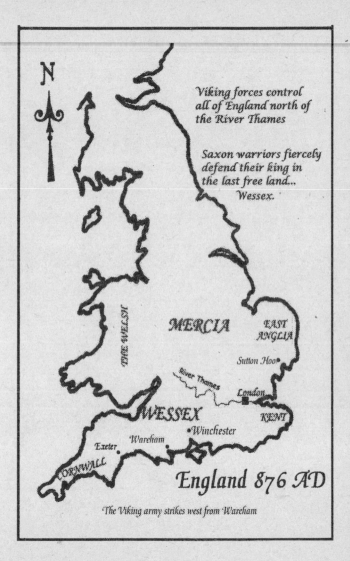

N

Viking forces control all of England north of the River Thames

Saxon warriors fiercely defend their king in the last free land... Wessex.

THE WELSH

MERCIA

EAST ANGLIA

Sutton Hoo

River Thames

London

WESSEX

KENT

Winchester

Wareham

Exeter

CORNWALL

England 876 AD

The Viking army strikes west from Wareham

CHAPTER ONE

Wareham, the South Coast of Wessex, England
A.D. 876

ROSAMUND SAW the iron chain first. Fire-hardened links snaked across the frost-whitened ground into the dark. The chain was attached to a man's hand.

They were surrounded by a Viking army preparing to withdraw from a fortress—better described as fleeing through the night before the West Saxon troops could fall on them.

He must be dead. Surely?

A thick metal band encircled his heavy wrist. Her gaze followed the shadowy length of an arm. It was solid, encased in a deep blue tunic sleeve that had once been fine. She could see his skin through the ripped material. The torchlight turned it to molten gold. Like fire.

Who was he? All the Saxon prisoners had been given back—a requirement of the truce now about to be broken in a mad dash to reach Exeter. Exeter held Rosamund's only chance to escape. She could not do anything that might jeopardise that chance. Not just her life, but Merriwen's depended on it, Merriwen with her helplessness.

Her foot brushed the chain. The cold iron, hard, roughly fashioned, completely confining, made a small deadly sound. Her heart tightened.

She withdrew her narrow, gilt-decorated shoe. The chain clinked. The fine hand on the ground did not move.

Rosamund's mind filled with what it must be like to be trapped and held down in such a way. She had been a prisoner of the Danish Viking army for three years, but never like this, never bound so that all but the most trivial movement was impossible. The chain between the fetters around the man's wrists was perhaps three feet long. It was stapled to the ground.

She stared at the metal hoop driven into the uneven frost-hardened earth to pin down the chain. Gooseflesh rose on her arms. Such a measure could not be necessary. It was barbaric.

Torchlight flickered over the unmoving flesh. The prisoner's palm was broad, the heavy fingers curled inwards, solid and well-shaped, gold skin and shadows. The smoky light showed the richly curved rise at the base of his thumb. Such a hand should have been as passively beautiful as a sculpture—it was a fist.

Someone shoved past her, cursing in Danish and trying to stuff a silver necklace and a looted piece of cheese into a bulging leather saddlebag. The way things stood for the fleeing army, the cheese was the more valuable.

Rosamund had her own store of hidden provisions. She had planned for her escape with the meticulous care of the desperate. She had no protection now and she had to defend Merriwen. The world crushed people who were defenceless. It had the power to crush Rosamund herself if she made one wrong move.

She stepped over the chain in the wake of the departing army.

Her embroidered skirts, bead-sewn and scented with Frankish lavender, trailed across forged iron, then a veined wrist and she looked back, caught between shadow and smoking flame, her gaze drawn by that unmoving gilded flesh, held fast. The prisoner had hit someone so hard he had skinned his knuckles. The motionless hand radiated trapped fire, the kind of fire she had once felt…the untameable kind that got fools like her into too much trouble.

No. She could not involve herself. Merriwen would die without her. Besides, the fire in her was extinguished.

She took one last look. The veined wrist had small bloodied marks where the iron fetter had broken through the skin.

"St. Chad's spotless coffin." The words did not come out in Danish, but in English, Mercian.

The prisoner had hit someone while still *chained*.

Something inside her, the long-lost dangerous fire, stirred. She leaned over the fist; she would not call it a mere hand, and looked more closely. There was no more blood now. Probably because he was too cold to bleed. Dead.

No one got in the way of the Viking Jarl Guthrum's will. She glanced round the moving army. Earl Guthrum had killed half a score of innocent people to secure this escape. He was breaking not just the truce with the king of Wessex, but his word of honour, and honour was the only thing that kept the world human. She could still scarcely believe he had done it. The flames inside rose. The Viking earl had hanged the West Saxon hostages given into his hands. All those deaths, and now one more.

Perhaps.

She knelt on the frozen ground. The cold struck through her decorated skirts. Jarl Guthrum's men streamed past. Of course, there was nothing she could do to stop an army. And there was Merriwen to think of....

She saw the chained man's face.

Her gaze fastened on a perfect profile made out of fire and shadow. Dreams. Such creatures as him did not exist on middle earth. He had fallen out of the heavens and come to grief in the firelit dark.

Somewhere in the blackness someone was speaking. She could not make out the words. She did not bother. Her attention was fixed on the sight of the shadowy creature before her, all of her mind, like someone possessed. Thick wavy hair spread out from his head across the frozen ground. The loose strands trailing the crushed earth showed deep copper in the torchlight. Rich. So fascinatingly bright and luxuriant she wanted to bury her achingly cold hands in its light and its deep black shadows. Now. Because it was full of fire. She touched it.

"...will pay for such madness..." said the voice above her head.

The hair felt like the threads of silk that traders brought from Byzantium, so smooth, almost heavy with that impossible smoothness against her naked skin. It was cold. Small shivers passed through her. Her gaze travelled over a light-gilded cheekbone, a straight nose, the solid thickness of a square jaw...the skin was dusted with a dark stubble already dense enough to blur the strongly carved perfection of that outline. Living flesh, male. If he belonged to the realm of dreams, it was the world of night dreams that were heated, erotic.

She snatched her hand back.

"Of course, you know where he comes from," said the voice at the edge of her perception.

She was mad to touch him. There was a quality of toughness about him that was stunning, at violent odds with the deeply compelling attractiveness. Or perhaps part of it.

She moved back. She was proof against the flaunted charms of any man on earth. She had been taught only too well that commerce between the sexes was no more than that, a matter of bargaining in which women generally had the weaker position. Women needed their wits.

Rosamund watched the brilliant motionless body chained on the ground before her.

She touched him. Just to see whether the man was truly still alive. Nothing more. Her hand settled. He did not react.

The brilliant flesh was so cold, even to her chilled fingers—cold as death. Her heart slammed against her ribs. The sharpness of the reaction stunned her senses, choking her breath. Then the rush of dizziness cleared on the realisation that the man she touched still lived, despite the coldness of his flesh, the coldness in the air around them that cut the lungs like ice shards.

"Alive." Her artistically reddened lips stumbled over a word that was totally inadequate to describe the strength that poured from the stranger, forcing its way through the thin skin of her fingers with the steady movement of his breath. So powerful. But it was human strength. The cold would kill him. She had already moved, when the voice out of the dark began again. She heard a snort that expressed pure contempt and then a word.

"Mercia."

Her head turned. *Mercia*. That was where the

chained man came from, the wide rolling country north of Wessex which now belonged to the Vikings. It was where she had been born.

It meant nothing. It was not a bond.

She had every reason to hate her fellow Mercians. They had sold her to the Viking army which had conquered them and then turned its attention to invading Wessex.

The voice said, "He should not have interfered with an execution."

The hostages. The prisoner must have done something that concerned the hostages.

It could mean nothing to her.

She found she was touching the fist with its skinned knuckles. Her fingers closed over the bent fingers and the strength flowed through her. It seemed to penetrate her heart.

What have you done? She almost said it aloud, as though the man she touched could answer. But she already guessed. She held on to the stranger's clenched hand, with the iron chains dripping off his bruised and lacerated wrist, and in the deepest part of her she knew. *You tried to help someone, somehow, even though such things are not possible, not in a place like this.*

"I should kill him."

She recognised the voice. Its owner was fully capable of doing what he said, without a moment's remorse.

She let go of the hand.

"That would teach him to try and escape down by the river. *Mercian scum.*"

The harsh voice, so well known to her, should not have said that. The flames inside her ignited. She hardly knew where the fire came from, because of the name of the lost land north of Wessex where she had been born. Or from the man she had touched.

She stood up and with a swish of her bead-sewn skirts she planted one painted shoe squarely into the patch of torchlight that held the speaker.

It drew three pairs of eyes directly to her. Her mantle still swung with the force of her movement, her decorated skirts showed through the opening of the bright blue fur-lined cloak. She adjusted the fall until it was perfect. She had been brought up alongside a member of the royal kindred. The first rule was simple—always appear impressive.

She smiled.

Thorkill, the speaker, Earl Guthrum's most loyal *hersir* and captain, returned the favour. It was like watching a wolf unveil its fangs. His gaze locked at the level of her delicate rose-coloured skirt. She realised he was in a good way towards being drunk.

"The lady Rosamund, the *princess.*" The sarcastic emphasis had no effect on her. She was used to it from the Vikings. Besides, it was not her title. Thorkill merely believed, like everyone else in this place, that she was King Ceolfrith of Mercia's niece. She had begun the lie because of Merriwen and she had stuck to it.

It was possible that the Mercian at her feet might be someone who knew the royal kindred by sight, that if he regained consciousness he might betray her.

The risk was lethal.

She stepped around an elbow and some more chain. What was life without risk? Liveable, that was what.

"I thought you would be packing up all your little feminine trinkets." Thorkill's voice, ale-blurred, managed to make something indecent out of that. There was laughter. "And maybe something to keep you warm at night." His narrow blue eyes stayed fixed on the pale slash of her skirts visible through the parting of her mantle. "It is a long way to Exeter."

"I possess spare cloaks," she said blandly, "and I have already packed."

She resisted the desire to pull her mantle tighter. Earl Guthrum's captain managed to wrestle his snakelike gaze as high as her face. So she widened the smile for him.

"You, however, seem to be still rather untidy." Her cool, rallying tone was perfect, even though her heartbeat was too fast. She added the haughty arching of one carefully plucked brow. "Perhaps because you have so much to take with you?"

Rosamund's gaze swept over a pile of baggage, stuffed with heaven knew what West Saxon plunder, and came to rest on the lump of shadowed fire in chains at their feet.

"And this?" She stepped around the unconscious man and selected a small iron-bound chest to sit on, narrowly avoiding treading on the prisoner's coiling hair. There was little room.

Od, Thorkill's companion in crime, hooted with laughter.

"The new prisoner is *hersir's*. We might get a ransom for him."

The other side of the Mercian's face was a mess, the gilt skin dark with bruising. She swallowed.

"Worth something." Od stabbed at the heavy form on the ground with one boot, catching the elegant shape of a thigh. "And he was quick enough when he dealt with you, Arne." The renewed torrent of laughter was directed at the third man of the party.

Arne said nothing. Rosamund could see why. That was where the fist had connected. She averted her gaze.

"Or maybe there is no useful life left in him after Thorkill brought him down." Od, howling at his own wit, spilled ale while she stared at the hard-fisted prisoner.

Thorkill watched her.

She tilted her head, keeping her gaze directed towards the shadowed shape at her feet. The Mercian was dressed in a rich, dark woollen tunic and trousers. No. *Dressed* was too strong a word for it. The ripped tunic gaped across his body. Her gaze fastened without her will on the gleam of uncovered masculine skin.

"Meat for the ravens, now," asserted Od. He passed the drinking horn to his commander. "That is the use for prisoners. Like the West Saxons you sent to their exec—"

"Hold your tongue."

The sudden violence of Thorkill's response shocked her. The word *execution* sent frozen shivers across her flesh beneath the sumptuous clothing. She risked a single glance at Thorkill's face. The disposal of the unwanted hostages had been a secret deed, not known until it was over. But Thorkill was the earl's trusted man.

Od's gaze, which had instinctively followed hers, slid away. He picked up a pair of dice and made a great show of tossing them from the bronze cup he held onto a makeshift gaming board, right hand against left.

Thorkill drank steadily. He wiped his mouth with the back of one bearlike paw. "Silent, princess? Will you not give me your opinion of the prisoner?"

She watched the half-drunk eyes ripe with secrets. He did not want her opinion. He wanted to turn the subject to safer ground. Had he acted for Guthrum as executioner? Or perhaps such a crime had revolted even a man like Thorkill. She thought that last hardly likely, but she was not one to let a chance go by.

Forcing her breathing to slow down, she drew her fine brows together and extended one foot towards the chained man, rather more delicately than Od had done. She selected the other thigh.

"I disagree." The neatly shaped toe of her gilded shoe insinuated itself under richly curved muscle. Her skirts brushed the dark trousers. The dangerous, ale-soaked gaze of three warriors followed that small deliberate movement. She shifted the decorated shoe, feeling solid flesh press against the dyed leather, her stockinged foot. The man's thigh was heavy beyond expectation, thick with saddle muscles, the weight unexpectedly intimate against her light bones, another person's flesh. She caught her breath.

"I think there may be a little life left in him yet." She slid the foot higher. "A little strength."

Thorkill spat into the frost-rimed ground. The silent Arne shifted.

The chained man's muscles were obvious. The ruined tunic strained over an impossibly broad pair of shoulders and a massive chest, the narrow leather belt drawing the wreckage tight at powerful hips.

Her breath skipped again. But there was no going back now. She had begun this and she had to go on. Under Thorkill's dangerous gaze, she slid her foot round.

"Some…useful…life there yet." The toe of her painted shoe came to rest against one heavy, taut hip-bone. She rocked it gently. Her kohl-rimmed eyes beneath their arched, perfectly shaped brows were directed at Thorkill. Her face gave nothing, but inside, her blood pulsed too fast, quickened by the primitive lash of fear mixed with the unbidden stirrings of something else, something equally primitive, equally strong.

"Such a man might even serve to keep me warm on the way to Exeter." The words, like her actions, were no more than a necessary part of the strategy she had so recklessly begun. But despite herself, her mind made the unwanted leap to what it might be like to have this fire and shadow creature pinned in chains, this man, in her bed, warming it, and her blood surged.

She felt painfully alive, filled with a startling, tense anticipation—as though the dangerous heady vision might become real, herself and the brilliant stranger. Even as her mind shied away from it, her tumultuous senses were caught, the rush of feeling like nothing she had known, the fine heat tingeing her cheekbones, visible for all the world to see.

Od made some drunken sound. The third man stirred in the shadows and muttered a curse under stifled breath. Neither she, nor the Viking who must have arranged an execution for Guthrum, broke their gaze.

"What a woman like you needs, *princess,* is a true man, not some crawling prisoner." Thorkill's opaque gaze moved from her flushed face and her burning eyes to her body, abrupt as a physical assault. "You need someone who knows exactly what you want."

There was a small pause while she was assessed,

the carefully draped clothes fashioned for entice-
ment, the silver and copper jewellery, the seduc-
tively made-up face. And the intense, starkly
complete response to an unknown man that she
could not disguise. Her body burned and her foot
rested where she had placed it, flat against the
stranger's hip, the sleek, virile line of power.

"People will take advantage of those who are
alone." Thorkill's breath hissed sharply. His tone
chilled her more than the frost. "And you are quite
alone, Rosamund."

Her spine stiffened under the threat. It was as un-
nerving as the unadorned use of her name. Thorkill
already coveted her, because of who she pretended
to be, because he had never been able to have her
and he was a man who took what he wanted. Until
now he had never stepped across the invisible line
she had set around herself. But she had never before
been quite so defenceless.

And she had chosen this moment to change the
precarious balance. For the stranger.

She tilted her head back. "No one can consider
themselves alone when they have the earl's favour."

Yet she hardly knew whether that was still true
of the increasingly desperate and self-absorbed
man who had just resorted to murder. And it
seemed Thorkill had carried it out for him, with the
hands that had brought down the disturbingly dangerous prisoner, this Mercian in chains who had in
some way interfered.

Her breath nearly choked her but her foot kept its place against solid flesh and all at once she was aware not of the coldness and the confining chains, but of the fire, the sustaining life of it and the stubbornness. It was as though she was not alone, the way she had been for three full years.

The fire started to spread through her veins.

"You need a protector."

Her lips curved. "I make my own choices."

That much was still true. It had always been so. It was the only piece of herself that remained. If that was lost, she might as well be dead.

The fire inside her burned higher. The dice clicked in Od's hand.

"Choices," Thorkill spat.

She moved her skirts out of the way.

"The world belongs to us now, to the men of the North."

The Viking army surrounded her and all the world belonged to them. But she was touching the stranger and the mad, heady possibility existed that somehow it did not.

Rosamund rearranged the beaded linen of her Danish concubine's clothing. It showed a glimpse of ankle.

"Shall we see?" *You are, after all, dealing with a Mercian. With two.* The prisoner's strength touched her in the dark, deep and dangerous.

"You cannot survive without a man like me. Shall I teach you that?"

Torchlight glittered off the knife hilt at Thorkill's heavy hip as he moved. He leaned forward. So did she. The night breeze ruffled her heavy mantle and touched the chained man's hair. Just as Thorkill moved again, she reached out.

Od spat ale down his beard when she touched him. "What the…"

But she had already let go of Od's bony fingers. She had what she wanted. She ignored Od, all her will bent on Thorkill.

"I will play you for him," she said to Thorkill. *"What?"*

She kept her gaze on the suddenly unsheathed knife. The blade was a foot long and stone-sharpened. *You are mad, Rosamund, crazed.* Thorkill's hand tightened on the hilt. *Why should you do this?* She tossed the small carved dice in the bronze cup that had once been the property of Od. They made a rattling noise.

"The Mercian," she said. "I will play you for ownership. You do not want him. I do."

The blood-quickening vision filled her head. *I want him….* She choked off the hidden, unacceptable meaning for the words. What mattered was that she was not going to let Thorkill's murderous hands touch the prisoner. "So…"

Thorkill was drunk, the knife in his hand unsteady. It was an insane risk. *She* was insane. But for the first time in more months than she could count, she was tingling with aliveness.

"So," she repeated, while the blood pounded through her veins and the brilliant body lay at her feet, light and fire and dense male shadows. "What do you say?"

"You mad bi—"

"I do not have much time." Her voice drowned his. It had to because there was no way she could repay the insult once it had been spoken. She had no greater weapon than bluff. She used it.

"I have commissions to fill for the Jarl before we leave." She presented Thorkill with a cool look. "He is of uncertain temper." She had not seen Guthrum for days, but this last had to be true after what Thorkill's commander had just done. "He would not wish to see me delayed."

Then she sweetened the empty threat with the beginnings of her most serene smile. It was a balancing act, always. She had no real position here, except what she created for herself.

Thorkill leaned back, careless, as though her words meant nothing. But the insult was not repeated. The earl's temper must be worse than she had thought.

She tossed the dice as she had seen Od do it, right hand against left. She flicked her wrist and the colourful sleeve of her gown fell back. Her fine bracelets clinked, catching the torchlight. The autumn frost in the air touched her bared skin, as did the more bitter cold of Thorkill's gaze. He had not sheathed the knife. One of the carved bone dice dropped onto her skirt.

It rolled slowly across the long decorated curve of her thigh. She reached for it. The air left her lungs as the Viking's hand clamped down on her wrist. She pulled back, but it was too late. The shocked sound that choked in her throat was pitifully audible. She had not seen him move.

"So you wish to make sport with me, princess?" The smell of ale from Thorkill's hot breath fanned her cheek. A strand of her blonde hair escaped the knot at her neck. This was not in her design. No. But she was sporting with a killer. She had known that.

"What else?" She tried extracting her wrist. It would not budge. His forearm, enclosed in a leather arm-guard, pressed into the top of her thigh. The metal studs embedded in the leather pushed through her skirts into her skin.

"Ah," said the executioner. "That is the question. The bet has to be…" the sharp studs ground briefly into her flesh "…worthwhile for me."

Her breath tightened hard in her throat. She could not speak. The unbreakable grip of his hand changed and his fingers moved higher across the exposed skin of her arm.

"You see, the fate of one Mercian slave is not enough."

But it was.

Rosamund saw what night and distance had hidden from her before, the purple welt across the side of the Viking's neck. It was long, dark, not the kind of mark to be made by a fist. The chain…

The unknown man, her Mercian, had struck him, Thorkill the invincible.

"Are you backing out of a wager?" She leaned forward until her foot made contact again with the heavily shadowed figure on the ground, touching the flaring line of his side. This time it was for strength, the bitter kind that she needed, the kind that would still strike out from a position of weakness.

She arched her neck, the way she had seen it done by the usurpers who crowded round the traitor King Ceolfrith at Repton.

"The *hersir* does not have the stomach to take up a wager with a woman?"

The response was a show of pale teeth in the tangled black beard.

"Perhaps it is you who does not have the stomach for a real wager, princess. You want something warm in your bed, you shall have it. This piece of carrion—" the fire-hardened chains clinked "—or me."

Her heart was thudding inside the tight wall of her chest. Thorkill's massive form blocked out the torchlight, the knife still in his free hand. She knew what he was like. Cold sweat touched her skin and it was impossible to move.

"You have not the stomach." He let her go. The breath of relief was still in her mouth when his foot lashed out at the still shape on the ground. The blow connected across the ribs with a concentrated viciousness Od had not achieved, the kick only slightly off balance because of the amount Thorkill had drunk.

The unconscious figure jerked.

"Careful," said her voice, its cool tone and its cultured Mercian accent utterly composed. "You will damage the goods and then what will I get for my winnings?"

Guthrum's captain stopped, his broad back in its huge shaggy cloak towards her.

"Shall we?" She was aware of noise behind her, the hissing of voices. She glanced over her shoulder and saw they had attracted attention. People, servants with baggage, warriors armed like Od and Thorkill, had stopped. A female figure, Olga, her friend, hung back in the shadows.

Witnesses. The hot blood flowed in her veins.

Thorkill turned and saw them. She smiled.

"Best of five throws?" The dice rolled across her damp palm. She dropped them neatly into the bronze cup and set it on the board, which had been balanced on another small chest filled with plunder. Some of the curious moved on, intent on their preparations to leave, but others stayed. She was sure she caught sight of Olga's bright green skirts.

She touched the Mercian's cold skin. Her hand buried itself briefly under the trailing mass of his dark, fire-streaked hair, seeking the slightest trace of warmth. The strong curve of his neck filled her palm. Her breath, already too fast, became painfully shallow. It was hard to swallow.

Her fingers slid round the strong supple line of his throat to find the hidden pulse of life at its base. The ripped neck of the tunic fell back and she found what she sought, the deep secret flutter of his life against her fingers. She released her breath.

Then she looked up at Thorkill.

"I accept the wager. You see…I have no love of cold nights." Her fingers moved upwards, over a firm stark jawline, and the exquisite roughness of stubbled skin abraded her fingertips. She touched well-shaped lips, just slightly parted, felt the faint reassuring whisper of his breath, still warm and faintly moist against her skin. Her own breath left small puffs of whiteness in the air.

"I may find it an interesting gamble." Her eyes were fixed on Thorkill as though her thoughts were directly on him. But her fingers traced the clear lines of the Mercian's face, deliberately slow. Her fingertips retraced their way lower, across the curved throat, the fine rise of a collarbone, finding their path by the pure, intense sensation of touch.

Thorkill's face tightened, his hard-boned fist set round the silver-wired hilt of the fighting knife. She ignored that, letting her hand slide over the torn tunic, flesh, a broad deeply-muscled torso. Every small touch scored through her. She bit her lip. She was mad to do this, mad to get involved with such a man. Her hand stayed, touching the stranger on the cold ground. The pressure of her fingers increased, trying to find whether any of the ribs were broken.

Thorkill, furious and fuddled with ale, terrifyingly dangerous, stared at her.

She found skin, the gaping tear in the stranger's ruined tunic, the end of the powerful ribcage, the sleek turn of his side, the rich flexible skin of his abdomen. She lightened off the pressure. Her hand moved gently, like a caress. She kept her gaze locked on the danger in Thorkill's pale eyes, the anger and the greed. Her hand stroked.

She could not see. She did not dare look at the shadowed motionless creature under her fingers. She knew there must be bruises. She tried not to cause damage. The Mercian could not feel what she did. But his fine living skin filled her hand, supple and dense and intensely sensual to touch. So cold, but he warmed under the touch of her hand. Her breath skipped and the sharp, intense sensation blossomed like something that would possess her—tightened body and aching, desperate soul.

She knew how to touch. Her slender fingers with their silver rings, her narrow palms made supple with rose-scented oil, moved slowly, seeking bare flesh beneath the ripped material, the hidden contours of masculine bone and muscle, the fine, living, intensely beautiful skin. The circular movement of her hand was slow, light. Fascinating.

She watched the small shift of Thorkill's eyes, drawn by that rhythmic movement and she knew that what he saw in his harsh devious mind was that skilful touching on his own flesh. He stared, eyelids narrow, black hairy jaw slackened. Hand suddenly loose round the knife hilt.

Rosamund's heart beat out of time. She hardly dared breathe. Someone cursed. Od's voice. The highly charged moment broke, with what must have seemed like the shattering of a spell.

Thorkill moved. "Give me the dice."

CHAPTER TWO

THORKILL SNATCHED the dice cup out of Rosamund's slackened hand. She let go. People shifted, craned through the dark to get a better look, jostled and swore again. Thorkill saw only her. Her and the unconscious man under her hand, the dangerous prisoner who had hit him.

Rosamund straightened up. The dice crashed onto the wooden gaming board.

"Four." Thorkill had put the knife down. "And three." The Danish voice was flat.

"Seven," said Od. His jaw, under its scrappy red beard, was tight. It was a reasonable start. Thorkill's henchman leaned forward, hands clasped. "Seven."

Thorkill said nothing. There was no expression on his frozen, heavily-bearded face, only in his eyes.

Rosamund let go of the Mercian.

"Princess?"

She picked up the dice cup. It was heavy, with an irritating cross bar inside that got in the way of the dice. She hoped, above all things, that her hands would be steady.

Please let me throw well.

She tipped the awkward cup, fighting the sudden urge to shut her eyes. One of the dice rattled to a stop on the wooden board. A five. Higher than either of Thorkill's numbers. It had to be possible to succeed, *had* to be. The second cube was still spinning. It dipped, stopped. Four.

Her heart expanded. Nine. It *was* possible to succeed. She could win. Truly... The small crowd whispered and the first round was hers. She fought down the wild beating in her blood. Not a trace of triumph showed in her face. The danger was still there. It seemed to fall on her skin like frost.

She had to get through this with skill.

She did not insist on a winner's precedence for the next throw. She gave Thorkill the bronze cup. She did not touch him. His thick-fingered hand reached out, dripping with warrior's gold. He grinned.

Her own fingers clenched, tight over her scented palms, as though there were still some trace of the brilliant living captive on her skin, traces of the long-lost fire which had sprung to life the moment she had seen him. Life where there should be none.

There was a flash of gems as Thorkill threw. Three. And then a five.

"Eight," muttered Od under his breath. He did not look at his commander. His fingers scrabbled furtively at the leather purse suspended from his belt.

She had to beat it. She would. She had thrown well before and it was possible. She cast the dice.

Three. The same as Thorkill... She stared at a two.

Od made a breathy sound. Like Thorkill, she said nothing. It was the best of five throws. They had both lost one. She was still in the game. She could claw her way back from a single loss. Surely. She edged along her makeshift seat, closer to the Mercian. The wind cut through her, straight off the unseen harbour where Guthrum's longships lay, raising shivers across her skin. It was as though she could see death in Thorkill's face. Death and destruction. It flowed round them in the ceaseless movement of the Viking camp.

Her gaze fell to the heavy form at her feet, the still face, and all the time, despite the bitter fire in her veins, she was aware of the unforgiving cold, of its grip on the motionless body and the half-exposed flesh. Such cold leached the life out of whatever it touched.

"Thorkill?" She did not want to speak to him, to call that dangerous attention to herself. But she had to go on with this and time pressed at her, the urgent need to find some shelter for the prisoner before he died, to have this over before the Viking encampment dissolved into total chaos.

"Will you—"

The ale-smirched gaze clashed with hers. She

caught triumph, waiting, violent. She almost shrank back. Od was leaning forwards, muttering. He had some unseen object clutched in his sinewy fingers.

The black-haired hand shot out and this time she did jerk back. Thorkill snatched the dice, his eyes on her face, drinking in that sudden involuntary movement of her body. She caught the gleam of his teeth in the dark as his thin lips parted. It was not a smile. He threw.

Three and one. She exhaled, careful not to let her reaction show, lowering her eyes under their kohl-darkened lashes. Four was achievable, beatable. The luck had to be even. She could do it. The hidden fire inside her burned higher. She extended one jewelled hand and took the cup.

Her opponent straightened, flexing thick mail-clad shoulders under the shaggy cloak. But it was Od who drew her attention, the half-hidden movement of his stringy fingers, the rhythmic sound of his voice, more confident now, like chanting. She caught the shape of a word.

Sigurd, and then other Norse heroes' names, evocations of figures of power steeped in legend, and she knew what he held in his grubby fingers. He was scrabbling at a silver coin. She had learned quite enough about Vikings to realise the significance of what she saw.

He would have wrapped his piece of silver in parchment, buried it in the earth before midnight in some dark spot and then dug it up again the next day. Some idiot would have written runes for him on the parchment. He had a talisman, a secret weapon that gave its owner a sure-fire method of winning at games of chance. Except that was not a proper purpose and stupid to boot. The under-handed, moon-witted—

"Princess." The honour-word cracked like a lash. "No stomach?" Od's commander picked up the knife, digging with the sharpened point at the wooden edge of the strong box. The impatience, the reined-back fury, hit her across the two feet of distance.

"Just assuring myself of my luck." She rolled the dice in the cup, ready to throw. She set her gaze deliberately on Od with his attempted rune-charms, and that was how she missed it. There was only the quick flash of pale iron through the flickering light and the shadows. She actually cried out as the dice spilled from the cup.

The blade of Thorkill's *sax* vibrated in the night air beside her feet, buried for nearly half its length, point-down, in the frost-crusted ground. It had passed straight through a ripped sleeve.

She thought her heart stopped.

"Did you speak, princess?"

What she had said was one of the gutter words she had heard around the stables at King Ceolfrith's hall. It had come out in English, but she doubted that a single one of the Danish soldiers around her would mistake its meaning.

"Indeed, you startled me."

"So it seems." He slurred the words.

She must have slid down from her seat because she was on her knees on the cold, churned ground. She could not look at Thorkill. Her eyes were fixed on the silver-wired knife hilt reflecting torchlight, on the dull gleam of the blade.

"The knife slipped."

It pierced the costly dark blue wool of the prisoner's sleeve. Two inches further right and it would have maimed. She did not know whether missing that solid swell of muscle had been deliberate, or whether the "slip" meant Thorkill had aimed straight for the Mercian's outstretched arm. She looked up at the opaque eyes. It was impossible to tell. Perhaps he had just thrown regardless. Perhaps he was too drunk to care.

"I shall enjoy startling you again. You are…interesting in that state."

She thought her eyes narrowed to slits. They stared at each other across the fine fallen body like two wolves disputing the spoils of the hunt.

There was silence while the cold crawled over her flesh, finding its way beneath the rich clothing and raising gooseflesh on her skin. She would not give up now. She could not. She touched chains, then skin, the solid shape of the Mercian's hand. The fist.

Her gaze fastened on the Viking's heavy, black-bearded face, the cold eyes and the livid mark across the strong neck. *You are not invincible, Thorkill, Guthrum's man, and neither is your desperate earl. The king of the West Saxons will find him. You will not always be the master.* The thought struck through her as though it came straight from the man she touched, burning with the warmth of something forgotten, something she had long discarded. Hope.

"Then shall we play on? Who knows, I may startle you in my turn." She tilted her head. His cold eyes watched the movement, his stone face, and then he reached out. The black-haired paw closed on the fine knife hilt, jerking it out in one single savage movement. The steel blade came free. There was a small trace of blood.

"Clean it." He stood, thrusting the blade at Od and startling his partner out of his trancelike crooning. *Oh, perfect chance.* She surged to her feet at the same moment, stumbling over her skirts and landing one gilded shoe firmly on Od's boot. Od, already unnerved by his commander's blade, let out a small howl and dropped the coin wrapped in charms. She kicked it into the oblivion of outer darkness where it belonged and sat down again, rearranging her flowing gown.

"Well, I am the clumsy one." She turned her gaze on the gaming board, on the results of her throw. She stared at the face of a small bone cube with a single circle incised into it. The other die showed a two.

Brilliant. It really had been possible to come in under Thorkill's four. He now had two games to her one. He needed only one more win and the match was over. She could not think on the consequences. He need only… He threw. She stared.

"Six," said Od flatly. He wiped the knife clean of blood using his tunic and then began working the blade softly with the whet stone of banded slate suspended from his belt. His gaze flicked to the dark and his lost talisman. But he did not move.

Four and two. It was a moderately good score. No. Considering her own luck, it was more than moderately good. It probably did not matter whether Od retrieved his dangerous talisman or not.

She thought of all she had staked on this game, of Thorkill, of her duty to Merriwen who waited for her even now, alone and nervous. She thought of the man held down in iron chains at her feet. She threw.

Five. And then three. She could not have seen properly. She looked again. The crudely carved circles shimmered before her eyes as though she would faint. Eight. Round four was hers.

She and Thorkill were even. She had forced one more round—the last game that would decide the match.

She swallowed, calming her breath, trying to order her tumultuous thoughts. But she had no time even to guess at Thorkill's reaction. There was no pause now, no interruption, only the danger that hung on the last throw, the prize. Her opponent caught the dice cup out of her hand. The bone cubes rattled, clashed against solid bronze with biting force. Her heart beat out of time, hard, as though it were stuck high in her throat, choking her.

Beside her, Od muttered, hairy-jawed face watching his commander. Her gaze flicked from him to the darkly-shadowed face of the Mercian prisoner, so death-still against frost, then to the ripped tunic that showed finely-turned muscle, bruising, the thin streak of blood across one arm. Thorkill looked only at her. She knew that without even seeing him. He watched her, not her eyes but the blanched, moon-shadowed curve of her throat above the beaded dress, the pale slash of her skirts at the parting of her heavy mantle.

She did not look at the dice cup. She could not. She saw Thorkill's wrist flick. She heard the crack of bone against the wooden board, a ripple of sound from the crowd, Od's quick breath. She turned her head and saw Thorkill's hard-boned face, his eyes— anger and drink, impatience, the thwarted instincts of a beast on the spoor of its prey. She did not think he would be able to hold that violent force in check.

She looked at the dice.

Five. And six.

It was outstanding, the best that he, that anyone, could have hoped for. Only one combination could beat it. Od did not say it this time. At a single glance from his master, he handed across the cleaned knife.

Rosamund's was the last throw. There were witnesses, a small crowd round them in the shadows, doubtless hanging on every movement. She was known. She had a position. Mercian princess.

But that position, created out of pride and anger and the sheer force of stubbornness, out of desperation, rested on the favour of a Viking earl who had broken his word and committed murder. More than that, it was in itself a matter of trickery, empty in a way Earl Guthrum, with his Viking warriors, did not dream.

She picked up the cup. Thorkill turned the knife in his hand. He knew he had won. The straightness of his shoulders, the tight, arrogant tilt of his head expressed it perfectly. Viking warrior, *hersir,* a master within an unbeatable raiding army and therefore a master of the known world.

The torchlight flickered in the wind, dancing off the carefully honed steel in his hand. She thought of how fast the blade had moved through the cold air, how powerless she had been. She had not even *seen.* She touched the Mercian, her foot just glancing against the deep, rock-solid wall of his chest. She wanted strength.

Chad's bones. It seemed to flow through her in waves. Such power—and the dangerous edge of fire. That terrible strength seemed deep, limitless. Yet there would be no mercy for him if she lost.

As for her fate, Thorkill was so volatile, so tight with tension, he might force her even if she won.

She would fail if she let such nightmares into her mind. She tilted her head like a royal woman of the court.

We are together in this, Mercian, win or lose, even if you are one of Ceolfrith's men, she said in her mind to the stranger. *Give me your strength.*

The dice flew out of her hand.

Rosamund heard the intake of Thorkill's ale-soaked breath. The dice rattled across the makeshift gaming board and rolled to a stop. She stared at the small round marks carved into the bone faces of the cubes.

Double six.

That was impossible.

Thorkill got to his feet.

Victory—she had won. She had command of her own fate. And she owned a man in chains.

"Twelve." Her tight throat choked her. "Double six." She repeated the unassailable numbers out loud.

They did not mean anything. Naught, because the mad greed, the thwarted fury in Thorkill's eyes would not be stopped. He put one foot on the prisoner's chain beside the staple that pinned it to the ground. The knife was in his hand. His gaze, that appalling gaze, was on her.

She got to her feet, but his free hand shot out, warrior-fast, fastening on her arm, the grip punishing, painful.

"You are still mine. You and that Mercian carrion both. I take what I am owed—"

In the shadows beyond the circle of torchlight, people had begun yelling. She thought at first it was something to do with the dice game, with her and Thorkill. But the shouting had spread too far, was too loud, too confused. She could not make out the words. The crowd of warriors surged, not just the small band gathered round the scene playing out over the unconscious prisoner, but what seemed like Guthrum's whole army, as though it were a single being, a giant beast with one collective mind.

The sudden yelling from so many throats shattered even the frozen horror of the moment. She felt the same instinctive reaction jolt through Thorkill's body where he held her, the response primeval, old as humankind. Shared fear. His head turned.

He was staring eastwards and her gaze followed his, drawn like that of every warrior in Guthrum's army to the night sky beyond the walls of the fortress at Wareham. A dull red glow filled the horizon where before there had been nothing, only space and the stars and the black shape of the rising ground behind the heath. It was no natural sunrise. The timing was wrong, and the colour eerie, somehow sinister. Man made.

It was a beacon fire.

The vicious, frightened sound of Thorkill's voice cut the air. His body was rigid. "The West Saxons. *How?*"

He let go of her arm. But he made no further movement, his gaze fixed on the red horizon. She could hear the sound of his breath. "No one knew we would move tonight. No one beyond the Jarl's own men. *No one*."

"Saint Chad's bones. He—" She stopped speaking. But no one paid any heed to the name of the sainted Mercian bishop. Not a single Viking noticed. She sat down again on the wooden chest. Her legs were shaking so hard she could not stand, her whole body. She reached out in the shadows with a bruised arm and found a damaged fist. Her hand closed over it.

It could not be. The prisoner could not have... Down by the river, Thorkill had said. Mercian scum. She watched the fire spreading its crimson stain across the night sky, Thorkill swearing, an army on the edge of panic.

"There was no one," repeated Thorkill. He turned his head and saw her. She kept her hand plastered over hard knuckle and damaged flesh as though that could hide it from the Viking's sight, as though it could hide everything. His pale gaze travelled over her, over the shadowed form of the prisoner. Then it locked on their hands.

He had the knife in his fist. She flung herself over the body, the impulse stronger than thought, mad, as though she could shield the massive frame of the Mercian with her own slight form.

The blade did not fall. She turned her head,

sprawled with the prisoner on the ground, pressed against that other living flesh, chest and hip and leg tight with that other body, at one with it. Her heart beat like a savage's with fear. She did not want to look at Guthrum's man, but her gaze sought the banked fury of his eyes. The suspicion about what the captive might have done, the near certainty that had sprung so horrifyingly to her mind, did not seem to be there. All she could read was the anger, the unappeased greed. She would swear it....

"Then take him, princess." Thorkill's eyes were utterly opaque. "Take all you want. But you will regret what you have done. I will have that piece of carrion back, that mercenary who fights for the Saxons and was King Ceolfrith's man, and I will have you and you will regret then that you cheated me."

There was a far-off cry, not a warrior's deep-throated curse, but something closer to a scream. Thorkill looked up. Then she thought she heard the earl's voice cutting straight through that desperate noise, shouting. Its unmistakable tone was furious and filled with force, more than that, with an implacable authority—the consummate commander, in victory or loss, honour or treachery. Unyielding.

Thorkill turned and ran toward the voice. Od followed with Arne and the rest of the men, snatching up their possessions and yelling.

The red glow seemed to intensify before her eyes. Somehow that deadly warning had been set in motion by someone who knew Guthrum's army was leaving the fortress at Wareham. The fell tidings leaped in flame, a message that would now be carried onwards in an unbroken chain from high point to high point across the hills of Wessex until the king saw it.

Alfred of Wessex would regather his forces and he would come.

Rosamund lay still on the ground with her new and disputed possession. She had just rescued something that had the power to kill her.

She buried her face in the smooth hollow between the prisoner's shoulder and his neck, and shut her eyes. A mercenary, Thorkill had said, and before that King Ceolfrith's man. King Ceolfrith had given Merriwen and herself to Earl Guthrum without a second thought. That was what being Mercian meant.

She should get up and go. She should leave this stranger with the brilliant body and the dangerous secrets. He was more than she could handle.

She found she was shaking, not with cold but with reaction. She had done something so foolish. Thorkill would not let her go and she had little defence, nothing beyond a risky plan to escape, made doubly dangerous now. Thorkill would be watching her every move, thanks to her own reckless decision.

And she had done it for a man who was Ceolfrith's.

The panicked army streamed past her and she could not so much as raise her head. She heard shouting, the whinnying of an infuriated horse, and further away, an inarticulate yelling that held no discernible human words, only the primitive shape of fear. It was a sound of despair, so familiar. It had washed over this land for seven winters. No one stood against that.

She turned her head. She was lying so close with the chained man that the tendrils of fair hair that had escaped the knot at her neck mixed with his. With dark burnt copper. His hair trapped fire out of the torchlight. It reflected small shards of light as though it were something living.

The tangled threads wound round her fingers, streaked with mud and frost. She touched his cold face, the stark lines and the pale skin gilded by flickering fire. The madness lay in the fact that she did not feel the coldness, only the life, the strength that had caught her from the start, and had taken her and held her in thrall as surely as the iron chains that bound him.

She breathed the frigid air, clear and crisp and tinged with smoke, perhaps from King Alfred's beacon fire. It seemed impossible that the smoke from that dangerous flame could reach two English prisoners together in a camp full of Danes. But the familiar, brutally hopeless bounds of what was possible had been changed the moment she had seen the Mercian.

You did that, she said in her mind to Ceolfrith's man. She took a breath scented with frost and woodsmoke and man. "So, tell me the truth, devious Mercian. Are you responsible for the fact that the West Saxons now know what Guthrum's army is attempting?" She watched the beautiful silent face. It was brutally tough.

"I rather think you are. You interfered with things and you were down by the river, Thorkill said, trying to escape."

Her hand settled on the graceful curve of his neck, the bruised cheekbone. "Thorkill does not seem to realise, otherwise that rune-carved blade would have spitted your heart." She could feel its steady beat against her own, that awareness of life, fierce and so deeply exciting. "But we know better, you and I, don't we?" Her hand traced an arresting profile, its pure lines and its bruising.

"I would say that not only did you interfere in some way with an execution, but you broke the news of this strike against Exeter."

His breath touched her moving finger, the intensely fine, sharply etched line of his mouth. Her other hand was still clamped over his fist.

"So tell me how you managed it. Did you have an accomplice? You must have. There had to be someone else outside this fortress who could slip back to the West Saxons with the message." Her fingertips rested at the finely flexible line of his lips. "If I had been Thorkill, I would have ended your life without a second's hesitation. As for me, I should leave you here on the ground, right now. I should let you take your chances with a Viking army the way I had to."

But he had already taken his chances and done something so overwhelming, so deeply imbued with risk that she could not even contemplate it.

Her body was stretched out over his, so close, nothing between them except her fine layer of clothing and his rags. She could feel the tight shallow movement as he breathed. The sensitive swell of her breast pressed hard against the wide solid wall of his chest, her thigh was entangled with the heavy muscular line of his leg, her hips lying against the fierce, taut, masculine shape of his.

The fire burned her blood, the fire that had come from him, full of the same defiance and...the desire. It had taken possession of her in a moment she had hardly known, between one breath and the next, through sight, through the first touch, through... some bond that did not exist. Mad and dangerous and complete.

She desired him, this stranger, Ceolfrith's man or not, dangerous as he was. She desired him, and not in a simple way, although that basic simplicity between woman and man was there. She wanted all that hard masculine beauty, the muscular body and the virility that heated her blood. But she wanted more, the very life that poured from him in waves, the aliveness that the last three endless winters had taken from her.

She was caught.

She swore under her breath, moving, all the time intensely and shockingly aware of him, of the fast slide of her tight flesh against his, of the fierce life. Life that hung by a thread.

She pulled away, but not far. Her hand was still round his like a pledge.

CHAPTER THREE

WHEN BODA WOKE, he knew it must be already past dawn. The only sense that functioned was the awareness of light against his closed eyes, the brightness—and the crippling pain.

The light was what mattered. Daylight and... beacon fire?

He could not open his eyelids or move his head. He could focus on nothing. The fingers of the dark still dragged at him. He thought Ash had managed to get away with the message, with the devastating news of Guthrum's breakout from Wareham. He remembered Ash's dark, silent shape gliding down the river's edge. Ashbeorn and the message were safe, surely....

His mind sorted through what had happened afterwards when he had let the Danes recapture him. Thorkill... Something moved him. The pain in his head burst and he fell back into the dark.

When he woke the second time, he surfaced further back towards rationality. Possibly. Thorkill was bathing his brow with a damp cloth.

That was novel… He smelled of flowers with a hint of spice, which was an improvement.

"Of course he will wake." The cloth-wielder's hand moved. She spoke Danish that was not quite flawless. If he thought about it, it made perfect sense. He had been in a Viking encampment when he had died and so he had ended up in Valhalla. And this was a Valkyrie with a foreign accent, but a shield maiden nevertheless, who would provide him with cups of ale and… The light hand drifted across his face…the possibility of more interesting things.

"He will wake soon."

Some still functioning part of his aching brain recognised what her accent was. The jolt of disbelief hit him as hard as the pain. But there was no mistake. It was similar to his own native speech, the accent he had striven so hard to overcome when he spoke Danish. But her accent did not quite match his. He was a peasant. If you were charitable. There was worse underneath. He closed his mind on that thought with the ruthlessness learned long ago.

"You will see," insisted his high-born Mercian Valkyrie. She touched the cloth to his head again. Too near to the place Thorkill had clubbed him. He nearly lost consciousness.

"He is strong," she said. She was an optimist. He could not so much as get his eyes open.

Another woman's voice answered, her accent different, so strong his scrambled mind could not follow it. The other woman's mangled reply stopped. The only word he had recognised was *stud-horse*.

So.

It was good to know she and the Valkyrie thought well of him. Even in this state.

"It is not my fault he is beautiful," said the Valkyrie. But that was too much. She had not only imperfect Danish, but defective eyesight.

He had little idea what the remains of his face looked like after the fight that had resulted from felling Thorkill with a chain, but it was hardly likely to be appetising. There had been nothing extraordinary to start with, only some quality that made people decide to back off and was largely nameless. He assessed the damage. There had to be a black eye at least, although it did not seem to be swollen shut. He still had the same number of teeth, which was a matter for wonder.

"I don't like him," announced a third voice. Saint Chad. How many female companions did Thorkill have? This must be the sensible one of the party. "He is too…too big."

"Merriwen…" Soothing noises were made.

The new speaker sounded more like the Valkyrie. If the Valkyrie had been about twelve winters old and…frightened? The poor daft wench. He had readied himself for some serious attempt to move, when a sentence in mangled Danish stopped him.

"You could sell him."

The movement froze as it was made, each aching muscle in his body rock solid.

He was not for reselling.

He had not risked death and maiming to lose sight of Thorkill now. He thought of his mission, of what Thorkill had done and the deadly anger inside him leapt. His mind saw the dead bodies of King Alfred's hostages in the moonlight and the empty gibbet intended for the one who had not been there, who was still alive. Perhaps. Gainmar, who had been prepared to sacrifice everything. Gainmar to whom he owed a debt.

The Valkyrie's fingers had stopped moving at the word *sell*. Because she was so close to him, he heard the slight catch in her breath. It was involuntary. It would be inaudible to the other woman.

"Perhaps." He caught the small hidden change in her breath again. She suppressed it. But the unsteadiness of whatever emotion had been reined in by the considerable barrier of her will vibrated through that small female hand touching his skin.

"I am sure," said the Valkyrie, "that either the West Saxons or the new King Ceolfrith would pay."

The last came out with a bitterness she took no pains to disguise. *The new king.* Mercia was a treacherous mess of shifting loyalties. The Vikings had known it. They had used that weakness, playing one royal dynasty against another, setting up Ceolfrith so they could take what they would. So where did his Valkyrie fit in?

Thorkill's Valkyrie.

Thorkill's woman. He was intensely aware of her slender hand against his face, the small fingertips at his cheekbone, the scented palm just brushing against his mouth as though she would block the words he could not say. She was so near, slight fingers touching the painful breath that seared his lungs and was too shallow, out of rhythm. She was close enough to sense that if she was clever. She might have felt him move.

She made no attempt to pull back.

"Od was hopeful enough of getting a fair ransom for all…this." The slender hand suddenly moved. The delicate fingers found their way across his face, his throat, the touching different, deliberate as a caress, slight enough that it should have been at the edge of sensation. The light trace of that delicate hand burned him.

Indeed she was clever, and she possessed some considerable skill, the Mercian Valkyrie who must be Thorkill's mistress. He would swear she was aware he had regained consciousness and that he felt the slow touch of her hand.

Her fingers landed neatly in the centre of his chest and stayed there. If she was Thorkill's mistress, Thorkill must be a more liberally-minded man than he had thought.

"I am not sure whether I will sell. It would depend on where I got the most benefit," she announced calmly. "If he is cooperative—" the sharply-nailed fingers dug into his flesh through the tear in his tunic "—I might keep him."

The brief pressure eased off as suddenly as it had come and that smoothly provocative hand moved across skin tightened by cold, by her touch following the shape of his body. Her fingertips grazed the edge of one nipple. He controlled his breath. She leaned closer. Her hand moved. Stopped. As though her touching held no thought, was incidental, might not be repeated. Unless she wished it.

That sense-maddening, accidental caress was loaded with the intent she had given expression to from the first moment and encapsulated in the word *stud-horse*. The small hand of Thorkill's mistress traced its deliberate path, flawless. Yet inside, he thought she was shaking, with that terrible unease he had sensed when she had spoken of Mercia, of payment. Her hand moved over his suddenly warming skin. She had nerve. It caught him, against his will.

"You truly mean to keep him, princess?" asked the other voice.

The Valkyrie's hand encountered bruising, presumably where someone had kicked the hell out of him while he had been unconscious. Her hand stopped.

"All this talking is upsetting Merriwen," she said abruptly to the other woman and then, "Merriwen, will you go with Olga? We will be on the move again soon. Olga, do not bring her back until I ask."

He would swear there was that sudden betraying catch in the princess's breath, but the narrow hand, neatly avoiding the bruise, slid with as much delicacy as before over his flesh. Expertly following the shape of the chest muscle, she pushed whatever remained of his tunic aside so that he felt the cold air hit his skin and the fire from her touch.

"Very well, I will take her. If you change your mind about the prisoner, I could help you arrange something. It would be no trouble…remember that, princess."

The slight tremor in the fine hand intensified. He heard the sound of the other woman leaving, presumably taking the poor nervous little wench with her. The word *stud* drifted back to him. He bit his lip under the scented closeness of his devious Valkyrie. He was most assuredly not dead. He opened his eyes.

Disbelief stabbed inside him. The shock was followed by something savage. It was like watching moonlight, something that delicate. His gaze took in her thick ash-blonde hair, the sleek curves of her body displayed in fine clothes beneath a heavy mantle, her slanting green eyes dangerous as a cat's.

She was very slender. Thin. Wareham under siege had been disease-ridden, and had not been the most desirable place to be, even after the truce and exchange of hostages, and with a Viking fleet in the harbour.

It was impossible that a creature off the dunghill like Thorkill could have got his hands on the woman who still touched him. Unacceptable. Her fine Mercian accent echoed in his aching head, mixed with the brutal denial and the aftermath of that sharp desire she had already aroused by her presence, by that deliberate touching.

Thorkill's mistress made a small sound like shock. Her slender hand withdrew in a reaction so sharp it had to be real, as though his still half-chilled flesh had burned her. She recoiled. Even though she had created the response in him that she wanted.

Still she watched him with her green eyes wide, their black centres blurred, as though all the ungovernable feelings that existed in him lived in her. Behind that he saw the unmistakable trace of what he had already guessed at—fear.

He remembered the disquieting fright in the other girl's voice. He forced himself to raise his head, move.

"Lady?"

"Princess." Her light voice with its educated accent was like winter's frost, the kind that had always damned him. "You should address me as that. I am King Ceolfrith of Mercia's niece."

Chad's bones. He had got as far as one elbow. Growing sunlight stabbed into his eyes. He appeared to have been loaded onto the back of a cart. Probably well on the road to Exeter. He caught a glimpse of what must be Earl Guthrum's baggage train, doubtless struggling as fast as it could after the mounted army. The heavy chains attached to his wrists spilled over the edge of the cloaks and the furs she had covered him with.

Full daylight, which meant he had been unconscious for hours. He calculated all that was possible, trying to force back the pain and the edge of sickness that had come with movement, saying nothing, the silence a means to force the woman who said she was Ceolfrith's niece to speak. He knew his face was in shadow to her. He had had four years of training as one of King Alfred's men not to show what was in his mind. And rather more unsubtle lessons before that.

The piece of moonlight sat next to him in the back of the cart, her widened gaze fixed on him, on whatever might still be readable in the mess of his face. Her own heart-shaped face was equally expressionless. Now. She had covered the betraying flash of fear by reaching for a glass beaker beside her.

"My name is Rosamund."

Unusual. He thought about it. The legendary King Cunimund's daughter all those years ago in the story.

"Didn't she kill her husband?"

"Absolutely. He deserved it."

For defeating her people. He hoped Thorkill had heard the story. He got a smile.

"Her lover did not fare much better. Poison." She held out the fine beaker like the honour-cup at a feast.

"There are all sorts of royal names in the family. Afraid?"

"Should I be?"

He took it from her slender fingers without the slightest hesitation, the movement brutally controlled. He made sure his hand touched hers and watched those incredible green eyes narrow. The instantaneous, highly visible response kicked through him in a reaction that was equal, as unwanted as it was violent. Hell. He had just enough control left to mask it. Then he changed his mind and let it show.

The slender, silver-ringed fingers that had played over his skin clenched. His own fist was tight around the cup, the expensive green glass coldly smooth against his palm. He wondered briefly who that had been plundered from. Probably someone he knew.

Her eyes flickered. "It is a herbal draught. I had one of the healers prepare it." She unclenched her hands. He drank.

"It will help you," asserted Rosamund.

Someone had drained it off the bottom of a midden. He choked, remembered she was a king's kinswoman and he was a king's man and forbore to say what rose to his mind. He took one more swallow. It made some slight difference. He swallowed again and set the finely-wrought glass down. She moved it carefully out of the way. They measured each other.

He was still alive.

"I believe you are a mercenary for the West Saxons. And that you were one of my uncle's warriors," she said to fill the silence he had left.

Which was what Thorkill believed. The next step into the dark waited. Did the Lady Rosamund expect every warrior who had once served her uncle to recognise her? She had no recognition of him, which was hardly surprising since he had never been within fifty miles of the unenviable Ceolfrith. And how, in the name of all the saints, had Ceolfrith's niece come to be Thorkill's mistress? Capture? And Ceolfrith, in thrall to the Vikings, had dared do nothing about it? He remembered her voice shaping the word *sell*.

Ceolfrith-the-ambitious should have been strangled at birth. If he had, indeed, been bartering his kin. The most likely time had to have been when the Vikings had first set him on the Mercian throne. Three winters ago.

"Is it true you were my uncle's man?" She switched abruptly into English as though to catch him out, into Mercian. It was not like West Saxon if you were a native.

"I was not in your uncle's service long." His accent was broader than hers. He watched her wide eyes with their exotically darkened lashes, seeking the smallest flicker of expression in their subtle depths.

"Two winters ago," he added, which was more recent than the most likely time Ceolfrith's niece would have left the Mercian court. Nothing changed in the fascinating snare of that cat-green gaze—and then he caught it. The stiff line of her shoulders suddenly relaxed, as though some unseen hurdle had been passed. The release of that finely-held tension seemed to touch his own skin. It was the slightest of movements, but she was sitting close to him and she had touched him. The aware-ness of her was startlingly complete, like nothing he had known. Like a fate thread.

He pushed the thought aside because it was mad. There was the missing hostage to be rescued and that was it.

Rosamund inclined her head with a dignity that would not have disgraced Queen Elswith at the West Saxon court, like someone with royal ances-tors named Rosamund. It was a gesture made with very careful skill. Perfect.

He had spent years achieving that kind of control in case his origins disgraced the people he knew.

It took a strong will.

"Then you and I should deal well together, since you owed loyalty to my kinsman," said Rosamund who had a very strong will. She raised her delicate chin and favoured him with a smile that should have slain him.

If what he suspected was true, the idea of service to Ceolfrith was hardly likely to be a point in his favour. He watched the smoothly curved body in the opulent clothes meant for seduction, the painted face. The green-grey eyes, tilted by the provocative smile, stared back at him. She had courage and undeniable beauty. She had more than that, the touch of fire that would drive a man mad with the thought of bedding her. The volatile reaction between them burned through the cold Wessex air, naked and dangerous.

She shifted in her fine clothes, dragging at the heavy mantle, letting it fall. She turned her head. "So what are you doing in Wareham, and what is your name?"

"Boda. I fight with the West Saxons. They took me out with the patrol." It was what he had told Thorkill. That much was the truth, true both for him and for Ash because they fought together when that was possible, like blood brothers. It was what had happened afterwards that defied expectation.

"I was brought in today. The patrol I was with was one of those detailed to check that Earl Guthrum continued to keep the truce and his word."

She actually flinched and turned her head, the moonlight-creature, Thorkill's mistress. She must know all about the executed West Saxon hostages. It was her bed mate who had carried out the earl's orders. The merciless anger, the unredeemed rage for what had been done, nearly consumed him. He beat it back. The graceful head with its heavy weight of ash-blonde hair was bent. None of it was her fault, whether she was willingly or unwillingly with Guthrum's captain.

"Princess?"

She looked up when the chains clinked.

Her eyes held the same kind of fury that rode him. All the fire he had guessed at was exposed.

"I know exactly what happened," she said in her flawless, high-class Mercian. "Earl Guthrum and King Alfred had declared a truce and exchanged hostages. The earl promised he would leave Wessex and go back into East Anglia. The king promised that Guthrum's army could do this unmolested. Guthrum swore on the sacred oath-ring. But now he has broken his oath." The smooth painted lips curled in a bitterness that seemed genuine. The remains of anger seemed to reverberate in the air.

"The earl has now killed his hostages and his army has not left Wessex," said the pure Mercian voice.

No. The earl had chosen not to leave. He thought of the fighting that was now inevitable, the bitter cost of it, and more than that, the loss. The loss to the land, to all the people who scratched out their living on it, the ones no one ever truly thought of, who lost their crops and had their wattle houses burnt and who did not die gloriously, but were cut down by someone better armed. Or who simply starved like a dog, or a slave—

"We are on the way further west," said the brilliant voice. "To Exeter, to that part of Wessex which has not been despoiled. Yet."

We. Thorkill's woman. Her small white hand reached out and pulled some sacking out of the way at the side of the cart.

"Beacon fire," she said. "The flames have been pursuing us since we left Wareham. They must be visible for twenty miles."

He blinked to clear the mess in his head, to focus on what was real. The reddened sunlight was enough to make his eyes ache. He made out the distant glow of fire, high on the ridgeline. Ash had carried the message, he was safe, and the king… The king would see—

"Does that not mean something to you?"

The advantage to having had your face thumped in was that it did a good job of distorting any expression that might have threatened to take life.

"Beacon fire. It's a warning system," he said blandly and considered for a moment that he might get the other side of his head knocked in. The princess restrained herself. Royal training, possibly. But she did have a handful of chain. Sudden pain lanced through him, familiar as gall. The slightest change in weight on the chain was enough to send the steel manacle into his already lacerated wrist. Any pain seemed worse when the rest of you was already racked with it. But it had not reached that point which was past bearing, so he gave no sign.

"I am sure you know all about beacon fire," said the princess. "I am only surprised that Thorkill did not kill you along with all the rest."

The more or less functioning part of his head noted the use of the word *all*. She did not know there was one hostage who had not been killed, who would fetch her lover a bigger ransom than he ever would. Assuming it was ransom that Thorkill had in mind. Assuming it was Thorkill, the executioner, who still held Gainmar. Assuming Thorkill's mistress—

"Thorkill must have thought he could get a ransom for you."

So he did. It was the only explanation for the fact that he was still breathing and moving, that nothing appeared to be broken despite the pain. Thorkill the ransom-taker. It was the only good sign for his mission.

"Since he kept you alive, you must be worth quite a bit."

I am not sure whether I will sell, she had said.

The princess took a small precise breath. The slight movement of the chain goaded him. "No wonder he was more than annoyed when I won you from him."

"When you..." The painful mush inside his head could not keep up. He tried to move, but the chain was taut. *"You?"*

"I won you in a game of dice." She raised one plucked and painted eyebrow. The small, business-like hand tightened on the heavy iron links. He fought for breath, not to make the slightest sound. How many times had he done this with someone else at the end of the chain? He pushed the memories back because they were worse than now. But they threatened to blind him, like the pain and the anger that smouldered beneath it, anger at the face of death and misused power, at the utter wrongness of it.

"You belong to me," said the woman at the other end of the chain. "You are mine to dispose of as I see fit. If you want to be ransomed, if you want to get away from this Viking army alive, you will do as I say. You do not cause any trouble, Ceolfrith's man who is with the West Saxons. That is over."

But it was not over. He could still see the bodies of the people who had been hanged, the distorted faces of those who had made the sacrifice, who had had the courage to walk into Guthrum's camp without arms because it had to be done, who had done something that was right and selfless and who had been killed for it.

Perhaps Gainmar still lived, captive.

"You have no choice," she said.

There was always a choice.

Boda's body moved, the response of each muscle fluid despite the bruising, the result of relentless training. And of something else he did not care to name, something deeper that ought to have been eradicated and had not been.

There was a choice, or life was nothing. Less than that. The existence of a slave.

She had pulled back. The chain was still in her hand and the slight movement of her body brought the fire-hardened steel hard into his arm. It had the power to force his breath short, a reaction he could not prevent, that sent his temper far over the edge, into the blackness he thought he had stopped four years ago. He choked back the damning sound in his throat.

His captor's studiedly precise voice did not falter. It floated over his head as though she had heard nothing, sensed nothing.

"You will do as I say. You will not do anything to endanger me or those who are with me. Is that understood?"

He shifted his weight, the kicked-in disaster of his body.

"I know what I am doing," she said. "I am not some drunken fool like Thorkill."

Thorkill was a cold-blooded executioner.

"I will show you."

The chain dragged at him like a goad, like something that might be used on an animal or an unacceptable creature. On a recalcitrant slave.

"I have my own position." *Reputed princess.* "I will make up my own mind about your future."

If he is cooperative, I might keep him, she had said. There had hardly been a doubt through her cultured voice precisely what she had meant.

"It is not your decision," said that same voice, cool as the moonlight she looked like.

He shifted balance. The chain snagged and since fire-forged iron was unbreakable, he did not move back, but forward. There was a trick to it, but he was an expert.

"Just as it was not Thorkill's decision," she said.

The raw mess inside his head struggled to take in the significance of the words. But he was too maddened and the black drive was strong. It had not died. It never would.

"Thorkill's decision?" he said in the accent that was like and unlike hers, a thousand times lower because it was pure peasant. Which was what he was in the end.

"I thought you were Thorkill's mistress." Except he did not actually use the word *mistress* because the peasant was in temporary control. He had already looped the suddenly slackened chain around his hand. He heard the sharp intake of her breath and would have called back what he had said but the words were far beyond that. She moved. He flicked his arm to spin the chain out of her grip.

"You—" The chain came free, but she did not move back as he expected, as even the most imprudent of warriors would have done. Her small ringed hand grabbed onto the chain again just as he pulled. Since she had no strength compared to him, even after Thorkill had finished with him, since no one had taught her how to keep balance and her weight was even lighter than he had thought, she came forward with the chain.

Her action was crazed. But then so was his. He moved to take her fall. She landed straight across his ribs.

"You…" The word she used was as bad as anything he could have come up with, even the blackened creature inside that he had been born as.

God.

He shut his eyes and let the significance of that wash over him with the pain and the blackness. He would have sworn consciousness did not alter. But when she shifted against him, it shocked him, dragging him out of the morass of pain and confusion that must have closed over his head. He had loosened his grip the instant they had fallen, so that neither his hands nor the chain would restrain her. She could have moved away.

She still lay with him, not as they had fallen, entangled, with her weight across the mess of his ribs. She was lying full-length alongside him, touching, her body smoothly fitted to his, curved against it like a lover's.

"Why did you not just kill me?" she asked. "When you had the chance?"

She was holding his hand. It was the strangest gesture he could imagine out of all that had just passed.

He turned his aching head and said the first

thing that came into it. Ready tongue and a glib remark. Never failed. "I always know how to work out my chances. There might have been unfortunate consequences."

The woman beside him made a small sound of derision that left the imprint of her breath warm against his cheek. "As if that would have weighed with you."

He focussed on the glimpse of sky. If the Vikings pushed the baggage train on again today, it ought to be soon.

The silken weight beside him stirred. The movement was slight, but the awareness inside him had already snapped tight.

"No," said Rosamund. "I mean what really stopped you, in your mind?"

How, in the name of every Mercian saint, did he answer that?

"It cannot have been because you were Ceol-frith's man."

Despite the fact that her command of rough words could match his, that was the first thing she thought of, the rules of honour. It was a code most men learned from the cradle so that it functioned like an inborn part of them, a set of rules that drove them whether they chose to keep or break them. He knew he did not think in such a way. Four years of training were not enough.

Since the workings of his mind were hardly something she would recognise, he said instead,

"The chains would have stopped me. Have a little compassion. They would slow down any man."

The impenetrable flippancy earned him another small sound of disgust.

"You are not any man."

No, indeed. He was not even in the running. He stared at the inexorably brightening patch of sky. The commander of Earl Guthrum's baggage train was lax. Not that he was about to offer a hint.

"You looked…"

Savage.

"As though you were somewhere else," said Rosamund.

She was a *hell-rune,* a sorceress. No one else had cut to the heart of the matter. He forced his head to turn and surveyed the enchantress with interest. She was watching the sky the way he had, her gaze fixed, as though she had not felt the moment his heart had stopped because of her words.

"You held back." Her voice sounded unsteady and he suddenly realised she was trembling. "Even though…" She did not need to complete it. The savagery must have been visible to her, the barbarian's quality. The disbelief in her voice had told him more than he wished to know.

"I did not understand." She turned her head, the pure decisiveness of the movement catching him off balance, so that for an instant he did not know what was in his face.

"I did not realise exactly what I had done." Her

hand tightened around his fingers and he realised his skin was damp with blood.

"I should have known what chains like that would do."

No. He watched the delicately shadowed face, felt the fine vulnerable contours of her body pressed to his. That kind of knowledge was not hers. It belonged to him.

"I saw what you did to Thorkill, the mark on his neck."

He offered no explanation. It was not possible, but the green eyes held his, oddly resolute.

"I saw…" Then her voice stopped altogether. The unsteadiness coursed through the slight body pressed against his. It flickered in the depths of her eyes, something she sought hard to hide.

"I am not planning on murder today," he said.

"No."

But the word took a long time to come. That could hardly be a surprise. There was no reason for the coldness that stabbed through his gut. She had every justification for doubt. And he had made no promises about tomorrow because he could not. Thorkill had to be stopped. That truth was already carved inside him. It had little to do with the shadowy concept of honour in his mind. It was the way things were.

Her slanted eyes were fixed on his. Then, against all expectation, he felt the soft exhale of the tense breath she had been holding and something changed. He did not know what. He could not even think about it. It was too deep, like a shadow of understanding where there could be none.

The closeness to the chance-met woman seemed suddenly unbearable, both the physical ache of awareness and the other kind of closeness, the one that had no material basis. That kind was impossible. But she looked at him as though she saw, in part, some of the things that drove him. Not the bitter struggle to push back the Viking invaders, not the present mission to save the one survivor among Guthrum's hostages, but other things, fundamental things that had gone into the making of the flawed creature he was.

That brief glimpse of recognition brought a moment that was like fire. The volatile force of desire that had caught life from the first moment of waking to her touch and the sound of her voice, drove into him. It was mixed with that impossible moment of recognition, doubled by it, by the leap of light in her widened eyes.

"You see," said Rosamund, "I live in an army full of murderers."

He had moved instinctively. The chain slid across his body, drawing her gaze.

"I have seen them not just here," she said. "The world is full of them."

"Aye. You do not have to be a Viking to murder, or to take prisoners." He watched her face, the tilted eyes under darkened lashes. "Or to give them. You can be Mercian, and a king."

They were lying so close he saw the reaction in her eyes, open and shockingly vulnerable. For that fractured moment it was beyond her ability to disguise, its existence a breaking in that strong will, or perhaps the release of something held back so long it could no longer be constrained. Her gaze stayed fixed on his. He sensed the rapidity of her breath, the sharpness that matched his own.

"That sounds almost like a criticism of your former lord's decision," she said. "Have you no loyalty?"

The last thread of sanity kept his response within bounds. "I have to be loyal." He was supposed to have been Ceolfrith's man. "But I am not blind." The sudden anger choked him, vicious and full.

What he had guessed about her was true. The desperate rat Ceolfrith had sold her to the Vikings in return for safety, for ambition, for a gain they would never let him keep. Bastard— A wholly cruder curse word had slid into his brain before he realised he should have reacted differently to what she had said. Malign a noble warrior's reputation for loyalty and they were supposed to respond by threatening death for such an injury. Code of honour.

It seemed a waste of time when there were so many injuries that were real.

Rosamund watched him, her vivid face, her generously curved mouth reddened with paint, with the deep flow of blood that he knew by instinct matched the fire inside him. Her eyes were bright, the emotions in them unreadable.

"The lord king made a politic decision," she said. "He received a throne from his Viking masters in return for offering them a fortune in gold and silver and grain and horses. And a kinswoman. You served a shrewd man."

He watched the proud arch of her neck, the taunting lift of her brow, her bright eyes. The show was perfect.

But she was still touching him and the tremor was deep inside. There was no barrier. In some ways there never had been, right from the start.

"Well, Ceolfrith's man?"

He heard the bitterness, the expectation that he would react according to the rules that governed her life and should govern his.

She was touching him. Her small hand rested on the chain. Outside, someone shouted in Danish through the frozen autumn air. She heard it. Her shoulders tightened. A small wordless sound escaped her lips. He could always recognise someone pushed past the limit of what could be borne. Experience.

He read the anger in her eyes, the harsh fear, the pride and its most bitter and inadmissible shadow, shame. He knew all those demons. He could not stand to see that last, not in a creature like her.

She was alone.

He did not give the roughest curse how Ceolfrith's man would have reacted.

He pulled her small, too-slender frame tight into

his body. He caught the gasp of her breath, felt her first instinctive reaction to free herself. He loosened the solid weight of his hands, waiting to see whether she would pull away.

She lay as she had come into his arms, full-length with him on the padding of furs across the wooden boards of the cart. Her hands rested at his head and his hip. Her long legs were entangled with his. She was pressed hard against him. The fire-hardened iron chain dug into his lower belly. His thigh was pushed between hers in the tangled mess of her highly-decorated skirts.

The position in which they had fallen together was invasive, blatantly sexual. He made no other move, but waited.

The first impulse to take her in his arms before she broke had been primarily for closeness. But the intense desire their own actions had called forth burned unappeased between them. His blood raced and his breath came short, shallow, hurting. Hers was as fast.

She shifted position. He sought to master the sharp awareness of her flesh against his, uncontrolled, mixed with the ache in his beaten body. The first pressure of even her slight weight against the bruising brought pain enough to tighten his breath further. He ignored it, knowing it would settle to something manageable. He did not care about the pain. He had had worse. All he cared about at this instant, with the Danish shouts around them, was her, the sudden sense-inflaming feel of her touching him, the despair and the fear and the threads of courage inside her head.

He said the name she had called herself.

"Rosamund." He did not bother to say *princess*. It had no meaning in this moment. Nothing did except the feel of her body and the things he had guessed in her mind.

She raised her head. Her eyes met his and the bitter shades of torment were there, the familiar demons. Mixed with them, was the desire. He held her gaze, the way he could not hold her with his hands. He was not Thorkill or some Viking, or even Ceolfrith's man. The choice had to be hers.

He watched her, letting her settle, feel him, his body spread out beneath hers. He sensed her warmth, the closeness of flesh through clothing, the harshly quickened beat of his heart under hers. He stayed, every last solid, blood-thickened muscle still, waiting.

Her hand fisted in his hair, the small sharp pain maddening, like an insect bite compared to the mess of the rest of his body. He controlled the impulse to move, the fierce reaction inside him, because there was something so desperate about the grip of her hand. He thought he must have shifted slightly, despite his will, because her gaze suddenly dropped away from his.

"Rosamund."

Her hand flattened out slowly, like the movement

of a creature that was blind. The slender fingers, so skilled at touching, found his face, their path halting and awkward, fumbling against his skin. Her hand was shaking.

"Rosamund..." He no longer knew whether he said it aloud, or just in his head to the bitter, pain-filled spirit he could sense. He hardly knew how to touch her with his hands still bloodstained and the manacles round his wrists.

She kept touching him. Her stumbling fingers found his lips, breath. The fire in his blood leaped, all the feelings locked inside that had no names.

He moved, his body tight and full and heavy round the smooth heated slightness of hers. His lips found her curved, painted, already desire-softened mouth and possessed it.

CHAPTER FOUR

ROSAMUND GASPED. Shock burst through her, desire underlain with the sharp residual trace of fear. An insatiable greed—deep and wholly unacceptable. The small fragile sound of her breath was taken by the man's mouth. He held her. She lay in his arms and her hands tightened on him.

Her lips plundered the stranger's, seeking warmth, touch, the living power.

She knew there was nothing in a kiss. She had learned that from the first. It required no thought.

But she thought of the catastrophic turning her life had taken, that had cut her off from her entire world and left her in complete isolation.

No way back.

She had not realised until this moment just how much she wanted to go back.

She felt strength surround her. Such strength, terrible, carefully bated.

As yet…

She was already in deep. Her mouth moulded to his, to that fierce, erotic, precisely-formed shape.

She had to touch it. She had to have it. Her head angled over his. He moved. She sensed the sudden quickness of his breath, the fast heat of his desire and she was maddened by it. She had never known such mad feeling in bedsport. It had come with a stranger. It pierced her heart. Her hand tightened on unfamiliar muscle. Her body sought his.

She drew in breath, the fine warm scent of the stranger's skin. His mouth moved over the vulnerable softness of hers and the need clawed at her, its very completeness a brutality. She could not give in to its power, not completely. She was afraid it would possess her.

The prisoner's hand settled at her throat, warm touch, the clink of iron, his fingers tracing the skin beneath the neckline of her dress. She made a small sound, her throat tight with it. But she did not pull away. His chained hands touched her and nothing existed but the kiss, the closeness, the smooth, careful, invasive touch of his lips. Their warmth. Enough to drive away the chill air laced with winter. She felt the touch of his tongue.

The response in her was instant, intemperate and unsteady with sheer pleasure. Her lips opened, parted wider. She sought the darker and more intoxicating heat of his mouth.

She still had control.

She had to have control. She had learned each move in the bitter game, every step along the path she so rarely wanted to follow for its own sake, just in moments of desperation, moments like this. She was giving in to a fractured instant of despair, nothing more. It had nothing do with the Mercian prisoner. With Boda. With his dangerous strength and his tough solid body. His secrets and his deep rough voice that spoke of home.

Her fingers bit into his shoulder. His huge, effortlessly capable hand cradled her head. She almost stopped breathing, her mouth still for a timeless instant against his. Then he drew her back into the intense, sense-maddening heat of the kiss.

Her body was already tangled with his, with the heavy chest and the long legs, the tight hips. Close as the shared touch of their mouths. She pushed into him.

She felt him react, the powerful surge that tore through that sheet of tensed, fiercely defined muscle beneath her.

Her fingers touched the edge of his hair, catching all that wild brightness that had dazzled her in the torchlit night. The tangled silk weight of it coiled round her fingers, flowed like water over her hand. She had touched him then on the frost-covered ground, just like this. Beauty and danger. Her eyes were closed.

His arms tightened, the demand suddenly urgent, a glimpse of fire. The first thing she had seen about him, the quality that had spoken to the deepest part of her and made her reckless. She responded. She felt the hard beat of his heart. She ached with desire and she imagined other things…connections of the spirit that were impossible.

She knew the rules. It was all a power play. Simple.

He touched her, the lines and curves hidden by the rich dress, and her supple body moved so competently with the smooth heavy weight of his, the response both flawless and intoxicating. Her skill fed the passionate intensity of the moment even as it cut off the future. She did not know any other way to reach the stranger. There was only this, the strong clever glide of his hands across the fluid lines of her body and the way she responded.

What else could there be?

His mouth left hers, touched her skin, the thin delicate line of her throat. Her body moved for him in a perfect rhythm, following the course set by the warm touch of his lips, the feel of his hands on her flesh through the thin barrier of her decorated gown.

The next step waited. She ought to touch him the way he touched her.

She watched the moving width of his shoulders and the golden skin half-visible through the slashing tear in his tunic, the deeply powerful shape of his torso, the sleek compact line of his hips, the curve of tight muscle.

She saw all that living power, the hidden fire she had sensed from the first, and the wanting of it choked her. She could do nothing. She took a ragged breath that stirred the rich tumbled mass of his hair, and the soft-fierce course of his mouth stirred magic out of her skin.

The desire was tearing at her and she was shaking.

He turned her so that she was beneath him, the movement effortless, the sudden glimpse of open strength deeply shocking. The next step on the path.

But it was not. There was the light touch of his mouth again, the sense-stealing gentleness on her skin, the intimate warmth of his breath. He made her long for things that no one could ever have.

The need cut through her and it was locked on him.

She wanted to touch the moving fineness of his body, to feel the dense living richness of his flesh mould and warm to her hand the way it had happened before in the frozen night at Wareham. Even to touch him in the way she had under Olga's cynical gaze. It had been bravado then, the desire something latent.

Now the desire was full and she, the skilled one, did not know how to act on it.

He was some unnatural kind of enchanter.

His hand touched her breast. Her body arched against him in a response that was not controlled or carefully contrived for the game, and she knew she would do anything for him. Anything for that warmth and that closeness and that bated, fierce, erotic enchantment. She would give herself.

She could not bear that. The horrified desperation escaped her mouth, a sound that was appalling and hurt and utterly vulnerable. Lost. Helpless.

She bit her lip, forcing back the terrible sound that held despair and madness. And longing. Her hands still rested on his body, on the finely bunched muscle.

It was he who pulled away, who ended what she could not bear. And still wanted. She had touched all the warm strength, the power that had struck her from the first and she knew now that she craved it.

She lay on her back, staring at the small glimpse of sky, not touching him and the brilliant aftermath of shared warmth still flowed through her aching body.

She had to regain herself. Men did not share with women. Each took. It was a transaction.

She stared at the small patch of blueness above her head and tried to fasten onto some thread that would bring her back to the ordinary world before she disintegrated. She was terrified of that.

"Do you think it is going to rain?" he asked.

"What?"

"Seriously. It is clouding up."

"Clouding…" At least she no longer wanted to cry. She wanted to hit him. She remembered the damage to his ribs with less than a second to spare and used her elbow instead to lever herself partly upright.

"What cloud?"

"Over there."

She did not look at him. He was lying close beside her, watching the sky, she hoped, as she did. She glared at a scrap of fluff against blue until her eyes stopped aching and there were no tears left. The cloud was scarcely visible, no more than a white wisp. Too thin for rain, and the air was too clear.

"No," she said. "You do not have a clue how to read the weather." Only how to create erotic magic and bring me to the edge of longing and madness. She blinked.

"Maybe it is for the best. Guthrum's baggage train might have got bogged down in mud and we would never reach Exeter."

"Not rea—" She had turned before she knew it. His attention was not on stray clouds. It was utterly focussed on her. She watched the fascinating eyes fix on her face, direct, fine, and surprisingly dark against fair skin marred by bruising and still flushed with heat from all that had passed... Her blood surged just from the sight of him. He looked at her as though he knew.

"Keen to get to Exeter, are you?"

He looked rough sprawled on the furs across the base of the cart, unusually beautiful and still aroused. Bed-rumpled like sin personified. The tiredness around his eyes, the ripped clothes, even the cold iron, were no counterbalance to the natural toughness, did nothing to lessen the attraction. He was appallingly dangerous.

"I do not recall that there was a choice about heading for Exeter," she snapped.

"No."

Rosamund looked at the chains and then she looked away. Mostly she looked away from his eyes because she could not cope with whatever expression might be in them. She would be perfectly all right if she could not see.

But she had not taken into account how close they were. She heard the faint rustle of his movement. She was terrified he would touch her. She wanted to pull away.

"You won me in a dice game?"

She could refuse to answer. She could get up and leave. He was a prisoner, her prisoner. She could do anything she damned well wanted.

"Yes."

"From Thorkill?"

What did he think? "Of course from Thorkill. Why? Do you believe I could not—" She realised what he thought about her and Thorkill. It had nothing to do with dice playing. The appalling word he had used when they had fought each other over possession of the chains…. Miserable barbarian. Miserable *Mercian* barbarian. She should have had him killed, not practically bedded him and let him seduce something shockingly close to magic out of her.

"You think it odd that Thorkill would engage in a game of dice with his…" she did not use the word he had "…with his mistress when you were the stake?"

"Aye."

It was straight. Rosamund could be just as direct.

She said with careful precision, "I am not Thorkill's mistress." She raised her head. She might not be royal, but there was the force of a dozen generations of thanes behind her, of noblemen, every last one a warrior. Her eyes locked with his brilliantly dark gaze.

"No," he said. It was a fighter's acknowledgement.

She should have felt triumphant.

The chains clinked with his restless movement. Outside, someone called out in words she understood perfectly because they were no longer foreign to her.

There was no triumph. That was long gone.

The Mercian prisoner glanced round. Iron fetters. Damage.

"You asked the wrong question. His name was Ingolf."

The bruised head with its gleaming sheet of copper-brown hair stilled.

"He was my lover." Keeper. She watched the arrested turn of his shoulders. "From the moment I was brought here." *Almost*. But she need not say that.

The choices had been set three winters ago by the Vikings prowling round the tombs of Ceolfrith's ancestors at Repton, coming to the nunnery to take Merriwen as part of their settlement with the new king. She remembered the hysterical fear spreading through the community of women and their royal pupil. She watched her hands begin to shake from it, even now.

The Mercian she had so nearly made love to, Ceolfrith's man, did not speak.

"I do not like seeing people sacrificed—" She cut it off because that was too close to the bone. It was not her intention to try to justify what she had done. She simply wanted him to see things as they were. The magic stranger, of all people, had to know. She could not ask herself why that was so. She had already brought some kind of reaction, a fast movement of that powerful body abruptly cut off.

Her rational mind had already figured out how dangerously clever he was. But the rest of her was too far gone in memory. The horrors possessed her, seeking their way out and she was walking again into a Viking army on that fine autumn day, so like this day, the sun beating down on her fine borrowed clothes, her royal mistress clinging to her, mad with confusion.

"I saw Ingolf on the first day I came to this army. He was the earl's kinsman."

She had picked him out of an army of heaven knew how many men, warriors, pirates. She had not been able to understand a word he said. She had only seen that he sat at the high table, at the earl's right hand and so he had to be the choice.

She had set out to seduce him. After she had seduced—

She made a small fist out of her unsteady hand. She had been so ignorant—a thane's daughter who had spent most of her life attending to a much richer girl and then had become betrothed to a well-born man, a handsome warrior who gave her presents and sometimes kissed her hand. She had known little of men. Apparently it had been enough.

She had won and not on a straight path. But she could not voice the rest, not to a Mercian. No. Never.

The isolation that he had so nearly broken waited for her. Her painted lips curled.

"I found Ingolf extremely useful. I might have been counted as a princess." She veiled her eyes from him. "But the princess came from a land as good as conquered. Ingolf gave me the protection of his status." She paused to let the damning implications sink home. "It worked."

And so it had. She had made very sure the earl's kinsman had fulfilled his side of the arrangement and he had done it. He had kept the rest of the wolves at bay.

And for three winters, no one, not even Ingolf himself, had laid a hand on Merriwen.

"You see, that is how things are." She turned her head. It was done. She was what she was, a woman of one and twenty, not a green girl. All those things she had been forced to learn were now a part of her and the thane's daughter was gone. Only the desperate deceiver was left, the eternal outsider with no home, certainly no connection to an earthy, dark-eyed prisoner.

"So, yes, I won you in a dice game." She watched the fine body sprawled across the bottom of the cart, the dense muscular shape and the fiercely carved lines, the toughness and the deeply sensual edge. Witchery.

"I am what you see." She had only to make sure that he understood. "I can always arrange things, Ceolfrith's man, I have had three winters to learn how. And I always win, even at dice games."

She waited for his anger, for the offended pride of a warrior. For disgust.

The exhausted eyes, darkened with shadows and secrets and the smoky hint of arousal, regarded her steadily.

"Well. At least you did not totally waste the last three years. It's a fair skill learning to cheat at dice."

Her mouth dropped open. "*Cheat?* I did not cheat."

"You did not? You have spent three winters in the midst of an army and you cannot cheat at dice? I could be at death's door with Thorkill right now instead of dallying with you."

Dallying did not describe it. She looked at the brilliant chained creature not two inches away from the bare skin of her arm.

"You may indeed believe you are fortunate," she said through stiff lips, "that fate was with me." She thought of those endless minutes on the frost-covered ground at Wareham, the horrifying possibilities for failure. Od with his runes and his enchantments. The click of the dice on the wooden board.

"You are lucky I could throw at all with that stupid barred cup. You are lucky I risked—" She stopped. She could not possibly say what else she had risked, not after all she had just confessed. It was not in her in this moment, lying stretched out next to all the heavy heated beguilement she had touched, not the sordid possibility of entering Thorkill's bed. She took a shaking breath.

"Aye," said the prisoner consideringly. "It was doubtless the cross bar in the dice cup that saved you."

"The…?"

"Some dice cups have them to stop people from sliding out the dice ready positioned to show the number they want."

She stared at the dark eyes filled with knowledge and the hideous possibilities unravelled in her head.

"I daresay Thorkill could not manage the cross bar."

"No." She watched bruises, a darkly stubbled jaw, clothes that ought to have been fine and were not. "Could you have managed it?"

"Oh, aye. Or if not, just a flick of the thumb and you're away."

She thought she would faint. He frowned.

"I do not—" she began as the dizziness welled, but he had caught her and she was lying hard against all that rock-solid strength, just as though the world were not about to fall apart. The bone-deep longing washed through her as though it would be reborn every time they touched. She shut her eyes, as if she could shut out the rest of the world and everything that had happened in it. Everything that would happen, Merriwen, Thorkill's malice, Guthrum's army, escaping into unknown Cornwall, every burden. If she could just lie here like this…

But she knew better than to think such things were possible. There were no illusions.

"You really are a mercenary, are you not?" she said into the blind dark. *A man with your talents must have suited an usurping king like Ceolfrith. He should never have let you go.*

"What you see," he said lightly.

Reckless mercenary with a low-class accent, unbeatable gambler, a man out for what he could get, clever and tough.

He might have been the perfect match for a scheming concubine.

She waited for him to start touching her again. She had just told him who, *what* she was, and the deep, fierce desire in him had by no means taken its satisfaction. She could sense it in the dense muscle sprawled beneath her much lighter weight.

She had seen it in the smoky, shadowed depths of his eyes. Her own actions had invited all that unslaked power, drawn him on down the familiar path.

And now she did not know what she would do if he took it. She could not move.

He held her still, while the desire thrummed between them like an uncivilized force.

The possibility existed that he had told her as much of the hidden truth about himself as she had told him of her own. She thought about beacon fire and Thorkill and dead hostages.

"I—"

"—talk too much." He sounded like sin-rich honey. No, darker, dark and unfathomable like the earth. He felt like sin, too, heavy and tough and beautifully shaped. Warm against the autumn air. The unexpected restraint seduced her as surely as the passion had. The dizziness slowly leached out of her limbs and her head.

"So where is Ingolf now?"

"Ingolf?" *You have no protector.* Part of her brain kicked back into action, driven by the now harshly-honed instinct to survive. The rest of her seemed to have been stupefied.

"Denmark." There was no hiding it.

"Didn't he fancy Exeter, then?" Deep voice. Calm. It was drugging. But he had still asked.

"Hedeby."

"Bit of a trader, is he?"

Hedeby was one of the richest trading ports in the world.

"No." But sometimes one wondered about Guthrum's kin. But never out loud. This was his campaign, dispute it and die. Speak of him and you said *Jarl*.

The other invaders of England, the sons of Ragnar, the ones who had got here first, were kings.

"Earl's kinsman."

"Aye." It was smooth. But something had jarred in the perfect body she touched. *Think*... She could not so much as raise the stone-dead weight of her head. It rested on warmth and muscle and rich beauty. His hair smelled faintly of woodsmoke and darkness, the kind of darkness you could fall into and never come out.

"So?"

She did not want to answer questions. Think. But he kept asking and she had to explain. Not too much. She had to be careful despite the tempting darkness. Just enough for him to know.

"Hed—" Her lips almost touched his warmly-scented skin, the long fascinating sweep of it beneath his hair, the indecently ripped clothes. "Hedeby." She tried to hold on to what it meant in this world, the Viking one, the only one left. There was no possibility of comfort, of trust in another person.

"Ingolf had a lot of treasure to spend." Plunder, riches stolen from East Anglia and Wessex. From

Mercia…but those particular riches had not been stolen. They had been given.

"But he did not have you."

"No. I—" She cut off the rest. No way out of the abyss existed. The only future for herself, and for Merriwen who depended on her, lay in escape. Alone.

"There is nothing else to say. Naught else to do." She had moved, but his wonderfully heavy arm was clamped around her and she could not get away, not without an effort. The necessary strength for that had flown far beyond her. Worse than that, the necessary will.

"Nothing else to be done," agreed the Mercian voice.

Rosamund lay still. Not far away, someone had begun singing in Danish about Sigurd the dragon-slayer. She felt the solid barrier of his forearm settle more comfortably across her body, the slide of chain.

Chad's bones.

She shut her eyes really tight. Outside, the song went on and the air ached with frost. He was so warm. She could not remember ever having felt the crippling tiredness she felt now, not even in those first weeks when she had been too afraid to sleep.

The same exhaustion was in him, a response that was physical, because of the head wound. But it was as though there was also something deeper, a hurt to the spirit, something long-held. She remembered the way his eyes had looked when she had taken hold of the chain in her fright and her madness. Like a doomed soul.

Nonsense. She was merely painting fancies out of her own experience. But the physical exhaustion in him was real, something that spilled over, breaking through the borders of control.

He did not try to control it.

Rosamund sensed the moment the unknown Mercian prisoner surrendered to it, the slight unconscious slipping of that heavy, chained arm, the deeper breath she felt like her own because they were so close.

No.

Surrender was not the right word. It was still a choice. That instant of shared breath, the feel of that small involuntary touch, was something permitted by that strong will.

Nothing else to be done.

They were both trapped for this moment. No useful action either of them could take in the middle of the flight of Guthrum's army towards Exeter. Not yet. And so there was this one stolen instant before everything began again. An enclosed space where the only thing that might be shared was this, the simple presence of another person, like the merging of self into someone else.

He fell, following the pull into sleep, into the loss of consciousness that took away the last mastery of self, into the dark. She felt the moment that it happened and the knowledge of it was far more intimate than all she had done with the passionate, half-frenzied touch of mouth and useless hands.

The drag of tiredness in her own body and her own mind was so strong she wanted nothing more than that same abandonment, the slow drift into the dark, as though he could lead her into the haven where there was nothing, just stillness and the prize that had become unattainable, forgetfulness.

Her body shuddered. The involuntary movement had as little control as the slide of his hand, the deepening of his slow breath, or the steady beat of his heart.

But the movement drove her awake, the acquired habit of poor sleeping that had been hers since leaving Mercia. She lay with her eyes closed and her hands curved round the stranger's heated, half-clothed shoulder, the massive wall of his chest, the softly moving swell of his breath.

Someone yelled out the chorus of Sigurd the Norse hero's song. And somewhere she distinguished women's tones, loud, Olga's strong accent and then Merriwen's voice, clear. Childlike.

She could not possibly sleep. She raised her head because she knew that if she rested her closed eyes for one instant longer against Boda's warm skin she would drown in the feel of it, sliding back into the welcome dark with him.

The coldness of the autumn air touched her

flushed skin. She fixed her eyes on the relentless light.

"No," said Olga, somewhere outside. Her limping Danish was harsh. Olga came from the cold lands of the East Slavs across the sea from Sweden. Where the Vikings traded…everything.

"Not yet. She is with him." That shivering word *him.* It faded into silence and the rest of the words were lost, along with Merriwen's answering complaint, confused and faint.

She moved away from the heavy body. He did not move, his stillness so complete that she wondered for one breathless instant whether it was unconsciousness and not sleep that had taken all that fierce life. But his breathing was even and the light showed the slightest edge of colour in the fair skin over the taut cheekbones. It showed more, the fierce quality she had glimpsed in that moment with the chains. She did not know the depth of that. She did not know anything.

Smoke rose from a distant hill, a lazy plume in the clear air.

Beacon fire.

She tidied her hair and swung herself down from the side of the cart. Olga was closer than she had thought.

"Lady?" The handsome, strongly-featured face was turned towards her. "Is everything all right?"

The flash of concern, the well-meant question, deserved an answer she suddenly found she could not give. Olga's kohl-rimmed eyes narrowed. "With the prisoner?"

There was nothing left either in the readjusted knot of her hair, or the smooth fall of her clothing to betray that she had nearly lain with someone. She thought there was nothing in her face. But she and Olga were in the same trade, experts both. And her own reckless bet with Thorkill, her own loose words, had set the framework. She sought for an appropriate sally, the kind of light remark that should rise so easily to her reddened lips. It would not come.

Merriwen, the span of her attention long since exceeded, launched herself forward and the moment broke.

"She wanted you," said Olga. "The baggage train is moving off again. Now. They are in a hurry."

The smoke drifted along the horizon, scarcely visible. She put her arm round Merriwen's shoulders to calm her, the gesture long-practised, so familiar. Her muscles moved like lead.

"You will have to be careful what you do with that man." Olga reached forward to untangle the folds of Merriwen's cloak. The sun caught her shining dark hair, the concubine's hairstyle plaited with bright ribbons.

"I—"

Olga's words cut across hers. "A Danish *hersir* like Thorkill does not forget. Like I said, watch yourself."

"Difficult loser?" said Rosamund lightly. She moved her free hand to help Olga with the cloak. "At least he is not on this journey." Their hands touched.

"Not here? Lady, I thought you knew. Thorkill did not go ahead with the earl's mounted troops." Olga's hand fell away from hers.

"He stayed with the baggage train."

THE CAREFUL SOUND WOKE HIM, slow, so stealthy as to be almost imperceptible. His brain registered that they had stopped again, the background of noises associated with men and beasts settling for the night. And this other sound, repeated. Close.

There was no weapon. None of the acceptable kind. His fingers closed over a handful of chain before he moved.

A stifled gasp split the air.

It was a wench. She was staring at him with her mouth hanging open. One small round hand clutched a thin tapering object about a foot long. Her other hand was buried in the furs somewhere beside his left ankle.

This had to be the third member of the party. *I do not like him.* Her mouth worked. Nothing came out. Heaven preserve him, it was the timid one.

"Merriwen?"

She nodded her head. A coarse linen veil covered her hair, not just that, but her head and her throat, like a nun's wimple. The trailing ends flapped. She looked like a nun. Except that the drab dress of undyed wool had been pulled tight, outlining the kind of unlikely bosom that formed the subject of conversation in cheap drinking-houses. She did not move.

He put the chain down, keeping his movements slow. She wanted to bolt. The enormous bosom heaved. But she stayed where she was. He was not sure why. Her left hand was still beside his foot. The other waved precariously in the air clutching its elegant shadow. He bit his lip. He had spent quite enough time at the court of Alfred of Wessex for his mind to unscramble what she held.

"A scribe?"

Her fingers tightened on the long thin shape of the quill box.

"You write?" He had instinctively used Mercian because her accent had been the mirror of Rosamund's. *Rosamund*. He lost focus for a moment. There was an unintelligible noise from the nun with her quill case. Her intent brown gaze slipped sideways and away from him and he understood.

The edge of a wooden casket stowed in the bottom of the cart was jammed against his feet.

She wanted it.

"The casket?"

The nun nodded. Her gaze flicked his, nervous as a doe approaching a water hole who finds the space already occupied by a boar with tusks. And a black eye. No one moved for a moment and then she frowned, less like the meek nun, more like the abbess annoyed by a dishevelled gardener. It was a princess look. Like Rosamund's.

He leaned back. But the control over stiffened muscle was not quite perfect. She made a small sharp gasp, but she did not fly. He watched her gaze flicker again towards the much-prized casket, to the solid shadowed lump of his feet in the way. She had not said a single word.

Poor daft wench.

He moved his foot. Every last muscle he possessed seemed to have locked solid. Pain shot through his thigh. He swore without sound. He had to get out of this as soon as it was dark enough. He eased further back. The little wench moved, her hand sliding through the furs towards carved wood as he moved back. Almost touching.

She was like a wild animal. "Got it?" A child.

She seized the casket. Stray light from the westering sun caught carving, the pure gleam of something that could only be gold. He sat straight, despite the stab through his ribs. The carving on the casket matched the pen case, something sinuous with rather belligerent-looking flying angels. His mind assessed the treasure, the way he had once learned, the thickness of the gold leaf, the filigree work, the many-coloured glass fragments and the hint of garnet. Something unidentifiable in green.

Chad's bones. If she took that outside the cart the

next Viking who was not stone blind would knock her skull in for it.

She clutched the box. He assessed the flat shape. It probably held his worst nightmare.

"Parchments?"

The wimpled face became prim. "Rosamund says I am not supposed to say."

Surprise me. He multiplied the cost of what she held in her hand by the number of weeks it would have taken to make. The result was impressive. The contents—

"I could show you," she offered unexpectedly. The lock clicked under the key held suspended from her girdle before it occurred to him that an honourable man might have drawn back at this stage. He did not have morals. The lid covered in avenging angels swung back on its brass hinges.

He stared, temporarily blinded. Then he swore.

"What does that mean?"

"I am not supposed to say."

She raised her eyebrows and he bit back the laugh while the riot of colour resolved itself into madder, verdigris, copper and lapis lazuli scored into parchment.

Rather plump fingers traced the glossed sheet covered in words, the eagle in precious ink and gold, the sign of Saint John, the most difficult to understand of all the saints.

"Do you read that?"

Her glance slid away. Pain made him careless

and the disbelief had stabbed through his voice. But St. John the Divine and this fragile waif?

Her large brown eyes became unfocussed. "I copy."

Neither yes nor no. What the devil did that mean?

She suddenly smiled. It was the first trace of enthusiasm she had shown. He watched the childlike expression in the round face half concealed by nunlike linen, the plain shabby dress and under it the fully curved body she had no awareness of. The smile settled. "I do let Rosamund help me."

Rosamund. Her fire and her quick mind that hid secrets. Pride and courage and enough determination to seduce an earl's kinsman. But he had been the witness to the near breaking of that perilous determination. He had taken the trembling of her slight body against his, all the bitter traces of fear and exhaustion, the physical reaction of someone pushed past the limits of what it was possible to endure. He had recognised that, although not all the reasons. He had understood it and the taste still lingered on his mouth and his skin.

Merriwen watched the priceless parchment with dreaming eyes.

What have you done, Rosamund? What have you taken on?

He had to get the truth out of her, just as he had to get it out of Thorkill. He waited for the dark.

CHAPTER FIVE

SHE WOULD HAVE TO WAIT for nightfall before she put her plan into action. Rosamund pushed her lagging steps forward. She had caught her glimpse of Thorkill, but she still had not found out why one of the best warriors was here, trailing along with the baggage, rather than hell-foot for Exeter and the next round of plunder.

As soon as there was enough darkness to hide her, she was going to shadow Thorkill and she was going to find out.

Thorkill's violence at her back and ahead... ahead lay the prisoner. Shivers coursed over her skin, not from the clear evening air and the falling frost, but from a world gone suddenly out of control.

It was like the formless fear-tinged chaos of those first days after leaving Mercia. Worse. Because she knew all the things that could happen—

She heard Merriwen's voice. *Merriwen.* She should have been safe in Olga's charge. The sound came from the lee of the cart, high-pitched, mixed with the darker, earthier tones of a man's voice. Whatever the man said was indistinguishable. But she hardly needed to hear more. There was only one man. The memory of his uncivilized eyes and his hot, desire-hard, powerful, unslaked body filled her mind.

She heard him say something, low, persuasive. No. He would not. No. All that terrible rough beauty…

He had been asleep. Injured. Drunk on exhaustion. She had left him in chains.

But she knew what she had touched. The power of it still scorched her skin.

"No," said Merriwen. "You must not."

The two shadows made one in the near darkness, Merriwen's small rounded silhouette and the denser, far larger shape of the man.

Merriwen had hold of his hand. "Let me."

Rosamund stopped, her spine jammed against the cart, the bowl of *briw* still clutched in her hand. Steam laced with wine rose, losing heat.

"Let go." *He* said it. Something shining flicked into the air, its compact shape and its erratic flight deeply and unexpectedly familiar.

The girl released his hand. Her voluptuous body snaked forward. The man moved back. Merriwen's outstretched fingers missed. Merriwen always missed. The five-stones had to fall into her hand.

Rosamund watched while the dizziness increased in her head.

Laughter stirred the frost-clear air, unaffected, free. Merriwen was also the best loser ever known, like a source of bubbling joy if you knew how to hold her attention.

The prisoner had the knack.

She saw the white stone retrieved and the two shadows merged once more into a single greater darkness, heads bent, dark unruly hair touching the trailing white wimple. The laughter welled out again, soft and full of that simple heedless joy.

"You do it."

She watched Merriwen give him the five stones, the flick of his hand as he threw, a hopeless throw impeded by chains and the handicap of damaged skin. By kindness. The stones scattered from his hand. He caught nothing. Merriwen had to pick up the mess, giving instructions like a princess, confident. They searched for pebbles in the dimness. He could not find them and she had to show him. The indistinguishable sound of his voice brought out the joy.

Happiness was shocking after a lapse of three winters. Rosamund watched the unlikely miracle unfurl, standing in the shadow of the cart with heaven knew what tearing at her heart. She realised she would give her right arm for kindness. She could hardly remember what it was.

Merriwen possessed four stones to his one. She

was still laughing. Their hands touched. There was nothing in it, nothing beyond the joy. Rosamund knew that without doubt. But at that moment, he turned, as though something had betrayed her presence.

She was not prepared. She stood, frozen to the spot, the wooden bowl in her hand, Ingolf's mistress. There was enough light left to show every last, hideous, tortured thought in her head and he read them all.

There was gratitude, yes, but also the more obvious and damning relief that he had not been forcibly seducing a helpless victim. Envy of joy. Despair and bitterness. An appalling jealousy with sexual overtones where there should be none.

Vulnerability. *Please, not that.*

He said nothing.

"Rosamund!" Merriwen launched herself forward. The unreachable joy was still on her face. "We were playing knucklebones. Five-stones because we only had pebbles. He got me the pebbles. Except I found one. Only it was small. What do you think?"

"Very...very good." She smiled. *Hide what a monster you are.*

Merriwen hung off her sleeve.

"Rosamund and I used to play, didn't we? Don't you remember?" The costly sleeve with its beaded decorations snagged tight. Idiotic games that belonged to a lost world. She could not even see that world, the quiet chambers and the fruit orchard at the abbey. The laughter. It was gone, cut off from her by all that had happened afterwards.

"Yes."

"Rosamund was good." Merriwen turned her head towards the dark shape on the ground. Rosamund did not look. Her hands clutched the wooden bowl with its carefully prepared food.

"Luck."

"More than that."

She glanced down. But she could not see anything, only a collection of shadows, the gleam of his eyes.

I brought your share of the meal. That was all she had to say. Hand over the bowl and go. There was no such thing as *more*. Her sleeve dragged.

"Why don't we play five-stones like we used to?"

"I brought your meal." She moved. So did he. There was a clink of metal. She focussed on the pale blur of his hand in the half light. Chains. "There is some meat. It has wine. And walnut oil." It had cost silver. It was good for invalids. He said something. She did not hear the words, only the lingering traces of the laughter.

Merriwen bounced, nearly knocking the bowl. "We could play five-stones again."

"We cannot. Not now."

The glow of delight was still in the wide brown eyes and Rosamund hated it. The saints take pity on her. She hated it.

"Afterwards?"

"No."

"Why not?" It was a question that could last for hours unchecked. To stop it required energy.

"Rosamund may be busy."

The stranger's voice did cut off the argument. Merriwen sighed. The difficult delight was gone. Rosamund saw it die.

"Busy," she said out of desperation. "Later on." Which was a lie.

After their meal meant finding Thorkill in the darkness. Finding the clue to a future that held violence.

She flicked a glance at the heavy collection of shadows.

"I have to go. Merriwen? Olga is waiting for you."

The prisoner's dark gaze followed her all the way until the darkness cut her off from sight. She did not find Olga.

GAINMAR LISTENED to the voices. They blurred in and out of consciousness, as though the speakers shifted like *shinna,* spectres who moved outside time, near and far at will.

He knew who they must be—the ghosts of hanged men, his own companions, war comrades. He should be with them, but the ghosts of the murdered hostages would not have him. He was no longer a fighting-brother because he had not shared their fate.

He wanted to.

Something touched him in the darkness, the slight contact enough to send the pain welling through him like a greedy wave and the sweat start on his skin.

"Wake him." The voice jarred his thoughts, insistent. *Danish.*

Only training made him respond to it, pulled him back out of the shadows, skills forced into him for so long they were now ingrained. He bent what was left of his will.

"He is not going to die."

The Norse words should have been encouraging. They chilled the marrow from his bones, the last vestige of warmth from shaking flesh. The appalling blankness took him out for what could have been moments or an endless stretch of days.

"…money…" shouted the same voice. It dragged him back, *shinn-seoc,* ghost-sick, spectre-ridden by the hanged faces that would not leave him.

"Money," said the voice again. And the present world with all its chaos crystallised into a single word. All the fighting, all the killing for conquest, even the English disputes for the throne that had preceded the Viking invaders, had been for that. Money and the power it brought. He ought to know. He was a prince of Mercia.

"The means is right here. Are you too stupid to see it?"

The second voice argued, too difficult and distant to hear through the strange pounding of blood in his head.

"Alive," stated the first voice.

Living and bound at hell's gate.

"Feed him. At least make him drink."

Someone picked up the useless body that did not belong to him, that should have been hanged with the rest. The voices disintegrated into confusion.

"He will still die." The other voice snapped into focus—a woman's voice, tainted with fear, sharp with resentment.

"Then so will you, little songbird. I must go."

"And so must I or she will notice," said the woman.

"The flask first."

Wine laced with herbs choked him and there was nothing. The black pit.

SHE SAW HIM. The brief yellow glimmer of the shaggy, weld-dyed cloak in a patch of firelight was unmistakable. He walked quickly, a darker and thinner shadow at his back—the gaudy bird of prey with his attendant carrion crow.

Rosamund stepped back into blackness. Her gilded shoes made no sound. But the catch in her breath hissed. She caught at her fear, forcing herself to control it. The last thing she wanted was to be seen by Thorkill.

She narrowed her eyes, focussing the exhausted mess of her mind. The swift, powerful figure showed no hesitation. Or did it? There was no reason why a warrior should not hurry through his own armed camp if he wished. There were campfires dotting the ground, the varied and brilliantly clashing smells of whatever food had been brought or looted. An obvious enough goal at the close of such a day. A hurrying warrior might even pause to glance over one wool-clad shoulder. The beacon fire had followed them and the Saxons were…who knew where?

Everything had its explanation. Yet not so. She knew how Thorkill moved, the biggest predator among a pack of lesser killers, sureness complete, a creature who killed in the open light. He did not need the cover of dark.

There was a different message here if she could read it.

She had plunged after him before she thought, sure in her own mind that there was something significant without knowing where the certainty came from. She pulled back quickly as Thorkill came to an abrupt stop in firelight. She was in the shade of a hazel thicket, more by luck than by judgement. She fought for silent breath.

This could not be his campfire. It was too isolated, nowhere near the captain of the baggage train, where the food was better and richer and the fires more closely arranged for warmth. And if the Saxons were mustering their own forces, who wanted to be in the most vulnerable place on the outer edge of the army?

But there was Arne, with his swollen face. Rosamund owned the man who had caused that. She sank down on the frozen ground.

"Still alive?" mumbled Arne through a thick lip. At least that was what the question sounded like, as though it were Thorkill and not Arne who was among the walking wounded.

"Aye." Thorkill sat, arranging the hairy cloak with unhurried precision, the slow movement a contrast to the rapid walk through the dark, another person—the familiar Thorkill with his unbreakable confidence. But the tension was there underneath. Od must have known it since he grabbed a bowl, dipping it quickly into the pot suspended over the fire and handing it first to his commander.

"What did you expect?" said Thorkill, the malevolence suddenly visible as though Arne's words had somehow offended him. But the food was there. Hot. Thorkill began eating.

Od ignored the unappetising smell of carrot stew and fiddled with his knife blade and a scrap of wood. He took a breath to speak.

Rosamund edged closer, screened by darkness and dried leaves clinging stubbornly to half-dead branches.

They were talking about Exeter, about the encouraging prospects for loot—and about the prospects of getting there before the regathering army of Wessex closed in.

"We still have a head start," said Od, knife point

snicking into the wood in his bony hand. She watched a diagonal line form, right to left. "We will get there before those Saxon lackwits have worked out which way they are facing." The knife point worked. "Dogs…" His voice trailed off into something indistinguishable. Arne snorted. Viking confidence. Limitless.

Od's knife dug left to right on the wood. She waited for Thorkill's answering boast, a battle-vaunt. He said nothing. Just ate his food. The silence stretched, rippling over the skin of her arms like frost. It truly hit her that Guthrum's army might be brought to open battle, not the bitter stalemate at Wareham punctuated by vicious skirmishes, but a battle that might sweep Merriwen and herself into its midst.

"Even Alfred could not do it," said Od, then looked as though he regretted that fatal word *even*.

Thorkill's hairy throat worked. "I always get what I want in the end, whether it is that whore of a Saxon *princess* who was stupid enough to wager herself or whether it is my rightful share of a war prize…."

She lost the rest because her heart was beating too fast. Her hand closed hard on a hazel-wood branch. The skin of her palm was clammy. She had to *listen*.

"I will get what is my due whatever happens. It is simple." Thorkill leaned forward. The others slid nearer, heads close, like conspirators.

She could no longer hear. Only snatches. Not enough. She pushed forward to the edge of the cover. Dried leaves rustled. She stopped, her body rigid, every muscle locked tight, too tight to bear. Arne's head moved.

"What?" said Thorkill. Arne's gaze flickered.

"Draugar," said Od, naming the walking spirits of the dead. The knife snicked, downwards, straight. "The spirits of the hostages have heard us." A small flash from the blade, slanting, then straight.

Bile rose in her throat.

"Stupidity. Listen, even if we fail…" Thorkill's voice dropped further. Rosamund's breath, like something long forgotten, pooled vapour into the air. She wanted to turn and run. But she had to hear. Her future and Merriwen's hung in the balance. No one but her to take it.

She shuffled forward, down the slight hollow of the ground. If she… Her foot slid on something unstable, moss, slick stones. She felt her balance slipping, like a weight at the top of a slope moving infinitely slowly to the point beyond control where it crashes headlong forward. She could not stop… She was dead, the next of the *draugar.*

Something slammed into her with the impact of an iron bar across her middle. The rest of the breath she had been holding vanished in a soundless white cloud, so painfully there was nothing left to release the tension inside her in a scream. She realised it was an arm only when she saw the pale blur of a hand on her dress. The arm hauled her backwards. She landed with a thud against solid flesh.

She could feel the fast heave of his chest against her back, the unyielding weight of a well-made body with the thickly flexible muscles of the battle-trained, the dense line of his hips, the push of his leg against hers. The scream swelled in her throat.

"Shut up," he said against her ear, if you were feeling charitable about the actual choice of words. Their intent was clear, just like the appalling strength. The faint whisper of his breath touched her skin.

"Back." The word formed in that spine-tingling whisper, as though it had no sound but took shape inside her head. They were so close it was as though she could not breathe air without the harsh, fiercely quickened push of his ribcage.

He drew her with him into shadow. There was no noise, just the smooth movement of living flesh, finely controlled, the sharp bite of iron against her spine.

"What was that?" said the ill-starred *hell-thane* Arne a dozen paces away.

The solid wall of moving muscle at her back became still.

"Spirits." Od's voice swooped sepulchrally. Rosamund held her breath. "Night-goers. Goblins. The terrors of—"

"Find out." The flat command, the fast rasp of

unsheathed steel, were unmistakable. Familiar. Thorkill and his knife blade… The mass of muscle pushed against her disengaged, swift, purposeful.

Don't. There were two. Armed. Three if Thorkill followed.

He was still chained.

She made a grab for a powerful arm. It eluded her, swinging in a perfect throwing arc. Something crashed into the bushes on their right, a loud scatter of stones drowning the fainter clink of chains, the rustle of his movement.

There was an irritated yip followed by huffing sounds and the cracking of twigs.

"A badger," said Od. "Arne's night-walker. The lackwit has woken it with his dainty feet. Look at it."

"Fools, all right," snarled Thorkill's voice. "Catch it."

Badgers were good eating if you had naught else in prospect. The pounding of feet drowned Arne's bitter complaint that something else had made the noise.

"Get out of my way." There was a thud. "Curse the thing. It slipped past. That way."

Rosamund lost the rest. Her own night-hunter dragged her left, forcing her down the other side of the slope and into the masking trees, across ground that was black, uneven, treacherous. She stumbled after, her finely-wrought shoes sliding, intent only on keeping her footing, her breath. Consciousness.

But it was probably impossible to fall. He would not have let her. Not just because his strength was implacable, but because all that powerful awareness was bound up in her. She sensed it through the touch of his hand, through a knowledge that had no name and was too deep for one. No.

She was no one's.

"Let me go. Stop."

He did neither. She could scarcely breathe.

They came to a halt only after what seemed an endless fear-filled eternity.

They were screened in a deep hollow lined with unidentifiable bushes and dead bracken, the scent of crushed grass and unnamed flowers sweet against the more distant tang of the campfires. Isolated.

"Will you let me go?" His presence was no more than a dark shape one aching breath away from her. She could not see him. It was completely black.

"Not yet," said Boda. His huge fist still dripping iron chains was clamped over her arm, the bitter strength palpable. Fury sparked off him like sheet lightning out of the dark. She had not expected the depth of that, sharp—like pain. There had to be pain. She remembered the bruising, the damage so recently caused by boots and hands.

"You... I did not expect—"

"What?" The hot fury struck at her. "You did not expect that Thorkill and his men would have ears? Eyes? The ability to think? Or did you consider yourself to be somehow invisible?"

The stumbling words of what might have become an apology died on her lips. She struggled for breath.

"Well? Or is it you who lacks the ability to think, princess, except of whatever mad whim you have in your head at a particular moment in time?"

A whim.

The cost of looking after Merriwen, the spectre of the future she had no control over and yet somehow had to master rose before her mind's eye. She thought of all that she had achieved so far, of all that could be lost, and her own volatile feelings broke out in a temper that matched his.

"I do what I must, what I *will*. Always. Nothing stops that."

"And just what were you trying to do?"

"I should have thought that was obvious. Trying to learn the plans of a man who has a score to settle with me. Precisely, I would presume, what you were doing when—"

"*Obvious* is the right word."

She took a breath filled with woodsmoke and darkness and the faint trace of his skin not an inch from her lips. Leashed power.

"Then perhaps I do not have your expertise, *mercenary*. You seemed to have no difficulty, whereas I—"

"I am not only talking about what you did just now. I am talking about what you chose to do before. Wagering *yourself*? What the hell did that

mean? What was it about this dice game with
Thorkill?"

"I—" But Thorkill's words had just told him.
Her mouth opened and shut. The closeness of him
breathed through her, heat and forced control and
fury, unknown depths where there might have been
anything, pain or hidden thoughts. Or just blackness.

"It is none of your business."

"Yes. It is my business. I was the stake, was I
not?" There was the faint, cold sound of the iron
chain as he moved his hand. She felt the snaking
metal touch her.

"Is that not right? The goods to be lost. Or
gained?" His uneducated Mercian voice filled the
air and it was not the cold iron she was aware of,
but the smooth flexible touch of his skin, warmed
from exertion, from running with her.

"You were Thorkill's prisoner. I saw you lying
on the ground in chains. I saw…" Her mind
filled with the vision and she was back in the firelit
chaos at Wareham, Thorkill's infuriated venom
ringing in her ears. She had looked at the chained
man at her feet and seen what? Things that had fascinated her, raw strength, rough, sense-stunning
beauty—all there bound at her feet and imprisoned.
And in her mind she had imagined this, closeness,
touching him, knowing how he moved and breathed
and spoke and the warmth of his body. Intimate as
this, and more. She had seen herself bedding him.

"You saw me?" His voice vibrated against her skin.

She shut her eyes. It made no difference in the dark, no difference to the feel of his hand on her arm, the pure dense weight of his body at her back, the solid strength she had been bespelled by, yearned for. He shifted, the sudden slight brush of his body sending shivers through her flesh, not from coldness, but from heat. Desire.

"Yes. I wanted…"

"What?"

Her throat was dry.

"What did you want?"

The fierce question burned through her, the very harshness of it part of the spell and the tough, beautifully balanced body touched her. It was not inadvertent.

He knew.

How could she even begin to imagine he did not? The fire between them burned high. There was the answer, *obvious,* blazing like a firedrake across the night sky.

A man to keep her warm on the way to Exeter.

She made some faint sound, wordless.

"Rosamund?" The rough-edged voice no longer demanded. It was a question. His Mercian accent was very clear. The strength, that bitter inexhaustible strength, held her and the answer was not obvious at all. What she wanted was in no way straightforward. She had risked so much to rescue him because it was right. Because of a thousand reasons she had stopped believing in.

She wanted impossible things from him, things that belonged to dead dreams.

Weakness. It would kill her.

"I told you. I do what I will and that means I get what I want." Her body turned, following the slight movement of his, her skill without thought, long-practised.

"You see, nothing stops me." She took a breath filled with woodsmoke and the sense of open space beyond the trees, the cold air of somewhere between the Dorset coast and Exeter in Wessex. She did not even know where. The man's body cut off the wind, the terrible awareness of space. Heaven pity her, she wanted that, the sense of closeness, of being held.

The need made her move that one last step that brought her close again. What could it matter? He already knew she burned. Entirely and utterly for him. She felt the sharp response to that knowledge in his powerful body. Her heartbeat was too quick.

"It was desire. That is a simple matter for trans-action." The silver arm-rings Ingolf had given her glided over her arms. She touched his shoulder, fully clothed. The flesh burned her through the fine material. Desire. He had kissed her mere hours ago.

He did not move. The small indeterminate pale-ness of her hand groped its way through the blinding dark, across the solid wall of his chest, nothing beyond touch to guide her, the intense awareness.

She felt the swell of deep muscle, the faint push against her hand.

"A transaction?"

Her own breath nearly choked her. She would not be able to speak. Her hand stopped moving. Ingolf's bracelets made a faint musical sound, lighter than iron.

"Yes…" Her voice seemed suspended. She watched her pale hand as though it belonged to someone else.

"Yes."

It was as though she could no longer feel.

A bolt of panic punched through her stomach. The nothingness trapped her. She was alone. That was how she ought to be, but at this moment she could not bear it. A small shard of truth came out, as though that could make her real again.

"I did it because you are Mercian—" She stopped the words. There was silence. Darkness. He moved. She knew it only through touch, through the faint rustle of his clothing. She was blind, adrift. And then his arms closed round her and there was the strength, complete and measureless. The first awareness, the thing she craved.

She felt his heart beat under her hand.

HIS MOUTH TOUCHED the wild mass of her hair, loosened and disordered from running, free of any veil. His lips moved, the sense of touch heightened by the blinding dark. Rosamund's hand tightened against his chest. His lips found her throat.

She stopped breathing, she who had lain with Ingolf a hundred times. Her free hand reached out to the blackly shadowed shape, encountering solid muscle, finding the smooth flexible line of his back, holding him. The kiss glided across her skin. *What she wanted*. She gasped, getting her breath, still too fast, not quite within her control.

She pushed her right hand higher, finding the curve of his shoulder, the edge of his hair, thick, silk-heavy, slightly tangled. His lips traced their way to her face, her mouth. Her fingers coiled round his neck.

The kiss started. Her fingers tightened, holding him to her. He had already drawn her closer. Her body came into the black engulfing shadow, pushing into him. Her slighter lines moulded to him, the melding with that tough muscular form complete, breast and hips and the long full curve of her thigh against his. But her left hand with the metal arm-rings stayed where it was, against the beat of his heart. She could not move it.

Her mouth cleaved against his, keeping her action carefully attuned to what he desired, to the slow, black-hot sensuality, the passion harshly leashed. She held still, the movement of her lips smooth, her tongue. Then she felt the quickening of his heart under her hand.

Her own heart leaped. Sudden, unexpected heat

engulfed her like a flash fire. She gasped against his mouth. The sound was pure need, her response uncontrolled and he was bearing her down. She followed into the greater blackness, the ground cushioned by springing bracken, the thickness of her cloak. Her senses swam. The scent of crushed growth, the cold autumn earth. The warmth of him. She sought it, her skilled hands finding his body, the roughness of wool over dense flesh, the leather belt.

But the powerful body eluded her, moving, heavy and full, too strong to confine, a black shadow. She felt touch, his hands on her, the unseen movement making her gasp, muscles tight. But there was such desire. It stabbed through her, fierce with need, blossoming where he touched. She sensed his harshly bated intensity. His warm flesh dripped chains. But it was the slow path of his hands that held her senses in thrall.

The sense-stretching touch moved higher. She knew the next move. She did not stop him, because she did not have the strength. How did she stop what she wanted? Her fingers twined with his, guiding them to the lacing at the neck of her tunic. There was no sight, only touch, the shared feel, her slighter hand under the broad-palmed strength of his. The suddenly fierce anticipation, sharpened by the blind forced slowness. Instinct honed by training kept her to the slowness, showed her the path that would most inflame the senses.

Their hands moved. Her only awareness that the barrier of clothing was loosened came in an instant that stole her breath, in the warm feel of his flesh against her skin. She arched into him and the broad hand took her shape, moulding the softness of her breast, unleashing need. Her hands dug into his shoulders. The curved width of his palm moved, lightly, brushing the already tightened hardness of her nipple, gentle, but repeated and repeated until her body writhed and there was neither artifice nor control, just the need inside her, desperate and blind as the dark.

The vulnerability appalled her.

She made a faint sound. He drew back. Her hands tightened on the corded muscles of his upper arms. There was a moment without breath in which she thought he watched her through the blackness.

She could not let him go.

Her hand slid down his arm, forcing lightness, a caress that would seduce. Simple. She was horrified to find her fingers were not steady. They grazed the hardness of the iron chain.

She knew nothing about him, only that he said he had once been a mercenary for the king who had sold her into a Viking army.

He was a prisoner.

Beside the chain was the warmth of his flesh. Her hand slid over it. The warmth filled her. She was lost. She moved into him and they touched, full length. She was in his embrace, in the overwhelming darkness. But the blackness let her do one thing. It let her imagine all the impossible things she wanted of him. It let her tell herself that she could feel all those things through the slow careful glide of his hand at the curve of her waist, her hip. On her thigh.

His mouth found the skin at her throat. His lips trailed lower, seeking their way by heightened touch, by the pale gleam of bared flesh in the darkness. She gasped as his mouth found her, then settled where his palm had touched her, settled and created magic.

Her body arched again and she pushed into him because she wanted more—more from the sweet tight pressure of his lips. The touch intensified. She felt the fast flick of his tongue and the threads of pleasure held her, held her in his arms, pressed hard against his strong body.

She felt his fingers move round her thigh, the warmth of his hand beneath her skirts, the intimate touching of flesh against flesh.

She let him touch her, lying on the ground, feeling his closeness, the nudge of his thigh against her knee. She had no protection against the consequences this time. It had no significance compared to the depth of her need. Her heart quickened, beating so hard that he must feel it.

The touch of his mouth changed, softened, the sensuality instinctive and complete. He gave her what she wanted. She felt his mouth withdraw and at the same time, his hand touched her flesh. He had brought her so close to the brink that her body came alive in that single split instant, all the mad tumultuous sensation he had aroused concentrated into that sudden touch of his hand on the most intimate part of her.

Nothing existed in her world except the movement of his fingers, achingly intense, charged with desire. She turned against the smooth erotic touch of his hand and heard the quick catch of his breath, felt the deep reaction and the sharp surge of the fire she had dreamed of when she had touched his body, seen him lying at her feet. Now it was real.

Her hands fastened on the thickly muscled shoulders, massive, warmly flexible, filled with power. Her own body trembled, helpless, wildly stimulated and caught on the edge of fulfilment, on the brink of the terrible nameless need.

He touched her heated flesh, the heavy hand with its bruising, locked in iron at the wrist, chains. The careful fingers traced her shape and she was moving against his touch, insane with pleasure as his finger slipped inside her, taking the heat of her. The need. The breath ripped from her throat, the small harsh sound abandoned, shockingly open, something from deep inside herself.

"Touch me." The Mercian words disintegrated in the dark. They could not contain what she felt or what she wanted.

She was lost in his closeness, the feel of his

body tangled with hers, the way his fingers caressed her, finding the point of pleasure-giving. Her body moved for him and the pleasure filled her, real. It broke over her in a wave and for that instant, there was no emptiness.

He held her and it was as though the shadows of all the other things, the unattainable things, were there in the blackness if she knew how to reach out. But she, with all her expertise, was helpless. She clung to him. His hands stroked the smooth curving line of her side, and there were tears at the back of her eyelids.

She lay on the ground tangled with him, the solid wall of his chest, the long, tightly muscled legs, the taut powerful hips. She was so intensely aware of his attraction, the power that had held her from the first moment. Bewitchment.

She shifted. The warm body moved to accommodate her, the strength effortless. It was impossible that something so tough, so harshly fashioned, should be capable of creating so much pleasure. Frightening.

Intoxicating.

She moved experimentally against that pure strength and the response was there inside her, the tightness of delight coursing through her body, little tongues of bright flame, as though the fire he had created within her was an ineradicable part of her and would flare again whenever she touched him. When he was near.

The fine warmth of his mouth brushed her closed eyelids, tender, like a dream.

CHAPTER SIX

THERE WERE NO DREAMS between men and women.
Rosamund knew that. The person trapped inside
her did not—the *fool*.

She still had a choice. There was always a
choice.

The fool touched him. Her fingers skimmed the
living wall of his chest, avoiding the side that was
bruised, seeking the outline of his body in the
darkness, finding, touching, the fine wool of his
tunic, the damaged folds drawn close at his hips by
the leather belt.

Stupid choice. The thick muscle bunched under
her hand, the fierce strength. Warrior's strength.
Rosamund was always aware of the greater
strength of men. She lived in a world where it was
used, the quickest decider in any dispute—her
fingers traced its shape.

He drew her closer into warmth, his hand sliding
up underneath the long curtain of her hair to settle
at her neck. She reminded herself there were fetters,
that she, Rosamund, was in control. The iron chain

brushed past her. He was still her prisoner—beauty and warmth and dreams.

She caressed him. Damaged wool slid under her hands, the leather belt at his hips. She sensed the shallow rapidness of his breathing, the insistence of his hand at her neck drawing her head down towards his and her heart quickened.

The carefully wrought buckle released.

She wanted to touch his skin.

His mouth claimed hers. Sensation washed through her, remembered pleasure and raw exciting newness. Her hands touched his muscular body beneath his clothes, rested one timeless instant in which her heartbeat pounded in her ears and she thought she would lose control. She forced steadiness in her breath. Her hand caressed the deep flexible line of his flesh.

She remembered touching him when he had been senseless, helpless. She remembered wanting. Wanting *this*.

His kiss deepened and her mouth warmed, flowered under the smooth relentless pressure of his. There was no separation. His size, the way he used his body to surround her, draw her close, overwhelmed her and the need drove through her. Her hand slid down, tracing the hot skin of his abdomen, then the barrier of clothing, gliding across it, moving, finding him, the rich masculine shape, the heavy blood-gorged flesh, the hardness of him. The small sound she made was lost against the heat of his mouth. She felt the reaction of that tough body, so fast, already deep.

But he did nothing to force her on. Her own need was enough for that. Her hand closed over him, touching him without moving, familiarising herself with the shape of his body while the twin threads of sensation ran through her, the sharpness of desire and its darker edge that could have been excitement or fear.

Not fear. Not from her. She let her hand move, deliberate—and achingly, purposely slow. She kept her touching light, intensely attuned to the reaction in that powerful body, not responding to it, not yet, drawing out the pleasure, prolonging it. She had such skill.

She let her touch intensify, the rhythm carefully balanced, using the slight friction of clothing to both heighten and deny sensation until the barrier became insupportable. For both. The kiss broke. She was terrified by how much she wanted him, powerless to stop the need.

Her fingers found the lacing of his trousers, sight blinded by the dark, only the faint gleam of his skin above the blacker line. The blur of his chained hand, the smaller paleness of her fingers. His big broad hand engulfed hers. But she was deft, always. She concentrated on that, like a shield. This was a trans-action. Her fingers moved to free him of the clothing.

Her hand would not move.

He had trapped her. Just the slightest change in the muscle of that heavy arm and she could do nothing.

She could feel him watching her in the blackness, as though he would read all that was inside her, as though he could taste how close fear was.

He was also utterly aware of her desire, in a way that was completely male. It was as well he could not truly see her face, the terrible vulnerability.

He drew her close and the desire nearly choked her, even as the sense of his power closed over her head. The first touch of her hand on his flesh forced a sound from her throat, harshly uncontrolled. She felt the fierce reaction in him, in the way he moved, the way his hands and his mouth touched her, the deep tension in his body. That tension drove her mad. It was what she wanted, to push that feeling deeper, to create it.

She knew how to touch. Her fingers explored him, moving across his heavy, heated flesh, varying the pressure of her fingers on the hot smooth skin, the way she touched that potent hardness, where, seeking his reaction just as she had learned—the only guide sensation in the dark, his harsh movement, slight sounds, breath. The fierce power of the man who held her, and the awareness like flame. It burned between them, holding her like someone enspelled.

Her own senses swam and she was lost in him, in the complete intimacy of the way she touched him, the urgent movement of his body against hers, the glimpse of rough power held back. He was adept at controlling that. Deep mind.

The hidden depths were what she wanted.

She judged the moment for him, slowing the smooth rhythm of her hand on his flesh, her heart beating fast, not knowing whether he would follow, feeling the moment of complete stillness between them in the silent dark, the unforgiving quickness of his breath and her own. There was nothing but the hot press of his body against hers, the tight hot flesh under her touch. She increased the pressure of her hand round the hardness of his shaft, bating the fierce urgency, waiting for instants that seemed like hours, her heart beating as savagely as his, knowing that way she could increase the pleasure for him, telling herself it was skill, knowing in her heart it was more, a gift to deepen the release of all that mercilessly leashed tension, if he would let her.

The bitter power and the hot flesh held still, just for moments, until holding back was no longer possible and his dangerous strength forced movement.

His mouth claimed hers briefly, the latent power open. Her control broke. The movement of her hand on his smooth skin, his heat, on his blood-tightened flesh, was unrestrained, feeling the power redoubled, far deeper, breathtaking. She was lost, so fiercely aroused she hardly knew what she did, all of her being centred on the impossible pleasure of touching him. She had no awareness beyond him, beyond the sudden, uncontrolled movement of his body, the sound he made, harsh, cut off—the bitter longing that was wholly hers.

She wanted to take his future.

"HEAVY-EYED THIS MORNING?"

Rosamund's carefully-scented hand froze over a casket containing kohl. She had not heard Olga's approach. Because of her own inattention and weariness? Or because there had deliberately been nothing to hear?

"I did not sleep well." Not a single touch shared with the Mercian would now leave her thoughts.

"Did you have a busy night?"

A stupidly reckless night. She had come to the women's supplies to cover the damage. In her hand was a bronze mirror, the front highly polished, the back rich with ornament. Scattered around her were pots of cosmetics with engraved lids, bronze flasks filled with scented oils, jars full of unguents for whitening the hands and softening the skin, a bone comb with teeth missing. All the pathetic armour of a group of women from all the corners of the world who were united in one thing. They knew what it meant to live with an army.

"Perhaps something kept you awake?"

A matter of hours ago, she would have joked with Olga, made some ribald remark that belonged to the world of the beautifully carved mirror. Now she said, "Not especially," and closed the lid on the kohl. The snap of wood was shockingly loud, as though something had broken in the silence.

Olga moved in the early morning light with the shadows behind her.

"Not especially? You surprise me."

"I do?" She still had the mirror. Her hand was tight round the elegantly looped metal of the handle. The animal face where the handle joined the mirror stared at her. Cat's eyes.

"Aye." The rustle of feminine clothing. The click of pots being restacked in one of the great oak travelling chests.

"You certainly do. I thought your new acquisition had more stamina by the looks of him. And you," the voice continued somewhere behind her shoulder blades, "there you were, taking so much trouble to snatch Thorkill's prize away from him."

Thorkill. Thorkill with his knife blade and his violent threats. The volatile mix of exhaustion and temper and fear made her speak.

"Do you think I should have left him where he was?"

A sharp click of pottery going into the chest. "Me? It was you who seemed so set on him." There was a rattle as though something would not quite fit. "It seemed getting ownership of a lusty man like that was what you wanted most in the world." Whatever it was rammed into place. "Beautiful, you said."

The morning shadows shifted as though they still held traces of night. Strength. Warmth and power and madness in the blood.

"You seemed taken with that. We all like a handsome man." The lid of the travelling chest clicked closed behind her, covering its cargo of seductive arts.

"There is no one else filling your bed at the moment, is there? I thought you might at least have made your new possession earn his keep since you have got him waiting there in chains."

Bile rose in Rosamund's throat, all the hopeless, mixed emotions.

Olga moved. She caught the quick swish of the green skirts.

"Is that not how it is?"

No. She felt like screaming it, hurling the mirror in her hand into oblivion. The polished sheet of bronze flashed, turning— It caught Olga's reflection. It showed the steady gaze fixed on her, all the dark intensity the jesting words had disguised.

She put the mirror down. Her movements were slow enough to give Olga time to hide the things that should never see the light of day. Olga was her friend. She turned.

"Have I got things wrong?" asked her friend.

"Nay." *It is I who have done that, all this time in this terrible place, you and I like* felagi— *comrades in arms.*

She shrugged her shoulders in her brightly

braided travelling gown, palms opened like a fighter acknowledging a hit in a practise bout.

"All right. You win. Last night was…suitably rewarding."

"I knew it."

Was it relief, that sudden release of breath, or something else? She watched her friend's face, the restless hands busy among the remainder of the pots and jars and expensive little bottles.

"A good investment on my part." Rosamund watched a bronze flask swept up. "After all, the man has talents that would be of no interest to Thorkill." It was a common enough jest, the kind they had always shared. The bronze container slipped.

It was a container for oil, after all.

"Let me get that." Rosamund steadied the tiny thin-necked flask. Not a drop had escaped the stopper.

"Thanks." It sounded natural. Their fingers touched. "We will be off soon. I can pack the rest of this away. Go and see whether your prisoner has dragged himself out of your bed, if you like. See whether he can still stand." Olga's laughter filled the air, rich, earthy and laced with irony. Like old times. Olga's hand was warm, almost hot.

"Aye. I will." Rosamund stood up, taking her time because her legs were unsteady. Her body ached as though it had been drugged, moved as though it belonged to someone else. *The prisoner*.

Her hand went to her lips as though she would find
them still swollen from the dangerous magic of his
mouth. They were cold. Olga was laughing.

"You deserve a bit of diversion. Nothing wrong
with using your opportunities with a man. They
are quick enough to take advantage of us."

"Aye." They both knew that. Her hand brushed
a loose bunch of dried herbs. Barrenwort. Protection from unwanted consequences. The scent
nearly made her vomit.

"But still," said Olga. "It never pays to overdo."
The quick hands hesitated. "It draws too much attention." The second chest was almost full. "But
then, you would not actually want to keep a
creature on a chain for amusement like that bed-
warmer, would you?"

She could not see Olga's face.

"It is as I told you," she said lightly. "I have not
yet made up my mind."

"Well, think on it."

Olga picked up the herbs. The mingled smells of
barrenwort and stinking iris surrounded her.

"I will think."

Rosamund walked out into the lightening dawn,
holding her elegant skirts above the dew-wet grass.
Her stomach heaved.

THE BED-WARMER WAS indeed awake and capable of
keeping his feet. He looked capable of any damned
thing you could think of, including black and

heated seduction. The growing light caught the varied colours in his hair, dark brown and chestnut and burnt copper. She was amazed by how much she still wanted him.

"Throw them."

Merriwen and knucklebones. Merriwen's persistence once she had latched on to an idea was mindnumbing. He bent down. Merriwen emerged out of shadow scattering pebbles. They had to pick them out of the wet grass before he could start. She watched his patience. She watched the pull of the dark woollen cloth across the smooth supple line of his side, the way his body moved.

"Now," squeaked Merriwen.

The pebbles flew, scattering in a perfect arc, effortless and controlled the way he had thrown stones to distract Thorkill's men. What was locked in his head? What did a man like him want? What in heaven's name was he doing here? The chain snagged, catching him unaware.

She walked forward.

"Oh," said Merriwen. "You missed them."

"Ill luck. You try."

"Later." The sound of Rosamund's voice made them both turn. Merriwen's mouth was a round O of surprise, but he already knew. He must have heard her approach across the grass or seen her, or both. King Ceolfrith would never have let him go.

"One more throw." He dropped the stones. "I can win."

"No time. We will be leaving any minute."

"Later, then. With him."

How could anyone promise that?

"Go and get ready, sweet."

Merriwen went, reluctantly. His huge shadow moved on the grey grass.

"Rosamund?" There was a clink of iron, the swing of the chain. The chain that had caught just now on the ground, snapping tight against his wrist.

She stared at the manacle. She was not entirely sure how you got such things undone. There was some sort of iron pin. Or was it a rivet?

"Rosamund..." He saw the direction of her gaze. His dark-witched Mercian voice stopped speaking—silence. Silence with such things hidden in it. She broke it.

"I have some things for you." She thought one required a hammer and chisel. Apparently.

His wrists underneath the iron bands were carefully strapped with linen. She and Olga had done that while he had been unconscious. She examined the pale linen for signs of fresh blood. There did not appear to be any, only the slight darkening of the herbal salve they had used. She and Olga had at least done that. Why did she not know how you got out of shackles? She stared.

"Things?"

He was angry. That was good. She might be able to do this if he was angry. Justifiably angry.

"In the back of the cart."

Half the contents of a smithy in case it proved useful. He was the kind of man who would know what to do.

"Rosamund, what are you talking about?" She caught the flick of black rage. "What—"

He was going to say something about last night and carnal madness. She thought he was trying to control the rage in case it hurt her. She had never wanted him so much. The chain caught the light. She had been glad it was there last night. Because she was still afraid of him.

Or of herself.

"You will find all you need." Her voice babbled, cutting off his. There was fresh clothing, a skin flask of ale, a leather bag containing strips of dried meat and a cheese, and a pouch with coins minted in Ceolfrith's name. Appropriate. "You can take it."

When he saw, he would understand. A clever man would pick his time, stray into the first patch of woodland, avoid the sentries and the scouts and be gone.

This man was particularly clever. Never see him again. Never have that touch. Things that had no right to exist. That were selfish. *Nothing wrong with using your opportunities,* said Olga in her head. *Using…*

"I have to go and see to Merriwen," she said. "It will be a while before I come back." She could not manage the word *later*.

IT WAS A LOT SIMPLER to move without chains, less possibility of some sudden betraying noise. Although since it was not the first time he had been stuck in fetters, he was adept at managing the restrictions.

Boda watched his quarry. The fast swish of her skirts vanished behind one of the carts. He gave her three seconds and then followed. She was in a hurry.

He gave no indication of haste, or of much purpose, nothing that would draw attention to himself.

She stopped twenty paces ahead, choosing a patch of shade even though it was still freezing out of the sun. She was no more than half-visible beside the trees.

She showed no signs of moving on.

Hang it.

He paused beside the ashes of the nearest fire and struck up a conversation with its owners. It was easy enough. They were belligerent with a Mercian on principle, but his deliberately accented Danish had them laughing. Then he helped them. He was a better hand than them at backing a reluctant horse between the traces of the cart.

He glanced at the woman without seeming to. *Move on, Olga.* She was reluctant. She had not seen him where he stood screened behind the horse and wagon. She simply did not want to go any further in the direction her hurried steps had taken her.

Perhaps there was no surprise in that. She was headed toward the centre of the train, the most heavily protected part, the section that held some of the earl's goods. Go near them at your peril.

He flexed his shoulders. His wrists ached. Someone made a jest about prisoners he was not supposed to understand. The familiar flicker of anger rose in his belly. He suppressed it, soothing the horse. Simple when your hands were unencumbered.

Rosamund's doing. She had set him free. It amazed him, the devices she had thought necessary to get out of chains. He was still not quite sure what she had imagined he was going to do with a rolling swage. But Rosamund hardly had his experience of escaping fetters.

Last night she had seemed afraid of him at first. Or afraid of what she did. And then there had been no fear, only a kind of compulsion. And he had not thought at all, only of the way she had responded, the urgent need and the pleasure that could meet it, if only for an instant without time.

But Rosamund was the kind who thought.

She had chosen to set him free, not for timeless madness, but because she wanted him gone. Because of regret.

The need had seemed real. The regret definitely was.

The horse tossed its head. The accompanying curses were in Danish, succeeded by speculation about the coming evening's foraging party and what might be expected in the way of local plunder.

In this world, timeless instants knew their place.

He wondered who was detailed to lead the foraging party. He worked slowly. Like most people, his companions considered stupidity and probable deafness went with powerlessness, so they talked in front of him. All he had to do was listen.

Thorkill was going to be a busy man.

Boda fastened the last buckle on the harness, glancing up. The woman Olga was gone. He drained the horn of watered ale he had cadged without haste and returned it.

She had not gone far. Not quite as far as the Jarl's heavily guarded possessions, but close enough that no one was going to dispute the details. She had made her way through tree-shadow to a covered wagon. She checked a leather pouch at her waist, the gesture nervous. A hand reached down from the cart to pull her up. The sleeve was heavily braided. Well, that was a lovers' tryst and a half.

The location was a good choice. Impossible to get closer to the cart without attracting the attention of the earl's guards. Not this time. Not yet.

"DO YOU THINK he is alive?"

Since the likely answer to that was not acceptable, Grimm did not give it. He belly-crawled the last few paces, avoiding a crop of thorn bushes. He reached the top of the ridge, keeping flat against the skyline, his body screened by blackthorn, holly and a crop of half-dead nettles.

"Good view," he said instead.

It was. The entire length of Earl Guthrum's baggage train lay sprawled across the Wessex valley below. Raidwulf's solid bulk landed beside him, flattening a patch of grass containing thistles rimed in white.

"This is comfortable."

"We should be down there round the campfire."

The answer to that was succinct. Both of them assessed the Viking force spread out below. The dawn light grew by slow degrees, the sky almost colourless. It was bitterly cold, but that was an advantage to the travelling army. Only the frost-hard ground made mobility for such an operation possible.

"Not a bad effort," said Raidwulf with all the understatement proper to a pithy northerner from York.

The baggage train was massive, larger even than Grimm had expected. "They have a lot to carry," he said. There was the booty derived from an invasion and the sweetener that had been part of the broken peace. Wessex had paid in carefully weighed silver.

"There are my silver goblets down there." Not to mention the rest.

"Could weigh them down, that," said Raidwulf. "You are a problem, you rich southerners."

Raidwulf had lost everything. York, great trading city of the north, was now Danish. The land of

Northumbria might never be recovered. Grimm knew all about that. Only Wessex still struggled in what sometimes appeared to be its death throes. Most people thought Grimm had always lived in Wessex.

Men and horses, beasts and wagons moved and reformed across the ground below.

"Orderly." The organisation was skilful. It nearly cancelled out the disadvantage of a cumbersome lack of speed. The seemingly chaotic lines were in fact held together. There were enough unencumbered troops to protect them, an advance patrol, a rear guard. He and Raidwulf had bypassed scouts.

The operation was as focussed and as utterly filled with purpose as anything the Danish earl did. Nothing stood in the way of that formidable will. The bodies hanging from the gallows-trees at Wareham attested to that. He could no longer see the moving figures below, only the distorted faces in the pitiless sunlight. Men he knew.

"Don't even think about it you daft beggar."

Northerners had a sweet way with words. He had to stop himself from being so stupid as to reply in kind. He carefully unwrapped his right hand from a sword hilt engraved with runes. The oath-ring suspended from the pommel brushed his hand. He had sworn himself to the king. What interested Alfred was not vengeance but the survival of a kingdom.

When properly viewed, war was a matter of

strategy, a great game where the pieces moved and it was the overall picture that decided survival.

"Back." He gestured to Raidwulf. They had their answer. Except…there was something about the moving figures. Perhaps there was a weakness. Grimm was good at puzzles.

They did not speak until they were back with the horses hidden among the stand of oak and birches. Well clear.

"So," said Raidwulf. "Too many for us until your king has the *fyrd* mustered again."

"Yes." Nothing short of an entire army would be any use. No chance for the small Saxon troop remaining in the field. Everyone knew that and now it was doubly clear. Everyone?

"They were nervous." Something clicked in his brain. "Nervous and—"

"Hungry," supplied Raidwulf in what he was convinced passed for southern English.

"Aye." The meagre supplies at Wareham had been yet another encouragement for the Viking earl to keep the peace and quit Wessex. "Guthrum would have counted on living off the land all the way to Exeter."

"But there is nothing left," said the northern voice. "Everyone in their path has fled. No more silver goblets and no food because that foreigner helped word get out before Guthrum moved."

Every mortal thing south of the River Humber

was quite properly foreign to Raidwulf. But there was only one foreigner in this case. The Mercian.

"Yes."

"You're thinking again."

So he was. A puzzle that made no sense. One missing body among the hanged and one missing man from the Wareham patrol. Both had to be lost. Logic told him so. Their own particular Mercian foreigner had as much chance of being alive amongst that massive, calculatedly competent army as the corpse of the last hostage.

"What was his name?" said Raidwulf.

"Boda."

Raidwulf grunted and swung himself into the saddle. "The most we could challenge would be a troop the size of a foraging party."

And so the first piece of the puzzle was about to fall into place.

"Just what I was thinking."

He got the kind of grin that spelled trouble. If Guthrum's baggage train was nervous now, it was going to become a lot more so.

And Boda, if he was still alive, would know where to find the king's men. He was already devising the message. The shapes of the runes flicked through his head, each in its destined place making an ingenious whole. Perfect. If only the messenger was there to receive it.

The only consolation was that Boda was the kind that was born to be hanged.

Like the hostages. His hand did not touch the sword. Not yet.

Raidwulf led the way back through the trees.

"You want those silver goblets back."

"What else?"

THE DAFT WENCH WAS IMPOSSIBLE.

"Are you listening?"

He was thinking of Rosamund. Merriwen, waving her blasted parchments under his nose, was a miracle of sense by comparison.

"This bit has to be blue." Merriwen's ink-stained finger pointed. "See? If you watch what you are doing, it all works out."

Boda wondered if she had ever given such helpful advice to her mistress.

He squinted against the low evening sunlight. Thorkill had to return from the northern path....

"Blue."

He passed the ink jar. The contents were mostly crushed lapis lazuli. Next to it was a stash of powdered gold. How in pity's name had she managed to get hold of such things?

Or how had Rosamund managed it.

Rosamund.

He wrenched his mind back to now, to the fading evening light on the pale ribbon of the track that led inland and northward, doubtless towards somebody's village and food, towards cover that might conceal game. Cover that might conceal...

"I need the other quill and the red. No, *that* quill." She had a sharp turn of command for a maid. He suppressed the grin, producing a cut goose feather and something that contained dragon's blood.

Colour flowed over blank whiteness. They were working on the eagle, sign of John, the most transcendent of saints… His own particular piece of transcendency approached. He knew. Without looking, he simply knew.

Damn it.

The inland track was still blank. He raised his head.

"You are still here," said Rosamund. The depth of her reaction was painfully unguarded, genuine. She sounded not so much surprised as stricken.

"I did not expect it."

She meant she did not want it. To him it was evident in every taut line of her small form. In her face. It was blunt enough. But that was how he dealt with things. She was as sensible as Merriwen, after all. It was only he who was the fool.

And Thorkill was out somewhere on the inland road.

She stood in the sunlight, every last inch the princess, wearing some fancy thing with multi-coloured braid and her rich hair wound round her head. She was desperate.

"You would miss your bargain. I can't go yet—" The first shout made itself heard before he had finished speaking. Hoofbeats pounded down the track.

He got to his feet without hurry. Rosamund stepped back, even from that.

"What is it?"

"What is what?" said Merriwen, deep in dragonsblood.

"I will see." And so it appeared perfectly natural when he joined the curious crowd pressing towards the track.

Chad's bones. The enemy really was out there, shadowing Guthrum's army. But they could not be many yet. Not enough for a major attack.

He assessed the strength of Thorkill's troops, the exact damage that had been caused and tried to calculate in his head. Inland and north.

He heard Rosamund's rapid intake of breath, suddenly close. She had followed him even though she must have wanted to stay with her charge.

"The Saxons did that." Her wide gaze fixed on the mauled remains of Thorkill's foraging party. "King Alfred," she said, as though it were a name to conjure demons and night-shadows.

"Well, someone spoiled supper." It could not be the king yet. "Go back." Thorkill looked fit to be tied, blood on one heavily-braided sleeve, not his own, judging from the ease of his movement. "I will—"

Thorkill saw her.

Boda shoved her backward and Rosamund's

small weight vanished as the sudden surge of the crowd swallowed her. Thorkill's deep-chested bay shied under the spur, temper as bad as its master's. The lashing hoofs missed him by a margin that held death and he rolled out of the fall, gaining his feet fast. But Thorkill did not pursue. The remains of the troop swept past.

"What is going on?" She had come back. That was unexpected. Senseless. Her jewel eyes were angry. "That was deliberate. He could have killed you."

"Nay. It was just a love bite. Thorkill has other things on his mind."

"Such as?" Her green eyes glittered not just with fury, but with the edge of recklessness. She was in an appalling position, most of it because he was here. She could not face the danger alone. The task stretched out before him, already set. He could not fail and neither could he turn away.

"Not here."

Her reckless gaze held his, feverish and over-bright like someone trapped.

"Later," she said.

Later meant the dark. It meant getting the truth out of her.

CHAPTER SEVEN

BODA WAITED until she was alone. The campfire at her feet was sullen. Merriwen was sleeping in the back of the cart. The princess appeared to have scorned it. A heaped bed of bracken waited by the flames. Thin cloud cover had made the night warmer, but it was scarcely inviting. He wondered what drove her. He would find out. Boda stepped into the circle of light.

She was wrapped in her heavy mantle, tidying ink jars into the oakwood casket. The parchment box lay close by. Even the reluctant firelight showed traces of the gold. She looked up.

The suppressed desperation was still there, like the shades of a nightmare clinging round her. Boda could sense it as though it settled on his own skin.

He began.

"She should keep that casket hidden." He took his place on the ground next to it, wrapped in the woollen cloak she had found him.

Her hands moved in the half light. "I suppose it is worth something."

"The gold is pure, well wrought. A month to

make all that filigree work. Three days at least to set the gems on one side. They have incised foil beneath to show the light."

"They…" Her hand stayed suspended over a jar and she was caught. "How do you know all that?"

"I had an acquaintance who was a goldsmith."

"And he taught you?"

The goldsmith had been female. What he had learned from Gemma was the depth of resourcefulness that women hid, the courage that matched men's. She had been an artisan, far beyond the reach of a creature lower than an outlaw, and he had been sixteen. Perhaps. He had understood nothing at that age. She had married the man who was his blood brother.

"We all learn as we go." He set the conversation squarely to its course. "Merriwen seems keen on her parchments."

"So she is." The jar slotted into its appointed place. "She should have been a Viking. She looted all this from a nunnery."

"Enterprising."

"I—you never—" She stopped, and even though he waited, whatever she would have said was held back. Probably as well. He tried to think like a courtier.

"You had your education at this nunnery."

"Of course."

He studied her, each flawlessly presented line, the intense, completely maddening beauty.

"So. Were you equally keen on parchments?"

"I never wished to be a scribe. But I have always read books and there turned out to be a good enough supply there."

Books at home before the nunnery.

"And what about you?" she said. "Do you read fine tales?"

Whoreson books. They were enough to drive him crazed, lying about wherever the king was, as often as not surrounded by drifts of loose parchment covered in trailing marks, in the king's own hand, or some scribe's. Traps just waiting to catch him out.

Rosamund's jewel-bright eyes watched him out of the dark, her sleek head tilted on an angle that was so graceful it had to be unconscious, part of her. Good family.

"I read nothing. I have trouble understanding how." It was not unusual for the mercenary she thought him. But it meant more than that. She ought to know the truth about him, where he could give it. The literary gems he was familiar with were not fine tales, but riddles and jests, guessing games of the more ribald sort that began with such immortal first lines as *a strange thing hangs by a man's hip*. Or the one about the drunk with two wives.

"The only proper tale I could listen to was the tale of the phoenix." He had no idea why that had come out of his over-loud mouth. It had no relation to his purpose in speaking.

"The phoenix," said Rosamund. "The creature whose life was renewed because it held the residue of fire in its claws. It sought its native land, its home filled again with sunlight."

Her green gaze caught with his and he could hear it in her fine voice, the sound of his home, the light in the dark.

"That tale, that…" The bright green gaze misted, like the onset of weeping. "I hated it."

The sheer violence of her words cut the air. The grudging light of damp wood on the Wessex earth flickered, other voices carried faintly on the night air. Someone swore. There was laughter.

"There is not much purpose in reading." She pushed the box away, the movement of her hand dismissive. "The least purpose of all in that story." Her voice in the darkness matched the dismissiveness of the gesture. The violent feeling vibrated beneath. That was the heart of the matter. That was what he had to take because there was now no other way. Thorkill's little tantrum had confirmed that.

"And Merriwen," he said. "What of her?"

She became still. "Merriwen has her own way of…her own talents."

"Aye." He watched the motionless figure, caught in midmovement, its tension and its unattainable grace. "Copying letters on parchment, creating pictures, takes a fair skill. Someone invested a lot of time in accommodating her interests."

She thought about her answer. He could see it in

the flicker of her eyes. He simply waited, the way he had been taught. *Never push hard until you have to. Always give the other person the chance to fill the silence.* Grimm's words, master of spies. But the unbreakable patience had been taught much earlier, in a far different way. It was now an ineradicable part of him.

"It is one of the few things she enjoys."

The sidestep was no more than he should have expected. She sought to block him from one line of questioning, but at the cost of opening up another, just as vital.

"It is one of the few things she is capable of doing. Rosamund?"

The criminally vicious depth of the need to hear her speak, the bitter desire for a response that was unforced, was something new. She was not looking at him. His lungs had filled with the frigid air when she spoke.

"Yes."

The release of his breath sent white vapour into the firelit dark, the reaction too strong. It did not matter. She did not see.

"Merriwen is… Merriwen does not…" He watched her struggle to speak.

"Does she read or not?"

"Yes, but…" The fragile line of her shoulders was tight, the tension enough to break. "You have seen…" The fine voice choked.

"What? That your difficult charge does not live

in this world? That she is no more able to fend for herself than a child. That the silly wench must be at least sixteen winters with a bosom fit for a drink-house jezebel and no awareness of that either? That a little daft creature like her is one step away from dead meat in the middle of an army?" Which was hardly the way a princess might have put it, but at least it was said for her.

The rigid shoulders loosened. "Yes," said Rosamund. "Chad's bones." There was a small silence. "Most precisely that." She stared at the dark.

Then she said, "Why are you like no one else?"

"Me?" The question took him off balance for an instant. *Because I am so skilled at pretending, just like you.*

"Must be mercenary's training," he said promptly. "It might leave something to be desired. But we do speak our minds."

It was only princesses who tied themselves in knots over the realities of life, kings and thanes. Noblewomen who were brought up in houses containing books.

"No. You are still extraordinary."

But that was too far-fetched to be serious. Underneath, he was bog-ordinary.

"But you are right in what you say," said Rosamund. "Merriwen lost her parents very young and somehow…somehow she never grew into this world as other people do. She does not know how to cope."

Which made an unlikely choice for a maid and companion to a princess. He made no comment on that. There was little point in forcing the issue. He wanted Rosamund's thoughts.

"So Merriwen is a liability." The graceful head with its rich, pale blonde hair turned. "But she is my liability. We came into this together, and together we stay."

And so he had reached it, a part of the truth laid bare in her reckless, steel-hard eyes. Poor, brutally trapped woman with her courage and her resourcefulness and her hidden anger.

He knew exactly what it was like to be trapped with no escape, a live beast in a cage.

He could not stand that.

He realised he must have shown some unguarded reaction only when her slight body stiffened like someone readied for sudden movement.

She was quite possibly still afraid of him.

He did not know what was visible in the bruised wreck of his face. Anger, and underlying it the marks of unrelieved bitterness, all the remembered blackness of his life, probably.

The barbarian's quality.

Rosamund made no further movement. Neither did he. It was hard enough to breathe, to force the control back over all she had seen.

"That is how my life is," she said. "There is nothing else. I would not be able to manage it." She took a breath that was unsteady. "You should have gone."

"No." Fool for saying that.

Rosamund watched him, while the harshness of the word vibrated in the air. She was tense, the slight curves of her body half-hidden by darkness and the heavy folds of her mantle, a secret richness to be guessed, shaped by thought and desire. By the harsh tension in his own body.

He still desired her beyond measure. He would never forget a single moment with her.

But he had no idea what was in her head. She just waited like someone who had little choice, because that was the way the entire world worked, whether it was Viking or Saxon did not matter. No one occupied themselves with the fate of the powerless.

Atheling sceolan to beaduwe and to beahgife.
Theof sceal gangan thystrum wederum.

At the top was the noble with the power of arms and the gift of riches, at the bottom the thief in the dark weather, right next to the demons in the fens and the muddy marshland. Everything belonged in its place. Never meddle with it.

"I am not going yet." He tempered it. "As I said, that would be a poor bargain."

The tired eyes in the pale face fixed on him. "You are mad." She spoke softly so that her voice would not carry too far. "Thorkill would like to hang you."

"Well, he is a dab hand at that." *And he was going to pay for it.* He kept his face expressionless. Her eyes narrowed.

"I would not worry," he said at his blandest. "I was born to be hanged, me."

"Don't." She was close, her voice and her gaze intent. "Whatever it is that you want, do not get in his way. He thinks…" She hesitated and the direct gaze dropped. Amid the exhaustion, he caught the sudden edge of fire.

"Thorkill knows the nature of the bargain. When I saw you in chains that first night at Wareham, I told him I wanted what was obvious to anyone who looked on a man like you."

The unexpected flame caught, burned him, his response unchecked, no less intense for the fact that it was mixed with the bitter remnants of anger. He sought to control it because she was so vulnerable. Lost. He knew it even through the anger.

"What I wanted was something to warm my bed," said Rosamund.

"The *stud-horse*."

Her voice filled his memory, the cool precision of it floating in a sea of pain. *It would depend on where I got the most benefit. If he is cooperative, I might keep him.* And her small slim hands on his body, the skilled lightness of her touch.

She had great skill.

"Yes." The precise single word excused nothing. She took a steady breath. "Thorkill believes that, I am sure of it." Her breath was not at all steady.

"After all, it is the way of the world," she said.

She, of all women, had been given reason to believe that.

"You do not—"

"I won a chained prize so that I could have my will. Is there anyone who would believe otherwise?"

"It would not be that difficult." Possibly not a noble *hersir* on the power-dispensing end of the equation. But a descendant of thieves scarcely one step removed from marsh-dwelling demons was another matter.

Her small scented hands fisted in the dark. "Thorkill has to believe it," she said rapidly. "*Everyone* has to."

That intense word, *everyone,* spoke straight through the screen of what she claimed she had done. She faced things alone. That was something he understood. So deeply that he hardly cared if everything she had claimed was true, if the glimpse of fire was for naught.

He closed the gap between them, pulling her into his body. She was so slight, reed-slim. Her startled breath made a sharp, shocked sound in the night air.

"What are you doing—"

"You just told me this is the only option. I thought we should sleep together."

Her softly curved form was rigid under the thickness of her mantle. He had brought her to lie on the ground with him, undividedly close. But his hand at her shoulder was light, unconstrained so that she would know she could move away. She did not. But she was trembling.

"It is not right," she said.

Moral arguments were not his strong point, so he said nothing to that. Since she had not moved, he pulled her closer, straight against his body, her back against his chest, her legs with his.

"There is no…" She did not complete the sentence because there was not the slightest doubt of the nature of the obvious bargain that existed between them. He made no attempt to temper the power of that. It was not possible. The fullness and the raw strength of it burned through every muscle, through his blood. But he made no further move, not as she expected. The expectations were what he wanted to break.

"I—"

"Do you not understand the word, *sleep*. Or will you be talking all night? I intend to sleep."

He held his breath, not knowing whether she would accept the only thing he could give. She did not say anything. Her hand was clamped across his arm. The separate fingers dug into his flesh through the woollen layer of his sleeve, the linen of his shirt. If anything had been wanting to assure his decision, that was it.

She lay still. He wanted to drag the extra layer of his own cloak over hers. Her hand would not release him. But the warmth of their bodies merged, complete where they touched, tinged with fire. The beauty of her, the richly curved shape of shoulder and hip and thigh burned through him, the soft feel of her and the exotic scent of her carefully wound hair, of her smooth skin. The subtle roundness of her breast against the confining band of his arm.

He held her close until the rhythm of her breathing slowed, the fine fast beat of her heart against his hand. She fought it for a long time because she did not believe his word. The bitter disbelief was not a surprise. He was patient.

There was silence and blackness, the hiss of the reluctant flames on the ground, and at last the final threads of tension vanished, so that he could sense the price of the burdens she carried, those she had told him and those he had not yet fathomed but would.

He caught the thought before it formed. There was no future, no time beyond this. Only the imperatives of what he must do.

The next move in the task.

For that he needed the beginnings of light. It was not long to wait.

LIGHT DRAGGED AT HER, growing light and the sound of a woman's voice. Rosamund tried to close it out, still half caught in the shadows of sleep.

"It is true."

Rosamund lay still, screened in the bed of bracken, oblivion still numbing her thoughts like a blessed release. She tried to hold on to the rare kind of healing sleep she had not known for three endless winters.

"You are sure?" A man's reply, light voiced, Danish. There was an irritating snicking sound, repeated, in some way familiar. The light pressed against her closed lids. She wanted the darkness, the dream in which she was not alone.

"A woman knows these things," said the first voice. *Olga*. "You can tell him. She is bewitched. If you are so keen to tell him something, tell him that."

Olga and— Rosamund realised the irritating sound was the cutting of a knife blade into wood. It made her heart stop with fear. She wanted to reach out, because she knew her lover was still there.

"Madness," said Od. *Snick*.

The word, like the sound, was laden with significance. The cold air raked her face, but she was still warm because the mercenary had slept with her, all the close press of his body like a wall, heavy bones and dense flesh and deep male lines. He had stayed. The awareness between them had been volatile as flame. But the closeness…the closeness had had the power of a miracle, a promise. If she could reach out, it would still be there.

"Thorkill will find out the truth," said Od.

"Thorkill has it. He can leave her out of the reckoning. She has her bargain. It is a passing amusement. Get on your way. You should not be here. You men, you want the wits to see what is plain enough..." There was a sound that could have been movement muffled by laughter that was as familiar as her own skin, part of the real world, her own world.

Her hand clutched air.

She opened her eyes on the familiar world. There was the swish of skirts, a fast step.

"Good morning. I did not see you wake." Olga walked towards her.

There was no one else in sight.

Dreams fled. She was alone on her uncomfortable bed of bracken. She tried to feel surprise. She unclenched her hand. Olga smiled. The brown eyes were dark. It might have been concern. The pain that had lodged round Rosamund's heart seemed too harsh to bear.

Women know these things. Sweet heaven, she wanted to speak. She wanted it so badly she choked on it. She wanted Olga to speak. She wanted the casual, earthy friendship she had always believed was there.

But in that moment Olga turned away. It was the sharp movement of someone who was afraid.

Rosamund sat up. The light strengthened.

THE STRENGTHENING LIGHT showed him. Boda stopped where there was still shadow.

The long narrow clearing was empty, silent except for the dim early note of a wood pigeon.

This was it, exactly as a group of savagely mauled raiders had described it last night, nursing wounds and disappointment and thin ale over the campfire. His gaze moved over the hastily thrown up fence of loose earth and brushwood and wattled hazel, now broken and showing the twisted boughs and dried bracken fronds behind that suggested a shelter. If you did not look too closely.

He assessed the space enclosed by trees choked with undergrowth that would have made it brutally hard for Thorkill's men to find the room to fight, the area of thinned growth where the Saxon warriors lying in ambush must have broken through, the smashed branches and crushed vegetation which bore unspeaking witness to carnage.

It was a good place for a trap.

He moved in, casting round like a hunter. There was the usual debris, dried blood, the gleam of a knife hilt with the blade broken, a lost belt pouch spilling what looked like the provisions for someone's breakfast and his amulet made of gilded copper for luck. Poor bastard.

Something moved with a faint crack of twigs. He made no obvious reaction, only his heart quickening like pain and every sense stretched. Overhead, the wood pigeon still droned its rising and falling note, undisturbed. There was the sweeter note of a blackbird and over to the left, the breathy sound of a wood animal, an intermittent kecker. The twig-breaker. It was irritated.

He made himself breathe, casting the search wider. Time moved on. The wood pigeon murmured. His heavy-footed companion snuffled and complained. Light grew. Naught. A place that kept its secrets well hidden.

He could hardly blame Thorkill for riding slap into this particular disaster. As far as Thorkill knew, his scouts had found one of those places where the terrified local population had hidden their beasts and their food stores from a passing army. Easy pickings and sorely needed. None of them had suspected Saxon warriors to be waiting.

Some enterprising Dorset thane and his local troop?

Or the king's men?

He stepped out of the supposed cattle pen. His companion shadowed him in the undergrowth. On impulse he pushed his way towards it. There was an annoyed rattling of twigs. He noticed disturbed earth, too much for his companion's clawed feet.

The low sun sliced across his eyes. Due east and he was touching hazel, which was fruiting wood. An alignment—runes.

The freshly cut sticks of equal lengths were scattered across the disturbed ground, scarcely distinguishable among the debris. He found the pale marks sliced by the knife blade. Straight vertical nicks and horizontal lines faced him blankly. At least it was not in Latin script, since the message was for him. He could manage runes even if it would take him half an hour to work this out in his head.

Grimm. It had to be.

Boda sat on his heels beside the message left by the king's men in runic code. His hand stopped above the first stick. Just in time. It was as though Grimm's voice, the relentless trainer of thick minds like his, was at his shoulder. *Look before you act.*

There was one plain rune. The sticks were not scattered, but arranged. *Rad.* The journey. The message arranged a meeting place. It had to.

He touched the hazel wood and something flickered inside him. Hope. For the first time it truly seemed that there might be a practical possibility of survival. He looked round the silent devastation of the forest clearing and his task was so clear, the shape of all that he owed. The shape of what had to be done.

He stood, stepping back across ripped branches and churned earth. Silence and the wood pigeon's chant, a scuffle from his fellow hunter. Large black eyes glared at him reproachfully out of a black striped face. There was the small matter of a flung clod of earth between them. Thorkill's badger, if it were indeed he, vanished into the hazel patch and the shadow, shunning day and what it might bring.

Boda placed the rune sticks inside his shirt against his skin.

Thorkill.

The day was already strong. Little enough time to get back to all that waited in the light. He began to run.

"So where is your bondsman this morning, princess?"

Gone, like the strong-willed, dangerous mercenary he was. Rosamund caught her breath, schooling her face into an untroubled mask, flawless. She had taken feverfew for the remains of a headache. She had to stop taking so much. There was less of a stash than she had thought in the small chest of herbs she and Olga shared keys to.

"Why?" she answered. She sweetened it with a smile. "Did you want him with us?" She was almost ready for the day's journey.

"Hardly," grunted Od.

Rosamund selected a ribbon of pale blue. It was made of silk. Luxury. Her uncovered hair slid through her fingers. She began to wind the ribbon through it.

"Well, then?" She turned her head, but only obliquely. It had taken Od far longer to approach her openly in the growing daylight than she had expected. His gaze followed the clever movement of her hand. She tried to keep it from shaking.

"It is just that they say you are witched with him."

She is bewitched. Tell him.

She threaded the ribbon into the braid. Od fiddled with the ever-present knife blade.

She slanted a glance at him, trying to assess. It was what Thorkill had to believe about her and the devious mercenary, or heaven help her.

Heaven help *him.* Her fingers caught.

"Perhaps they are right." She braided. *I am witched. Desperate. And it is likely to kill me.* "We all enjoy a diversion from time to time." Her voice was as light as her smile had been, as the movement of her hands in the sun.

"Why?" The knife struck into a piece of wood. It lodged. "Why not choose Thorkill over that... piece of Mercian scum?"

It was diplomatic.

She tried to get her fingers to work. The ribbon became tangled. What did Thorkill suspect? What in pity's name was the mercenary doing?

"A woman's fancy." She shook the braid out and began again.

"For what? The creature's brilliant looks? Even with half his face smashed in? Was that it?"

The almost violent intensity of the questions made her turn her head. Her hand stilled. Od's gaze was fixed on it, on the gleam of her skin in the light, the glitter of silver rings, the ribbon, the pale fall of her hair. His hard-boned face was stiff.

"I know I am not much." The thin lips twisted in the untrimmed beard. "I never expected after

Ingolf left that his woman would look at a man like me."

His woman. Od. *Od.*

She was an expert and she had not guessed it. She had seen him only in terms of the greater danger posed by Thorkill.

"Thorkill," said Od. "Thorkill is a *hersir,* one of the Jarl's captains and the Jarl listens to him. He listened when—" The belligerent voice stuttered, as though a word too much had been said.

Her spine crawled with dread.

"Listened when, Od?"

Thorkill's man was staring at her, narrow eyes filled with violence, the knife in his hand.

"Tell me." She wanted to turn and run, but she had to know. "The hostages. It was Thorkill who killed them." *And you.*

"Aye. Why not? They went to Odin in death. More than Saxons deserved. Who were they to stop us? And so Thorkill said to the Jarl and the Jarl acted as was right."

"Right? Earl Guthrum had made peace." She moistened her lips. "He gave his word that he would go back to East Anglia. He swore on the holy ring of Thor."

"Odin is the father, the old one, the lord of hanged men. He is for those who think. Thorkill is sworn to him."

And the earl? What did the dangerous earl truly think? No one knew. It was part of his power.

"We need to go on," said Od. "So Thorkill said, what can an oath matter compared to that? An oath to a foreigner? When Odin took the mead of inspiration he broke his oath on the holy ring because it was needed. We need to win. The Jarl had to break his oath in the same way and so the sacrifice had to go to Odin. Something to make it right."

"Right?"

There was a deep, deep silence.

"The Jarl kept faith with the needs of his own people," said Od at last. "You ought to understand that. You are one of us now. The Mercians will never have you back and the West Saxons would not want you."

The looted silk ribbon slid through her fingers.

"It is pretty, that. It suits a woman like you. Thorkill would always be able to provide you with trinkets and fine clothes whatever happens. Do you understand me? *Whatever* happens."

He was suddenly very close, a breath away from her.

"We are living in dangerous times, princess. You saw what was done to those who rode out in yesterday's foraging party. Alfred will recall the army. For all we know, he is here already. He is not going to give quarter now. Not to anyone."

She watched the embedded knife blade, the cuts in the wood. The steel edge vibrated as though it were eager for its next feed. Battle and counterstroke. It never stopped. It never let go. Od's hand curved over the knife hilt.

"Do you know the best thing about Thorkill? He can always find another way to get what he wants. Even if the Saxons should beat us, they will still pay Thorkill for the prize he holds."

"What do you mean?"

"You will find out when the time comes." The knife blade flickered in the red sun. The marks in the wood suddenly stood out in sharp relief. Runes. A triad.

Sigel, ger and monn.

"If you are with Thorkill. With *us*." His hand was not steady. That was why the knife blade flickered. "Think about it. You would not want the alternative."

The alternative. She arched her neck and the sun caught her blonde hair. "I make my own choices." Her hands were sweating.

"Then make the right one." The Danish boasting had vanished under a sudden earnestness, more chilling than threat. "Work it out, *princess*. You are a survivor. Calculate the odds." She heard his breath. "A woman like you knows how."

The knife jerked free of the wood.

"You did it on the first day you came here."

ROSAMUND PICKED UP the mirror. The face that stared back at her was compelling, every feature that might be considered good painstakingly enhanced with cosmetics and hard-won skill. The result was attractive, it might have been called beautiful. She did not know whether it was her face.

The eyes were feral.

Those were hers.

Think. Work it out.

She shut her eyes against the compelling stranger, but then all she could see in her mind was the unsteady knife in Od's hand...Thorkill's knife flying through the air in the dark, landing in a ripped sleeve.

Boda with his brilliant looks. His fine body with its rich, heavy-boned warmth, and the secrets locked in his head. Lethal secrets. As deadly as Thorkill's and somehow linked, she would swear it.

What?

Something the Saxons would pay for.

Think. Her life depended on it, Merriwen's. But it was no good thinking. She knew too little. She might as well cast lots onto a cloth or study the pattern of the birds' flight overhead against the sun.

The runes. Sigel, ger and monn. Sigel was the sign of the sun. It could strengthen whichever rune it was placed next to. The combination with ger and monn was powerful. But it had nothing to do with success in war. Why would a warrior like Od choose it? A *hersir* like Thorkill?

A triad like this one was concerned with restoring balance. It could help heal the sick, for example. Od was not sick. Thorkill had come through yesterday's fight unscathed. Arne had nothing worse than stomach-turning bruises from Boda's fist.

Boda. It always came back to the mercenary who thought like no one else and made her believe things that… She believed in nothing. The face in the mirror was the face of the world's greatest survivor.

Od might joke, but he was a believer when it came to the effectiveness of runes. He was a believer in getting what he wanted, like Thorkill… Thorkill's voice in the dark beside the campfire.

I always get what I want…whether it is that whore of a Saxon princess…or whether it is my rightful share of a war prize.

She had assumed *war prize* meant the Mercian she had won. Boda. Boda who had been standing in the dark, unseen, unguessed and listening like her, looking for some further secret.

She had never truly questioned him about why he had been there. When she had started, he had turned the focus neatly back on to her own actions and then…and then…

Madness.

She still ached with longing. She had wanted closeness. She had shut her mind to everything else. She was such a fool. She could not afford to be a fool. She cast her thoughts back to Thorkill. But there had been nothing else, just half a conversation, indistinct voices and the snick of Od's knife.

Down. Diagonal. Down. And then left, right—

She bent down and traced it on the ground at her feet.

Ur. Primal strength. It brought healing.

Then something else. Left, then right… Eolhx, then ethel and…what? She could not remember. Or she had not been able to see. A secret rune, powerful. Thorn perhaps? The demon and earth giant, the protective thorn. If it was so, the last three would offer protection against anything, even the bad consequences of a person's own actions.

Actions that had to be justified. Taking prisoners?

Hanging.

Something to make it right. Like a sacrifice for Odin. But where did Ur fit in? A rune for healing.

Still alive? Arne had asked.

No. It could not be. That was a flight of fancy. She stood up, brushing the dust off her hands, finding her things to tidy away, the mirror that had shown her the stranger's face, the cosmetics. The travelling chest of dried herbs. Feverfew. The key. Olga.

No.

But that was the way the world worked. The survivor in the mirror knew that. It was truly her face. She had begun braiding the last ribbon through her hair when the Mercian's shadow touched hers.

CHAPTER EIGHT

THERE WAS NO OTHER WARNING than the blackness, movement that disturbed light. The sharp rush of awareness that had no place. He spoke. Rosamund's fingers were tight on the ribbon.

"You are going to be late. The advance guard is already moving."

She tried to tie off the silk without fumbling it. "I thought it might be you who missed the journey."

They both spoke in Mercian.

"Nay, not me." That was all he said, her prisoner, no explanation, just three rock-solid words as though there could be certainty where there was none. His boots stopped beside the back of the cart, splashed with new mud and damp with dew. She could not raise her head to look at him.

"You dropped this."

A small glitter of light on the crushed grass caught her eye. One of her earrings. She had worn them last night and she had not remembered to take them off. She had been too lost in exhaustion. In bewitchment.

She moved, but the mercenary was quicker. He had the slender chains of silver.

"I can—"

The delicate links were pressed against her palm. He had hold of her hand. The feel of skin, the sudden warmth of human flesh, made her breath catch. She stiffened. She did not want this. It was a trap, this terrible sense that there might be a bond. It was a false step that could lead nowhere except disaster.

"You slept well," he said and it was not a question.

They had shared a night. He had felt her body relax into his and he had known that last unguarded moment when she had given in because the depth of her need had been too great.

"I slept."

"Well, there was naught wrong with that."

It was too seductive.

The sunlight clung to him, to the brilliant looks, to all the strength she had touched. Yes, she wanted that. Smashed face, borrowed clothes, richly tangled hair, the faint sheen of sweat on his skin. Her own war prize.

"You have to get some good of your bargain."

He was teasing her, with that kind of spare understatement that cut through even the black bitterness of war.

She wanted the way he thought. Her hand was suddenly tight against his and he let her hold him.

"Come on, then. Pack your things. We are keen to move this morning in case the Saxons come and plunder your earrings."

The smile had begun to touch her face when he said, "Or have you already foretold the future?"

The runes. She had been stupid enough and distracted enough to leave the marks on the ground, because her head had been filled with other thoughts. With *him*.

The small shapes dug into the dirt were no bigger than the prints of animal's claws, little scratchings already blurred and indistinct. But he had seen them.

Mercenary's training, which might leave some things to be desired, but not the sharpness.

"A distraction. I have no skill in divining the future. Have you?"

"Not me," said her hunter.

Ur and then eolhx and ethel and thorn.

Did he understand the meanings? Ur, the healing rune next to the powerful triad.

The fine, dark eyes flicked over the message.

"I take things as they are," said Boda.

And deal with them.

"Time to go."

"Past time." Her hand slipped from his. She did not ask where he had been, why the faint sheen of exertion was still on his skin, the rich russet hair tangled.

She would find out.

He moved away, the lingering pain and stiffness of bruising disguised under the power.

She turned back. Her foot touched the runes scored into the ground by her own hand.

Ur and eolhx, two runes of strength. Ethel which stood for protection and well-being but also for the *kin-fetch,* the ancestral heritage that could never be lost.

Foolishness.

It stood next to thorn whose other meaning was change, sudden and complete, the kind that was so strong it was violent.

She scrubbed the occult marks out with her shoe. She had work to do.

THE CODE WAS DECIPHERABLE. Boda considered the roughly carved hazel sticks, made with haste, but still precise.

"I want my new writing feather."

The little wench was engaged on the construction of a quill. Rosamund was with the other women. This was only a short stop, made for the sake of resting the horses, and possibly eating if you were lucky.

He needed speed.

"My quill."

"Take the barbs off the side first. No, the feathery bits on the inside of the curve."

The sticks he had rescued from the battle site were carved with hook runes—hooked lines that represented real runes. Each hook scored into the hazel wood was a number. The number recorded the rune's position in the *futhork,* the unchangeable list that was like the Latin alphabet. The strokes on the right showed which of the three groups within the *futhork* the rune belonged to, those on the left...

"I'm taking the barbs off now. You have to watch me."

Those on the left showed the rune itself inside the group. Most people used left to right, sunwise, not widdershins, against the light's path.

"Is this right?"

He glanced up.

"Yes."

BLECH.

That was helpful. Of course, the reading order of the three rune groups themselves could be altered. It was not necessarily one, two, three.

It might be three, two, one.

"I have started on the feathers. You have to watch."

KLOBT.

"How many?"

One, three, two, possibly. Why make it simple?

"How many barbs?"

It could be said that quill construction made a change from knucklebones. He looked up. She had chosen a long feather. Goose.

"The lot," he said without mercy.

Merriwen grinned. "Some."

It was two, three, one and then apply the key word, which he knew. The runes had then been shifted right by two. The result to be read widdershins, right to left. What did Grimm have against sunwise? Left to right, the way the sun moved, was the natural order of things.

"Nearly finished."

You and me both, wench.

"Two more bits."

The pairing of the last runes was indecent and nothing to do with the message at all. Better than a signature. It was Grimm. He choked. The rest of the message said what he had thought from the first. Unravelling the details merely defined the meeting place. Tonight.

"Finished."

The directions were exact, good enough even for a peasant who had never travelled further than Kingston in Surrey before he had seen Alfred. The precision made him wonder whether Macsen was there, Macsen whose family had owned large chunks of Devon since time began.

"Finished."

"Let me see, then."

Chad's bones. The feather looked like a dead dog's tail that had been out too long in the rain. A mongrel cur at that.

"Good?"

"The best. Pass me the knife. I've never seen a quill quite like that." He bit his lip. "We will do the nib."

She gave that silly grin, but handed over the small knife happily enough. She would probably take her hand off if she tried cutting the nib. Not as easy as it looked. You had to shave away the tip at a steep angle.

"Is it done yet?"

He considered the best way to get out of the camp, yet again, past scouts who were increasingly nervous. He must have used up a considerable quantity of whatever luck he had been born with. The guards were becoming a problem, but at least Thorkill had no idea what was going on.

Yet.

"Enjoying yourselves?" It was the other one, Olga. Rosamund was not with her.

"Yes," squeaked Merriwen and waved the chewed mongrel's tail. "I did this all by myself. Well, he helped," she added generously.

"Kind," said Olga in a voice that meant the opposite. "Merriwen? Rosamund wants you."

Boda stoked up the fire for their guest. Hazel sticks always burned well.

"Come and look at this first," crowed Merriwen.

Then she said, "I like making things with him," which floored him. She sounded blithe.

"Is it all finished now?" demanded the little wench.

"Not yet." He kept his gaze on Olga.

"We are going to make another writing feather after this one gives out," said Merriwen.

"Well, just think on," said Rosamund's friend, "how things can change."

"No, they don't," retorted Merriwen. "He is not going to leave us."

Olga looked as though she had been asked to swallow the contents of a stable drain.

"DESERTED," snarled Od. His irritation mounted. Not so much as a stray dog or a crumb of moulded cheese. The silent village at dusk had made the whites of Arne's eyes show. What you could see of the left eye behind puffed out eyelids.

But that made him think of the Mercian, which lashed his temper worse. He took care not to show it because Thorkill was black-mooded enough for the three of them. It had been the same everywhere. The Saxons had disappeared, leaving only what could not be taken away.

He kicked the door of the bower they had taken as theirs. At least there was somewhere to sleep tonight out of the cold. He kicked the bed frame.

"We could get ourselves a wench to warm it. Mayhap Olga when she has finished ministering to that living corpse." Olga was as good as Thorkill's now.

He needed a good bout to work off his frustration and Olga would do. This time Thorkill could share. It was only fair. "The corpse will do a strapping wench like her no good, so we—" But he regretted the words as soon as said.

There was only one wench on Thorkill's mind, the *princess*.

Od's foot lashed out again. He would have offered for her after Ingolf was done with her. He would have bid a substantial amount of what he had won from this war, rewards gained by his own efforts, at his own risk. He had goods. Not as much as Thorkill who always took the most—

"No women. I want you to watch the hill road tonight."

"What?"

Thorkill picked up the ale flask. "You heard. The hill road. There was something about that ambush yesterday. The way the Saxons knew what we would do."

"It was that cursed beacon fire."

"Maybe. And maybe it was something more. I want the road watched. If anything, any person, any message gets in or out of this encampment I want to know. I want it stopped."

"The guards will already—"

"You go with them. You stay where the valley narrows, where there is only one path you can take inland in the dark. I have told the guards but they are cowards about being too far in Saxon territory. You make sure they will be more afraid of the earl's wrath if this baggage train is attacked."

Odin's breath. Outside striking distance from the camp. Why should he spend the night freezing his balls off in Saxon territory when—

"Take Arne." The bullish head turned. "Arne can look out for his foreign friend. There might be a chance for repayment with interest."

Arne grunted through a squashed lip.

"That Mercian?" howled Od before he could stop himself. Never question Thorkill, but this time he could not keep the disbelief out of his voice.

"You will go," spat the Jarl's *hérsir.* "I want to be sure. If the Mercian is involved it is I who will deal with it, not the Jarl's guards. If the Mercian is there, you will take him and deliver him to me. Is that clear?"

As rank mud under a stagnant pool.

Arne had got to his feet, but he looked too sullen for revenge. Arne would spend the time with his bruised jaw hanging open looking for ghosts. Great company.

It was stupid. Thorkill was way off the mark, cut pride making him scent some conspiracy just because the hard-nosed bastard had lost for once in his charmed life. There was no more mystery about the fine princess and the Mercian than was contained between used bedcovers. He had told Thorkill so, and the truth was plain, not from her words, but from the heat that had been in her slanted, kohl-painted eyes. That was where she would be now, between bedcovers. With her precious *diversion* getting his—

"Move," said Thorkill, cold as a snake.

No choice. As ever.

But if, after all, the Mercian was there…well, sometimes parcels got damaged in transit.

ROSAMUND STOPPED. She chose shadow.

It was bitterly cold on the open hillside, no cover of cloud tonight to stop the frost falling. The sky was filled with pure white stars, high and distant, utterly remote from the petty, crawling conspiracies of men. The moon rode like a hunter.

Its light was both blessing and bane. She saw her quarry clearly enough, but the moonlight would also expose her. Rosamund watched the separate black shadow moving ahead of her, hugging the darkness, its tall form at times indistinguishable but always moving with a sure purpose. A second man followed, the pale blur of his face sometimes visible as he glanced back over his shoulder, half stopping, as though he were less certain than his companion. Arne, who was afraid of night-walkers and spirits. And Saxons. They were far from the camp.

She crouched down behind a screen of brush-wood to watch. The narrow track snaked away, an ill-defined ribbon leading inland and north into steeply rising ground.

Od called out, his voice soft, yet carrying far on the still air, further than he thought. Arne's head swivelled. But the greeting was answered as though it were expected. There was no challenge. *One of us.* The earl's guards were a long way from their base.

She listened with impatience while they spoke and the cold found every gap in her clothing. She had only a woollen cloak, not warm like her mantle, but it was dark and hooded. That was what mattered.

"…would have to come this way," said Od.

She tugged at the plain woollen gown underneath. It was Merriwen's. She had paid two of the women to look after Merriwen tonight. She had not trusted her to Olga.

There was no one left to trust.

Rosamund bit her lip and pulled harder at the ill-fitting dress. The billowing folds had to be firmly belted. The skirts were too short but that was an advantage for mobility. Besides, one could hardly use a concubine's clothes for this, not even if it involved tracking a lover through the night.

Od, she would swear, had the same quarry in view. The mercenary had eluded both of them. She had foolishly waited for darkness, calculating the mercenary would do the same. He had not.

"It is the only path…" Od's voice floated in snatches.

So she had looked for Thorkill and Od because she knew in her bones that there was some link between the mercenary's purpose and theirs.

She had seen Od leave the camp with Arne and she had followed.

Get on with it. They were talking now about nothing, about the disaster of yesterday's foraging party and the freezing night, in voices so low she could scarcely catch a word. She could hardly see them in the shadow of the rocks and the scrub. What in pity's name was Od doing gossiping when he should be searching for his goal?

The minutes flicked past. Neither Od nor the nervous Arne moved. Cramp started in her legs. The cold seeped up through her shoes. She shifted, terrified of making a sound, last time's eavesdropping disaster hideously fresh in her mind. No mercenary nearby this time, just cold and... They had stopped speaking. There was silence and the faint rustle of branches hung with dried leaves. No other movement.

It is the only path...

They were not going to move. The bolt of horrified comprehension nearly made her surge to her feet. Od and Arne and the earl's men had no need to move. Their quarry would come to them. The mercenary had gone on ahead, Saint Chad knew where, and he would need to come back this way. All they had to do was wait.

She crept forward, moving her weight with care, stiff muscles screaming like her beating heart. The pale ribbon of the road vanished into moon-shadows ahead, but she could still make out the rocks and the thorn brakes, the sharp drop on the other side.

There was no way past, not unless you climbed over crumbling rock in the dark, hand over hand, sending the loose shingle flying, outlined in moonlight.

If the devious mercenary had gone this way, if his objective had lain inland up this valley, he would come back through this path. A detour might take who knew how many miles and he had no reason to make it. He had no reason to think the earl's guards would be posted this far out.

He would walk straight into them and they would take him and possibly kill him.

She had risked coming here to gain information, so that she would know how to protect herself and her escape plans. She had to go on protecting Merriwen, otherwise everything was lost, everything she had done, the terrible decision she had made on the day King Ceolfrith had thrown his own niece to the wolves.

She had no way to rescue a dangerous mercenary. What she had to do was escape, reach Cornwall, fulfil her duty to Merriwen.

But there was a worse truth.

One she had not faced and which was now staring at her like a ghost in the dark. All this, the danger and the violence and the living on a knife edge of destruction had to stop because she could not take much more.

The path disappeared into the valley in front of her, into the patch of blackness where Od and Arne and the earl's men waited.

Behind her lay the relative safety of the camp.

That safety was fragile, but she had created it for herself out of disaster and it was all she had—that and the desperately longed-for prize of escape once they were far enough west. The distance shortened every day, with every step Guthrum's army took.

Ahead lay the blackness.

Blackness and fear and violence. And the mercenary.

She could not go near that. She could not do it.

She bunched Merriwen's dress in her hand.

"THE EARL'S GUARDS?"

"Aye. Has to be." Boda stared at the scarcely distinguishable shapes in the darkness of overhanging rocks.

"Confident," said Macsen, fellow king's man, whose own troops were in the hills.

"No. They are not." Guthrum's men were rattled, which was why it was odd they had ventured out so far. "Useful place to watch though." Perhaps that was the simple explanation. The perfect choke-point of the valley had been too good to resist. He tried to ignore the cold prickling of his skin, the tug that there was something wrong.

"We can still get past them." Macsen's hand touched his arm, to draw him left. Or as though his sole companion could sense what was inadmissible, the totally irrational bolt of fear that had just shot through him. The solid hand gripped briefly.

Macsen was the kind of person who sensed too much, whether it had happened yet or not.

He resisted the urge to ask for a prediction of the prospects of pulling Thorkill's guts out by hand.

It was a certainty anyway.

"This way. There is another path."

"How could I have missed it?"

"You are a foreigner." It was not even a gibe about being Mercian. They were in Devon, which had not always been part of Wessex.

"And I thought it was the thorn bushes putting me off."

Macsen's own family's lands were near here. Some of them. Macsen owned more than Boda could imagine without a sinking feeling in the guts, so he kept talking.

"At least I do not have to read Grimm's rune sticks this time. What kind of code did he think that was?"

"Grimm was worried someone might interpret the message."

"Me perhaps?" The glib words rolled off his tongue.

"If all else failed." Macsen's grin disappeared. "The poor devil was convinced some *hersir* was going to rip your...eyeballs out for breakfast. Could you not read the panic?"

Boda stopped moving. Grimm worried about *him?* Yet the information had come out with that utterly unself-conscious ease that had to be born into thanes and princes, and into descendants of long-lost emperors like Macsen. Boda did not truly belong to the brotherhood of such men in a king's service. He did not know how.

"Oh, aye," he jested and it sounded effortless. "I could tell by the fond farewell." Macsen had told him the unfathomable Grimm was already off on some other mission. Boda relayed the meaning of the last two runes. Macsen's grin came back.

The other man dropped down ahead of him into blackness. A hidden path. He really had to get out of here, back to the camp. His hand brushed hazel branches. The irrational fear burst through him. He stopped, looking back over his shoulder just as Macsen turned. There was nothing out of the ordinary. Only the earl's guards they had to evade. *Nothing.* Just one more step down and he was out of their sight range.

Something moved. The fear became real.

SHE WAS COMING TOWARDS HIM. The dark cloak engulfing her slight form was unfamiliar, but not the grace, not the way she moved. He could not at first figure out whether she had seen him, or whether this was the only way she could find besides the track. Or whether by some miracle she knew the hidden path.

"*Rosamund.*" The harsh rawness of his voice scarcely made sound.

"That is her?" Macsen had come back behind him. "That is Guthrum's Mercian prize?"

It was the accepted description, a few words packed into a fast instant. But the rage still slammed through him. No one owned another person. He had the knife in his hand.

"The princess?" asked Macsen.

"Yes," he said because it was quicker. Then he said the only thing that mattered. "We have to get her away from here."

Macsen had already moved to flank him. They pushed forward. Rosamund saw the movement and tried to run, as though she wanted to cut him off.

The violent downward gesture of his hand conveyed what he could not shout to her, that silence was more important than speed. The crack of a twig gave him a heart seizure. She pointed right towards where the earl's guards were, then at him and away.

She thought he and Macsen had not seen the Danes. She was trying to warn him. Shock mixed with the rage. His heart beat again as though it would choke him. Something moved in the direction she was pointing, a black shape. He dropped low and she had the sense to follow. The cover was good enough where he was, but not where she had stood.

He tried to get her to stay, at least until the guards relaxed again, but she did not. He could move far more quietly than her despite his heavier weight. He knew how to use the cover. She must have figured out that he was better at this, trained. It was logical.

But she came towards him as though impelled, as though she thought he still needed help. It drove the rage into a force that would kill him. She was too near the hidden drop. He caught her, but the inevitable happened, a small fall of loose earth and stones.

He heard each separate shard find its course all the way to the unseen depths.

"The guards," she mouthed, as though he was slack-witted. She was smudged with earth and leaves, but he would swear she was not hurt.

He said exactly what the guards could do with themselves, which was the only temporary relief for the volcano of fire inside him.

Her mouth opened and shut. He had hold of her. She felt as substantial as a green reed, breathing out of rhythm.

"Move left. Take it slowly. There is a path. Take it down and through the hazel trees. It rejoins the trackway. Go." Her fingers dug into his arm. "I will follow." When he had distracted the guards. When—

"Thorkill's men." He heard her breath heave. "Od."

Damnation.

"I will—"

"No." The second voice made her raise her head. Her frantic gaze fixed on the other man in the blackness beside them. "I will do it," said Macsen. *I will take the place of decoy.*

The decision had to be assessed and taken in less than a second.

"Thorkill has a stake in this." Boda knew Macsen understood the short cut in his words—the level of danger, the extent of determination that would have to be overcome.

"This is Devon," said Macsen. It was his home. He had the best chance of survival, just as Boda had the best chance of rescuing the living hostage, Gainmar. The mission always came first. It was how their brotherhood worked, how the king's purpose was met.

And there was Rosamund.

He dragged her away the split second after Macsen broke cover. She gasped. He pulled her with him over the drop.

They had perhaps four seconds where speed was more important than silence, when the noise of Macsen running and the instant's disorientation it caused would mask whatever noise was made by their own flight.

They vanished into blackness beyond the moon's reach. He did not see what happened above.

SHE HAD RESCUED a stranger, some kind of changeling in a familiar body. Or he had rescued her. It was hard to tell which. She was alone with him.

Rosamund regarded the flames in the makeshift hearthpit of what had once been a small storeroom in someone else's Saxon village. It was empty of anything resembling stores. She had laid out three shillings and a half cheese in bribes for it. They had eaten the rest of the cheese with strips of cured pork and dried fruit.

He had made a fire for her and now she was boiling water. Just like a settled married couple who had shared five years and trust. The water was slowly beginning to steam.

She looked up at Boda. The firelight gilded the rough stubble on his jaw and made moving gold out of the copper lights in his hair. He had a decidedly competent-looking knife sheathed at his hip—the very picture of a mercenary. He was not one at all.

"Are you really Mercian?"

She got the merest flick of a glance from his fine eyes and it was the most stupid question of all to ask, the least relevant. She had not even thought to enquire whether he had given her anything remotely approaching his real name. She waited for an answer. She got a question.

"Could you feign an accent like this one?"

"Yes."

"I could not." His unexpectedly dark gaze fixed on her. She would swear then that she could see all the depths she had sensed from the first, the shades that had caught her and reflected some of her inmost thoughts like a mirror.

"That much is true," said his voice with its accent so much stronger than hers, as though its owner could see straight through her head to what she wanted, the things she pathetically ached for. A companion. If she moved her hand a single span, she would touch him. Her cold fingers lifted.

Then he said, "Why would you doubt that of all things?" and she realised he was also assessing her.

Her hand carefully adjusted a basin beside the fire. How could she be so foolish? A spark of anger flared. She clung to it.

If her *companion* meant to string out more deception with her, he was well off the mark. If she did not know who he was, she at least knew the company he kept. The other warrior on the hillside, the one who was from Devon, she had seen before—in the middle of the Viking encampment at Wareham. She set herself to weigh the knowledge and the best use of its power. Just as he would do it.

She would let him know.

She fixed her gaze on the fire.

"You might have come from Mercia," she said to the stranger, "but you are one of the king's men of Wessex. I do not imagine that his most trusted followers, those who occupy what must be the highest ranks, are paid mercenaries."

She repositioned the bowl.

"I do not believe you and your friend are for hire. You can spare me whatever sham you gave Thorkill. I simply do not believe the king of Wessex could afford to buy, for example, a man like

Macsen, Prince of Lydnan." She looked up at precisely the right time. She had his attention. All of it. The most terrifying thing was that she could not read what was in his eyes.

She had produced a shock. She had faced him with knowledge that was as unexpected as it was true. He had not reacted.

Rosamund felt her stomach clench. The anger pushed her.

"You are not some hireling to be given orders to obey. Prince Macsen spoke with a comrade, an equal."

"Is that so?"

She caught the flash of what she thought of as the chained barbarian look, the fiercely murderous element she was not supposed to see. It did not stop her. She wanted to provoke him, to take some kind of reaction from him, even if it had to be that.

"I can work out how things stand in Wessex," she said. "Sometimes I get to watch Guthrum's men count the money that should buy peace. What is it called? Danegeld? Money paid to the Danes."

She watched the knife, the brilliant motionless body and the power beat at her. Yet what she thought of was Od and Arne and the earl's men waiting in the dark for him. The moment of sheer terror when she had seen him. Him and Macsen.

"I saw him when he came into Wareham, your Prince Macsen. He would not have seen me. He would not know that someone like me watched him cross that courtyard with the earl at his side. Tell me, since his loyalty now stays so strongly with the Saxon king, did the same loyalty apply to that woman who was so besotted in him?"

She watched Boda, the king's man, two firelit breaths away from her. "I saw her go to him at Wareham." *I saw the look in her eyes like someone taken by spellcraft. Perhaps my eyes look like that. Bewitched.* "Does he still keep with her?"

"Yes." His fine barbarian's eyes narrowed. Her heart clenched.

"You surprise me. I thought Macsen's talent for deception must be as great as yours."

"He will never leave her." His gaze fixed on hers and her painful heart beat fast, so hard.

"Why?" said the man who might be called Boda. "Who left you, so that you cannot now forget it?"

CHAPTER NINE

THE MERCIAN MADE SOME slight movement and her gaze followed it, trapped.

His rough voice said, "Who? Who was it that affected you so much?" Silence. "The Dane? Ingolf?"

Rosamund could hardly breathe. *Say yes. It will close the matter.* He looked at her as though her answer mattered. As though she, the mud-splattered cloak across her shoulders, the ill-fitting dress, the tight breath in her throat and the thoughts in her head were the most important things in the world. As though he cared and she could rely on that. Or even break it if she wished. She hated that. Hated *him*.

More than that, she hated herself, what she had become, all the things she would do to survive.

"It was a transaction with Ingolf. I gained status and protection. He gave me what I wished. Nay, what I needed and calculated and then took from him. In return…" Her voice stopped. She gazed at the king's man and it was as though the breathable air that separated them did not exist. Heat flicked her skin.

She forced her voice to work, to go on. "My return was that I gave him all the pleasure he could desire." *And it was nothing, bitter dust compared to the first moment I touched you.* He made some movement and she watched the fire-warmed brightness of his body with fascination, the latent power now so thinly veiled, clear as though it touched her. As he would touch her. One movement and it would be real. Inevitable. Like the fiery brightness of the sky covering the earth at the moment of light-change.

"There was someone else."

No.

He bent down. His shadow touched her beside the hearth. But not him. She watched his hand with the fading shadows of bruising across the knuckles, an older mark on the palm she had scarcely noticed before and which now seemed prominent. A stranger's hand. He sat on his heels, the compressed muscle of his thigh inches from her own.

"Who was it?"

No one.

His gaze caught hers.

"Edric." She had not said the name for three winters. "His name was Edric and I was betrothed to him. He broke the betrothal four days before Ceolfrith sent his Viking masters to take Merriwen and me from the nuns' school."

"So he knew." So matter-of-fact. He did not look away. There was no one like him and he was not for her. He never would be. She wanted him so much she could have wept.

"Edric's kindred had always been with Ceolfrith. He would have been there when Ceolfrith agreed his settlement with the Vikings and gained his kingship and, of course, power for his supporters."

"So it was logical."

"Yes. Sometimes sacrifices have to be made to gain power. Edric knew what Ceolfrith had promised." *He knew Merriwen and I were inseparable, that I was sworn to her. He did not want a scene, or to be tied to me. For all I know, Ceolfrith had already offered him someone wealthier in return for such support.* She wanted to explain even that, to tell him the entire truth, but it was not her secret. It was Merriwen's and it was dangerous to death.

"A good courtier does not embarrass his master," she said. "Edric was very good." She had not realised quite how astute until the message had come, incomprehensible at first and devastating. Then Guthrum's men had arrived to take the Princess of Mercia and all her rich possessions that had been safely stored with her behind the nunnery's stone walls. Then she had understood.

That was the end.

"I had thought that he…" *Cared.* She could not say that under the steady gaze of King Alfred's man. It was what she wanted from him, not from long-lost Edric. "The betrothal was an arrangement, of course, but I did not see it that way. To me it was, oh, like a dream." *Not terrifyingly real like what I feel for you, even though you are a stranger and not mine.*

"It was a girl's dream. Such dreams are not real. I just…believed it was. You only see dreams once. Then you grow up and you see what life really is, and what is possible and what is not. You do not dream again." *You might want to, but you are changed and you also hunger for what is real, like fated opposites, unless they combine in someone like you,*

"You understand." She knew that he would. "Boda?"

But he had looked away and he did not turn back at the sound of the name that might not even be his. She could no longer see his eyes and it was as though the impossible bond was broken, as though she had broken it because of who she was, *what* she was, the self she could no longer change or hide, the self that cut her off so that she was alone.

Desperation choked her.

Touch me. Body and mind ached for him. How could she say that? She turned away and carefully moved the pans of water from the flames. They would boil over.

"It does not matter," she said. Nothing did except her task. "You do not have to tell me anything more of who you are or what you plan to do. Do you know what I plan to do? I plan to escape from here with Merriwen. Not back to Mercia." She nearly choked on it.

"Not into your precious Wessex, but into Cornwall, somewhere not involved in this endless war. Guthrum and his fine army can take me west and when they stop, I will leave. I have enough money, off Ingolf, out of gifts and Viking plunder. I care not where it comes from, only for what it will do, because I will win my way out of this. I will take Merriwen back from them and she will be safe. I have sworn it…" She stopped. Too close to the bone.

She watched him, so near. She drew a shaking breath. It made a faint sound, desperate, weak, alone. *Touch me.*

"That is my future." Tomorrow, she would pick it up because she had no choice.

But in this moment she could not face it. *Share this moment with me. Touch me. Let me be with you.*

Understand.

"I have to go from here. When the time is right." She moistened dry lips. "That is not yet."

They were inches apart and the flame between them burned. She had seen it in his eyes, as clearly as she had seen the capacity to understand, the intelligence, the almost brutal clarity of thought.

She had touched him and known the fierce edge of fire. She wanted him. He wanted her, despite whatever else he planned. It was straightforward. There was no need for such desperation.

It was not as though she had never proposi-
tioned a man.

"Will you stay with me? We have this time
to…before…" She choked. He turned his head.
She saw shadows, the fire-bright hair, the rough line
of his jaw. Not his eyes. "Will you spend this night
with me? I want…" She collected the betraying
pause. "I would spend that time with you."

"With me? Why?"

She shrugged. "It is what I wish."

"To spend time? As you would, perhaps with
Ingolf?"

"There can be nothing else." Coolly decisive.
Loaded with the most fundamental sexual provo-
cation between woman and man. The words of the
most accomplished concubine.

The fierce power moved. She saw the solid thigh
muscle tense. She saw the blur of his hand. He was
angry, angry enough, perhaps, to flatten her with
one blow, but there was no place for the thought in
her consciousness. Mind and body were consumed
with the far more primitive terror that he would go.
She, the most accomplished prize for fifty miles
around, would lose him—

She looked up and saw his eyes. Fire. There was
no pretence. "Stay with me," she said. "I am afraid."

His mouth came down on hers.

She was aware of his raking anger. He held it back.
She was so desperate with need, she could not have
pulled away from him. He must have sensed that.

It took seconds for the need to spill over into pleasure. It was his doing. Deliberate. Like an act of will. He created that pleasure through the kiss, through the smooth touch of his mouth, the unexpected brush of his tongue against her lower lip, through sudden softness when she anticipated power. The pleasure caught her like a hunter's net.

Her lips moulded to his.

He pulled her down with him onto the floor, onto the pile of luxurious, skilfully made furs that were part of her riches, and she stayed with him, her body and her lips following his every movement because she wanted the deep pleasure of him. When her mouth firmed on his, the kiss became consuming—inciting a response out of her tumultuous highly-wrought senses and then taking all that she felt, the way a thief wrested gold out of the night. If he had been her husband of five years, it would have been possessive.

Tears spurted behind her eyes and she closed her eyelids. Her fingers dug into the solid thickness of his shoulders. His hands tightened but he did not just take, he gave what she wanted, in the warm power of his body and in his passion. Her fingers fisted in the softness of his hair, grazed the taut muscles of his neck. The kiss took her higher.

She was lying tangled with him in the warmth spilling from the hearth. His size cushioned her at the same time that it overwhelmed. She could feel each harsh living muscle. That he was already fully hardened.

Her breath hitched against the hot power of his mouth. His hands were caressing the curve of her waist, moving higher, the touching smooth and slow and inexorable, filled with intent. Like his kiss. It drew sharp sensation from her, even through the barrier of Merriwen's coarse dress.

She was intensely aware of his strength, his weight, the smooth glide of male muscle against her flesh. He held her close and when her body shifted she felt every nuance, the supple, flexible power.

She remembered touching him two nights ago on the dark hillside with Thorkill nearby. She had been lost in desire and desperate. She had not thought that need could increase. But it had. She wanted the outpouring of his passion in the same way, to feel the heat of his skin and hear the sharp sound of his voice, to feel the last movement of his body that was beyond control.

He knew how to take her desire. His hand was at her breast, the touch through linen enough to send her volatile, almost fiercely aroused senses spinning. The brush of his fingers against one hardened nipple shafting the sensation deep inside her. He knew what she responded to, after that one brief encounter on the dark hillside, and his touch gave it. Despite the anger and the deep, harsh emotions she could scarcely guess at. Her mind shied away from the implications even as her body moved, inciting his touch, taking all he would give. Wanting him.

Her fingers slid down the undamaged side of his torso, over the solid padding of muscle, the harsh fast swell of his breath. She could feel the savage beating of his heart. It was how her own beat.

The kiss broke. His thigh pressed between hers. The big hands at her hips, on the full curves of her body, held her even as she moved against him, taking her restlessness, subtly increasing the pressure until she was mindless with need. His hand slid between their bodies, beneath her crushed, ill-fitting skirts, and she gasped. Her face was buried in the coiling richness of his hair, the heat of his neck. Nothing else existed beyond touching. There was no world beyond the four walls of a stranger's bower, no war-torn country, no secrets. No other time. He touched her bared flesh, the inside of her thigh, her heat.

Her body responded. His hand caressed. Just as he knew how. The skilful fingers took the moist ache of her flesh, the scorching heat, the passion inside her that was truly his. She cried out. Her body moved and the pleasure and the desire crashed over her. The last conscious thought was of closeness, of the remorseless strength that held her.

What she wanted…

The clear certainty took her breath and there was no pause this time, no break in the fire. Her hands clung to him, her body rolled with his. Her mouth found his and the whispered words breathed against his lips, the words locked inside her head, *how much she wanted him.* It felt as though the words were scored across her heart, dangerous words, as dangerous to her as he was. She said one of the worst, *need.* It took shape against the warmth of his skin.

Her fingers dug into solid muscle through his clothes and he was holding her. She kissed the smooth dark heat of his mouth.

His hand caressed the rounded length of her thigh. Her own hands were already at the taut line of his hips and the sharp power of his reaction, the glimpse of the hidden things that lived inside him, drove her onwards.

She held him as he had held her, her hands curved at either side of his hips. The toughness and the unbated strength leached through her skin and there was a moment of utter stillness, laced with power and the sharp heat of sex.

"Rosamund…" The dark-rough Mercian voice made it a question, the only question there was.

His hot gaze held hers. His heavy hands on her body were tense, possessive but suddenly, intensely careful. Her senses were flooded with him, utterly aware of what they had once shared, of all that would be, now in this firelit bower. She could read the same awareness in his eyes, dark heat. Yet the careful hands still held her. He did not move.

She had said she was afraid. He was asking her what she wanted.

"This is what I want." *You* are what I want.

"The same touch."

"No. I want more." Her hand had moved, but his voice stopped her.

"There might be consequences."

She stayed, the slight movement of her hand arrested. It was impossible to move, breathe. Wholly unexpected pain drove through her heart.

She forced the necessary breath. "No." She was that much of a concubine still. "I will be safe." There were herbs, preventions a woman could take if she knew how.

Rosamund knew.

She could no longer hold his gaze.

"I can promise you that," she said to the swimming firelight beside the richly spread out beauty of his hair, to his dark shadow. Ingolf had never concerned himself with consequences. No man did who simply took what he wanted.

This man who held her had thought.

He had thought of *her.*

"No consequences." Her voice sounded cool as ever, a concubine's voice for a concubine's subject. She swallowed what might have been dangerous tears.

There would be no bond after this. His thoughts did not belong to her.

Her hand moved. Her breath quickened. Her whole being focussed on the aching movement of her hand.

He let her touch him. Her hand palmed the full, heavy shape of his sex. He let her feel the reaction and her heart started to hammer. Her hand settled over the blood-hardened length of his flesh. She was skilled at touching. The familiar path. But everything was new and she had no shield, only her need of him.

She said what might be his name.

He moved, this time the reaction so abrupt it was almost violent and she was caught in his embrace. She was deep in what she had wanted from the first moment, the fire. Her body cleaved to his, tangled with it. The frantic beat of her heart was matched by his. She felt so intensely aroused that the slightest touch of his hand on her flesh was enough to send her close to the edge. The sharp gasp of her voice was lost in the firelit air, against his skin.

Her own intensity was mirrored, shared at a level beyond thought. She moved for him, settling as the dark, fire-shadowed mass of his body covered hers, her thighs at the taut line of his hips as he positioned himself. Her body was scorching when he touched her, aching with need, a desire that was shared. That was all that mattered. He was with her. The heat of his lips brushed hers like a moment out of time and then drew back slightly. She saw the scratches at his neck from where he had plunged through the undergrowth in the dark to find her. He smelled of heat and strength and the kind of ruthlessness she understood. He had saved her.

"You are what I want. Now." She watched him, the marks of those terrifying moments in the darkness still on him. "Just like this."

His hands were at her hips, holding her to him. His eyes were black in the shadows, but she saw the pain, more clearly than light could have shown her because she was looking with her heart. She moved towards him, taking the heat of his body, the fiercely driven urgency of his flesh, the exquisite pleasure as he filled her, taking him inside her, the physical need—and the unspoken pain if she could. She would release him from that if she knew how.

Her body was tight round him, the closeness like an impossible bond as her body moulded to the power of his and he pushed deeper. Her hands fastened on the beautiful harsh line of his shoulder. At the first thrust, a jolt of possessiveness surged through her, both bitter and fierce. She leaned up. Her lips lightly touched the scratched skin.

There was nothing after that except the passion, the strength of his body and the fire, the intense hidden feelings that had no other expression. She felt them burn him, their strength almost savage. But she was not afraid. She understood.

She moved for him, giving the physical release, drawing her legs higher to take the deeper thrust of his body, inciting him, her own body as urgent as his, both of them brought to such a pitch of wanting that the pleasure suddenly spiralled over, deep and fierce, and she tightened round him, her last vestige of control broken, sensing the same break in him, the fast, harsh movement of his body. The moment that showed demons.

HE HAD THE SPAN of one day. Part of this night. Boda could guess the number of hours, priest-taught skill.

Rosamund lay so close they almost touched. Part of this night... The looted ashwood cracked in the fire. It caught his attention, as though he had slid out of consciousness without will, the way some integral part of himself had slid beyond him forever. Held with her.

The slight weight of her body was warm and infinitely fragile. He forced his aching eyes to focus. She was sleeping. Her smooth limbs spilled out of the coarse, ill-fitting dress. The unsteady light caught the ribbons painstakingly threaded through her hair.

He shifted, driven by the aching discomfort of bruised ribs, by heaven knew what. The nightmare that would come. He turned his mind from it, pushing his thoughts elsewhere, a matter of practice. If he moved away— Something snagged against his tunic. Her hand. Her long, slender fingers were tangled in the crushed wool, as though she did not want him to go.

He actually made a sound.

It was impossible to move. Impossible to breathe, even to feel the beat of his own heart. Light flared in the hearth as the ashwood burned through and her slanting green eyes were open. No way to tell whether the sound of the wood breaking or his own movement had woken her.

"Are you leaving?"

Speak. "Not until it is closer to dawn."

"Dawn." Her fingers clenched tighter against the mud-stained wool, the knuckles of her hand starkly white, even in the red firelight. He had touched her and he had felt every last thread of desperation that had driven her to him.

He did not fool himself that it was anything more than that, anything that mirrored what he felt.

There were a thousand ways to be a culpable fool and this was the worst of them.

"It is to do with Thorkill," she said.

He had a suitably vague answer to that already worked out. He took a breath.

"You want something he has. Someone."

There was no discernible tension in his body, neither was there an expression on his face. Five years of dedication to learning the craft. He had been the most dedicated. He had reason to be.

The perfect response that would brush her question aside was still in his head. It was, of course, the safest route and the right one. But he did not speak. Her green eyes watched him.

"Thorkill talked about a prize they held that was worth enough to get them out of trouble if things went badly for the earl. I thought at first they meant you. But then later Od spoke about something they still held, some*one*."

The next decision in the path spun out. She faced Thorkill, and she had no one, only him. He moved round, letting her slight weight settle.

"Yes. There is someone, another prisoner, and he is worth decidedly more than me."

"He—" The tight hand wrapped in his tunic jerked. She made some soft incomprehensible sound, and then she said, "Who?"

Of course, it was quite possible that she knew the surviving hostage, although he had not been in Mercia for some years. It was equally possible she did not.

"Gainmar." It took a timeless second for the clever, exhausted eyes to register a Mercian name with royal connections. A desperate person must have expended some effort at Wareham on avoiding a man like Gainmar, even though he had not been Guthrum's hostage for long. Gainmar would not have been treated as a common prisoner. Not until the end.

"Gainmar?" He saw her mind register the abrupt danger her hesitation had caused. "But I thought…"

She was simply too tired for games of strategy.

None of this should have happened to her.

The bolt of rage shot through him, unstoppable, as far beyond his control as any of his reactions to her.

"I th-thought…"

He glossed over it for her. "You thought he was killed with the rest of the hostages. He was not. Thorkill kept him alive, hidden. You will appreciate how such a man is triply useful—related to Ceolfrith, related to the Mercian-born queen of Wessex through her mother's kin, and related to Lord Athelred."

Triply damned dangerous. The man attracted followers like a lode star without actually trying. Only irredeemable misfits like himself refused. No wonder Ceolfrith had hated Gainmar.

"Related to Athelred?" Rosamund fixed on the name that was least familiar, grasping after safe ground she could reasonably know little about, now that it was too late and tiredness had tripped her into error. "You are talking about Athelred the young lord of Gloucester?"

"Aye." It was odd how one always thought first of Athelred, who was fifteen winters old, and not of his father.

"The Mercian firebrand," said Rosamund, working it out. "The one who said Ceolfrith had sold out when he took the throne. The one with a powerful family that frightens even the new king." He felt her take a breath. "A lot of people would be interested in Gainmar's fate."

"Aye."

She was a woman who had reason to understand the worst side of politics. He had no idea who she was. It was clear she was not Mercian royalty. But he had as good as guessed that from the start and it made no difference. He did not give a curse for the complicated weight of identity. He had never had one.

He watched the smooth, ring-adorned hand fisted in his clothes. She was still from the ranks he would never match.

"I have to retrieve Gainmar," he said.

"Of course." She made some slight movement in the shadows. "That is why you are still here."

It was hardly a question. He could not see her face. Because she had carefully moved. Because his own eyes were blinded by the flare of the hearth flames behind her.

"Aye." That was his task, simple and complete. Nothing more. He watched her averted face, the flickering firelight and shadow on her pale skin.

You only see dreams once... He had never dreamed at all. And then he had met her.

She was used to dreaming, his unknown noblewoman. The moment had already happened in her life, the one that could lift life from what it was into the impossible thing that you wanted it to be. It had involved the fickle thane Edric.

She looked up. "Did it ever occur to you that you have taken on rather a large task to accomplish alone?"

"Aye." He grinned, because it glossed over the inescapable fact that he did not know whether he would get through this. "Mostly after it was too late. I'm a bit slow on the uptake."

"Aye," she agreed. Her face was expressionless, which counted as a clean hit. He suppressed the next grin and looked hurt.

Rosamund curled her fine lips, princess-like, and he thought the subject turned, but she started talking again.

"You did not know, did you? It was just an ordinary patrol that brought you to Wareham, but you had picked the wrong moment. The Vikings had broken the truce. You saw the dead hostages and your companion set the beacon fires, but you did not go with him. I will bet that you could have got out with your friend.

"I am good with bets," said Rosamund. "I think you chose to stay. You took this mission on yourself." Which was not so much a clean hit as an elbow in the throat, the kind that left you without breath and wishing you would just die and end the choking. She regarded him steadily in the make-shift bed they had shared.

He could talk about West Saxon and Mercian politics, a dozen different reasons.

"Gainmar and I once ended up in the same fight," he said, which was part of the real reason. "It was just some skirmish. They happened before the invasion, but this one was difficult for us and he got stuck and I—" Time rolled back to a cold and grudging spring, the scent of May blossom and blood, black mud slipping underfoot, a broken-shafted spear in the hand of an eighteen-year-old, desperate and dead keen. Afraid. Afraid he would never be good enough.

"You did what?"

He had followed Gainmar because he'd been possessed with some thick-witted notion of heroically rescuing a grateful prince. Because the man was going to be killed. Because people always damned well followed Gainmar. And then—

"We got stuck somewhere dangerous. It took two people to get out of it." How the hell did you explain what it was like to rely on each other when your lives depended on it?

"I see," said Rosamund, as though he had explained the whole thing in a way that made sense— Rosamund who had stood with Merriwen in the middle of a Viking camp.

"You helped rescue the prince," she said lightly. "I am surprised that he did not offer you a place with him, that... What went wrong?"

He would swear he had let nothing alter in his face or a single muscle of his body. But he did not have a skerrik of sense with her. Little defence.

"Perhaps he is not generous?"

Impossible to let that go. None of it was Gainmar's fault.

"Yes, he did offer."

"Then?"

He knew this time he had his face closed off. "I did not accept."

She wanted to ask why, but she did not, and he

did not have the means to tell her. There had been the generous gift, the recognition that he had wanted, offered freely by a Mercian, and when it had come, he found he could not accept. Because it did not change the person he was and that might damage a Mercian giver.

He watched her pale hand slowly uncurl from the muddied mess he was wearing.

"You are a king's man after all," said Rosamund. "It was so from the start. I just had the wrong one in mind. You can see how I do not have much luck with kings."

This time, the lightness of her cultured voice covered things he recognised—bitterness and despair, things he hated because they crippled everything. There were places inside himself that were deformed and maimed and dead.

He tried to cover them over

"Not all kings are alike," he said.

"You think Alfred of Wessex is any different in the end?"

"Yes."

He had recognised that, even as a small thug of sixteen winters who trusted no one. He struggled to explain. He was clever enough with words. It was a survival trick. But they were everyday words, not for things like this.

"The king of Wessex wants people to live through this disaster. All sorts of people. He wants a kingdom that is whole." As far as anyone brought up in a royal hall could grasp the existence of the world outside it, Alfred did, because he was interested in so many things, too many for a man who seemed destined to spend his life fighting. He was more interested in building things. That was where his true strength lay.

"A kingdom that is whole means there is a place for everyone," he said. It did not make for much of a better explanation.

"A place for you?"

But he turned that thought. Peasant into warrior might be overlooked in time of war. But he was something else.

"Alfred would like Merriwen's books."

There was a pause while she doubtless thought about this bizarre piece of logic. Or realised she was lying with someone who was wit-sick.

"I see you are the perfect king's retainer."

"I have to be. Without the king's service, I would be nothing. At least, nothing a reasonable man would wish to recognise." Without the king's service, he would be following in his father's footsteps.

Rosamund became very still. She did not dispute his words because she could see well enough. He had the kind of quality that was bred into barbarians. In his case it had come from a father who had been hanged.

"This way, I would have a life."

"I see."

"It is like a debt."

He had to repay it. Alfred had given him everything, but there were some things even the king was not aware of, or even Ash who was his blood brother. For him, it was rather more than a case of being able to cheat at dice. Ash and Alfred had given him the way out. Not just the chance to do something that did not involve starving, but other things he did not know how to name, or whether they even had names.

Such things would have names in Rosamund's world, easily spoken and true, the right kind of ideas she had always lived with.

"I swore an oath," he said desperately.

There was the sharp sound of her indrawn breath, as though the words struck through to her.

"I understand that," said Rosamund. "I know what it is to give your word to someone, to something, to a purpose." Her eyes flickered with the light of the hearth flame and then were veiled. Like the thoughts in her head. She did not touch him. He fell back on the pieces of truth he could give her.

"What I told you at the beginning about being taken prisoner as part of the West Saxon patrol is exactly what happened. No one expected—"

"That the earl would break the peace."

"No." Regrouping in the safety of East Anglia had seemed the best option for the Danish army after a prolonged and draining stalemate. "Guthrum must be counting on the fleet. Or perhaps he has hopes of receiving aid from the north after all. Or—"

"He broke his oath," she said flatly. She was a thane's daughter.

The entire court had been thrown into a frenzy about the oath-breaking aspect of the disaster. Particularly after Alfred, torn between devoutness and a restlessly inventive mind, had taken the unprecedented and bishop-panicking step of getting a Viking to swear like a Viking.

"An oath made on Thor's arm-ring," said Rosamund. "Not on Christian relics that would mean nothing to him."

Something in her voice sharpened his attention.

"If the earl was going to continue the campaign, he was going to break the oath," he said. It was the practical response.

"Yes. The Jarl kept faith with the needs of his own people. That is what *we* understand."

She had slept with Guthrum.

CHAPTER TEN

HE SHOULD HAVE KNOWN. The Viking earl. What the hell else made sense of her position, her freedom?

The word *we* jolted its way between them like a lightning strike and it was not a slip made out of tiredness, but something deliberate. *The Jarl kept faith with the needs of his own.*

"Do you know why the hostages meant to secure the peace were killed in that particular way?" asked Rosamund.

That particular way swept him back to the riverside at Wareham with the sight and the smell of death all around him. It dragged Boda further back, to the only image his well-schooled mind could not block out at will. *That way.* The moment the breath left the body, the violent struggle of someone doomed. Memory. He wanted to throw up.

"It was the double sacrifice to Odin. They had to be stabbed first and then…"

He did not hear the word *hanged.* Perhaps because the terrible things inside him prevented it. Perhaps because it was already in his mind.

"It had to be done," said the girl lying with him.

It had to be done, they had said to the boy in his mud-stained tunic. And his father's patched leather shoes had climbed up the steps of the gallows tree at the crossroads while he had watched.

"I saw," said Rosamund. "Just a glimpse of the bodies afterwards. After…after Thorkill and his men had finished. I was not meant to see, but I did and then I found out it was Thorkill who killed them. He wanted them dead. Od said it was Thorkill who persuaded the earl."

Thorkill. The dead bodies. Thorkill taking him down with the chains because he had been mad enough to get in the way—mad and filled with the ineradicable rage. The same black fury that choked him now.

"Is that not so?" she asked.

"Yes." His voice was harsh, black.

He heard her move.

"But if you are the earl, it is your own decision in the end. Is that not so?" she said and the rage-filled answer was at his mouth.

"I trusted him," said Rosamund. It was like a declaration of war, the short, deadly words defiant. Defiant…and stubborn.

She did not have to say what she had.

That kind of defiance was so familiar, like the stubbornness. It had made him spit out the worst things about himself before someone else could say them for him—things he feared.

He took her hand. Cold. He knew he had let her see the traces of the black, deep-seated rage locked inside him. He expected her to pull away.

"Tell me." The words were all he could manage, but she did not move away from him and he felt the small tremor of her body. She spoke to him.

"The first moments of something new are important. When I was taken from the nunnery, I was...angry." Her fingers firmed against his flesh. "You know that kind of anger."

She had seen it in him. He watched the small pale blur of her hand in his. A connection that was impossible.

"I had both the anger inside me and a sense of...of things being unreal. Nothing like this had ever happened to me. I had my share of grief because I was an orphan. My parents had died of the fever and I went to the nunnery with Merriwen, but this... I did not believe it could be real. It was the unreality and the anger that helped me. I arrived behaving like a princess of Mercia who would make her own choices and the earl backed what I did. You have to understand that—no one gainsays him."

Alive, or dangling on the end of a rope.

Her slender fingers with their copper and silver rings moved against his. He was so blind that was all he could see, not her face.

"Guthrum helped me," she said and because he had fallen past the nightmare edge, it took him a moment to realise she had stopped speaking. Her cold hand was still. He forced himself to focus on what the words meant. What her silence meant.

Who such a woman could turn to and what the price might be.

She used his name, *Guthrum,* not *the earl.*

A lone woman and a wit-sick waif. Rosamund would arrange the protection of the waif.

"Guthrum—" said Rosamund. *Guthrum the killer.* "I had Ingolf, of course." Silver caught the light. "But behind Ingolf was Guthrum's influence. It never failed and I thought it was reliable. So...I closed my mind to the rest, because of what I wanted, something for me. That is how low I have sunk. But all the rest was there, all the horrors."

Corpses in the air. The things he could not shut out.

What memories did she have? Edric who had abandoned her. The ambitious earl. Ingolf. Himself...another man in the line that spelled desperation. What she wanted was to find a way to live with memories. Otherwise they would maim her as they had maimed him.

"I told you," he said. "If the earl was going to pursue the campaign, he had to break the oath."

"But—"

"It was a matter of practicality." Practicality was his strength. He concentrated on the man he had seen at the peace negotiations, the Viking earl, harsh, filled with volatile pride.

"Do you know what happens to Viking leaders who do not win? Who do not bring in enough loot every time? They run the risk that their own captains will turn on them. Enough disappointed *hersirs* like Thorkill can destroy an earl. Guthrum had to decide, either press on through the unplundered half of Wessex and push himself perhaps as far as a crown, or return to East Anglia with what he has. Even the safety of East Anglia changes as the different Viking war bands come and go. It was a practical decision."

He forced his breath into evenness. He focussed on what he could see, what he could feel here and now, her hand in his, the glitter of the hearth fire. All he had to do was work it out, find the right words, and the horror would lessen for the woman he touched. The words floated out of reach, above the crippling weight of memory, the mad anger that had begun at Guthrum's execution ground.

That rage had come close to undoing everything, not only for himself but for Ash. Never again. You could not let the dead harm the living.

Life and death.

He remembered what Ash had said about Vikings.

"Life and death are threads to a Norseman. The end has already been fated. The true choice is to press on with courage."

"Yes." She spoke, just that word. "The oath on Thor's truth ring was..." Her voice stopped again.

"Was given to a foreigner. In the end it became a ruse of war, a leadership decision…" His voice choked. But he had to find the right way to help her, someone living. All that mattered was that he did not let her down, that she was not alone.

Let me find the words.

"We all face decisions we would rather not see. God knows there are some decisions in my life I would not have wanted to take, but I did. I will go on taking them. Just as you will. Because you have courage."

He watched her slim fingers tighten on his. "We make the decisions we must, at the time we have to."

He sensed the soft exhale of her breath. His own was ungovernable, but she breathed softly, deeply. There was silence, the warmth of the hearth, the flicker of flames. She might have slept in her exhaustion. He let go of her.

But when he moved, her opened eyes fixed on him.

"What if Gainmar is ill?"

"What?"

"Od was carving runes. I saw him. Some of them were charms to ward off enchantment. Some of them were triads that would give you protection against things—even against the bad consequences of your own actions." *The kind he could do with.*

"But there was one rune that kept recurring. It was Ur, strength. Or healing. The protection runes would serve for healing, too. And then...some of the herbs are missing from the store, feverfew."

Merciful God.

"What would you do?" Her green gaze fixed on him, wide, dark and unwavering. "If that was the case?"

"The same. The decision is made."

Gainmar being ill would make the hand-over difficult, lengthening the moment that invited second thoughts, volatile greed and violence. Broken oaths. He did not say it. He did not even touch her.

The plan was made now and she was part of it. Her chances of successfully escaping on her own, with the little daft, uncomprehending wench clinging to her, were nonexistent. She was part of whatever he did, even though afterwards she would go her own way.

The nightmare that was the next step in the plan waited and he would walk into it because it was completely and utterly suited to what he was. But he did not want the nightmare to touch her.

He wanted her to come through this without harm. The imperatives tied up in that were violently simple, and at the same time so complex he could not look at them.

He watched her fineness beside him, close as a breath, the smooth exquisite skin he had touched.

She did not look at him. The future stretched out, with its fate threads and the burden of all that had to be done.

"You do not regret your decision to give your life to the Saxon king?"

"No."

Rosamund thought that of all the many differences between them, that was the one with the power to sever her impossible connection to him.

OD WAITED, black shadow sharp and slanting in the grudging morning light, motionless.

Rosamund knew he was waiting for her.

She stayed hidden in the lee of the cart. She thought about watching Od huddled down with Arne beside the moonlit path, gossiping and complaining, the blindingly fast, shockingly accurate rush of that tall frame when he had caught the sound of her movement.

One could underestimate Od. She thought she never underestimated what a Norseman could do. But she had.

She did not go out into the early sunlight and braid her hair. She had a lot of the answers she had sought, as much information as her supposed mercenary was going to give her right now.

The true answer was the response to the question she had not even known she wanted to ask. Only fools needed to be told what they had already worked out for themselves. She was very foolish.

Someone like her did not have a future with a good man. It had been lost with one footstep outside the nunnery walls. She had thrown it away herself.

She wrapped her arms around her body for warmth beneath the costly fur mantle.

Od turned his head. His hand went to the knife sheath slung at his hip.

She stepped back. In the same moment, she saw what had drawn Od's attention. *Who*.

Her other piece of knowledge was that she knew what the stakes were.

The newcomer stopped beside the black, angular shadow. Inside two minutes he had the restless Od talking to him as though they were at ease. The first touch of sunlight made fire out of the copper glints in his hair. He said something. Too far away for her to hear. Od spoke at length. He might have had everything to say to his casually attentive listener. She watched how the trick was effected. It was effortlessly clever. Skin-clammingly risky.

You do not regret your decision to give your life to the Saxon king?

No.

Boda laughed, the sound clear and uncomplicated on the cold air, animal good spirits. Faultless.

There were things he did not know about what was in Od's head.

Od gestured. The knife was in his hand. She walked forward.

Boda became aware of her first. Like one of his fate threads.

He did not look at her.

He already had Od turned away, one hand briefly round the other man's arm. There was some jest, the easy laughter. His back to her. The laughter echoed. Sun glittered off the blade.

"A fine morning."

They stopped. The Viking Od with his knife turned first, the proper order of things. Besides, he was surprised. King Alfred's agent turned next. She looked at the fading bruises on his hand. She did not look at his eyes. Could not. Ought to. There were things about Od that she had not told him last night. She watched the loose curve of his fingers. Too beguiled. Desperate. Lost.

"It was better staying in a village last night," she said to Od. "Do you not agree?"

Od's eyes were bloodshot—a night spent watching on the road. His gaze fixed on her. The slightly swollen lids narrowed with the sting of shortened, irritated temper. With something else. Her mantle was not fastened closely. She did not touch it.

"Then you should be comfortable enough again tonight, princess." Od's bloodshot gaze moved. She forced herself to stand still. She was utterly aware of Boda's closeness, the solid bulk between her and Od. "We should reach the next settlement. Though doubtless it will be as deserted as this place, as useless."

"More use to us than to the Saxons." The breeze made her cloak flutter, the hem of her skirts. "A matter of advantage."

You are one of us, now.

"Aye." Od's eyes flickered. Alfred's man watched. Od caught her reference to their previous discussion, like a hound on the scent.

"All you have to do is work out where the advantage is," he said.

A woman like you knows how.

"Perhaps." She smiled. She kept her voice cool, steady, calculated. It might mean whatever Od put his mind to. Od measured the smile, the possible acknowledgement of the moment he had told her where her best interests lay. The things he could report to his commander. Dutifully done.

The eagerness was his own, personal and utterly disquieting, so brief in its moment of life that Boda might not have seen it.

"So—" began Od. Someone shouted ahead of them. The baggage train was moving off. Idiots left behind could take their chances and be cut down by whatever unseen Saxon force lurked in the hills and the woods.

"Time to be away." Od turned and the fleeting moment was gone, irretrievable.

Boda had seen—King Alfred's agent who planned deception and stood on the edge of death. The man she had slept with had understood the volatile secrets she had to show him in Od's mind. She looked at him and something she did not intend sprang to life in the same instant that Od turned back towards them. The touch of flame.

THERE WAS A REASON thieves chose dark weather. Boda waited patiently for the blackness to become intense enough to hide what he had to do. Night fell in shifting shadows over an encampment that was restless, nervous and inclined to draw weapons.

For the first time on the journey, there was a rising wind that would mask the slightest betraying sound. He watched the moment of light-change when everything altered shape, even luck, and he saw what he wanted.

The female figure hesitated, bound on what must have become her daily ritual. He understood now, why she was so necessary. She took a step into shadow. Prudent. Or frightened.

But still she went on.

He followed, moving easily until he found a patch of blackness. Then he waited. His quarry had gone to the familiar covered cart placed again near the earl's. Near enough to be protected, but not close enough to attract too much attention from the earl's guards who did not answer even to someone as useful as Thorkill.

They had not moved Gainmar. It might mean any of a dozen things. The woman still hesitated. This time there was no helpful arm in a finely braided sleeve reaching down to help her. He weighed the possibilities.

What he wanted were the few moments it would take to see Gainmar for himself first, to assess the man's condition, to speak, if it was possible. If not… He did not let his mind touch the rest of the plan, not until it happened. Survivor's trick. But the consciousness was there underneath. The nightmare.

Olga took a step. What he did next depended on who was in the cart with the prisoner. The only certainty was going forward. Unpaid debt. He would—

There was no distinguishable sound in the windswept dark, nothing to warn her of the other man's approach, but her head still turned. After a moment, she put out her hand. It was taken. Rosamund's friend, Olga, disappeared into Thorkill's embrace.

There would not be another chance. Boda moved—simple enough to turn through the blackness to the back of the cart. To his surprise, no one stopped him. The slight sound of his movement was masked by the restless wind, by a more than adequate distraction for Thorkill.

Luck.

He did not know how long he would have before Thorkill moved from lust to the business of the hostage, whether there were other guards inside the wagon, what he would find. There was only one certainty. Once he had got himself into the cart and seen Gainmar, he was not going to escape.

He swung his weight up and over the wooden side.

"Where is Olga?"

"With the other women." Rosamund had seen

her join them. She stirred what passed for food in the copper cauldron over the hearth pit in tonight's looted bower. Merriwen was throwing pebbles. Five-stones. She could not stand the next question, because she could not answer it.

"Where is B—"

"This is nearly ready. Supper."

"Oh," said Merriwen, successfully distracted. The stones scattered. Rosamund watched their flight, but in her mind it was another hand she saw, bruised and in chains.

"What is for supper?"

You do not regret your decision…

"What is it?"

There was never any room for regrets. They killed you.

"What *is* it?"

"Briw."

"Briw?"

It was always *briw,* which had become the catch-all term for whatever could be scavenged and put together in one pot.

"Why—"

"It has bacon," Rosamund said. It was in there, somewhere. *What was he doing?*

"Why does it have to be *briw?*"

The shreds of meat swirled past. "We do not have anything else."

"Why?"

The same question. Every day since the first

month of successful raiding round Wareham, since the Saxons had forced a siege and then a truce. The king's men who did not give up when they ought to—

"It is difficult on journeys. You understand that."

"Can we have bread? Or roast meat?"

"Later. Later when we get to Exeter." *And then Cornwall. Another journey with winter coming closer each day.* She thought about it, about all the things she had been so sure she could manage. Fear closed round her heart. Suppose she could not? Merriwen was sixteen now. Not a child.

"You always say *later*."

She would manage because she had to. She could talk Merriwen round.

"Come on. This smells good. You like bacon and you can have the biggest—"

"No, I do not." The stones hit the floor. It was a shock. Merriwen had been so good, so happy, so much more confident since—

She shut her mind against the thought of the king's man, the risk-taker, the wreaker of unknown magic. Her shoulders were stiff. She turned her head.

"I want bread," said Merriwen, who had such a precarious grasp on reality. "You never let me have what I want. You always stop me. You always get everything for yourself. You got presents from Ingolf. You get all the nice clothes and then you went and got mud all over *my* dress."

Rosamund's hand tightened on the wooden

spoon. It was unsteady. She was so tired she could hardly see. The copper and silver rings glittered in the firelight, stinging her eyes.

"Presents," said Merriwen. "It is not fair."

She looked at the stormy face with its pouting lips, the beautiful figure half-guessed beneath the plain gown, youthfully mature now and full, far more voluptuous than hers.

"Why do I not get presents?"

Try it. Just try it for one day. There are enough of Guthrum's men to oblige you, and then you will see— She put the wooden spoon down. It seemed to be stuck to her damp palm.

"I have looked after you."

"Because I am the princess. So I am supposed to say what happens. You are not supposed to tell me what to do. I do not like it."

The decorated fingers of her hand uncurled from the wooden spoon handle. It was a long way to Cornwall, a road filled with dangers she could not foresee, that would take Ceolfrith's niece and swallow her whole. Dangers even Rosamund hesitated to face. *But she could manage it.*

"I am the princess."

She could manage it if she was alone.

The base, cowardly thought reverberated in her head. She sat down. She could not get as far as the wall bench. She just sat on the floor and put her head in her hands. Her fingers were shaking. She heard Merriwen move, the rustle of skirts made out of coarse plain wool. She did not know how it was possible to love someone as much as she loved Merriwen and at the same time feel such things that ate at her now, bitterness and rage and despair.

"I am the princess? Aren't I?" The footsteps halted. "Rosamund?"

The interchangeable name hung in the air between them. She raised her head from her hands. It was not a declaration of hostility, it was the question of the mysterious stranger who lived behind Merriwen's eyes.

"Aye. You are the princess."

The mysterious stranger watched her. "But I am not supposed to say so."

"No. But it is because…because…"

"You should sit on the bench. It has a cushion."

It did. Someone, in their mad flight to escape invaders, had abandoned that.

"The bacon will be ready. I can dish it out."

Merriwen always made drips and lost half the—

"The ladle slopped."

"Let me." She got up. One step at a time. She took the ladle. "I'll help you." Always. They were friends. She got a smile that brought her to the edge of tears.

"We have to leave some for Boda," said Merriwen. "He is one of us now."

Rosamund stopped, with the ladle dipped in bacon and boiled peas.

"He—" She choked on it. *No.* But she could not face that explanation, not even to herself.

"Boda wants to play five-stones with me. I hope he comes back before Olga."

"I told you, Olga is with the other women and then she—"

"No, she is not. I heard her talking. She went to meet Thorkill."

"Thorkill?"

"Olga said Thorkill was going to see the sick man tonight."

IT WAS NOT JUST BAD. It was worse.

Boda slid through the dimness of the cart. The interior was lit by a single brass lamp burning cheap oil. The sour fitful flame glared directly into the man's face and the fickle luck turned in his hand.

Ill was not supposed to mean dying.

He knelt beside the unmoving figure wrapped in furs.

"Gainmar."

Or dead.

God's breath. He touched the exposed skin of the neck. Freezing. Chad's bones—

The dark-ringed eyelids flickered. The blood-shot gaze wavered then fixed on him. It took a moment before the recognition clicked home. The effect of deliberate estrangement on his part.

"You?"

The effect of disbelief.

"What the...are you doing here?"

It always amazed him how well princes could swear. He explained—keeping to the barest essentials, watching the forced breath, the glasslike skin, the glimpse of bandaging, aware of the precarious timing, the wavering attention in the fever-clouded eyes. Of Thorkill half a dozen paces away.

In the end, he could not stop the question.

"So how did you become quite such a mess?" It came out with violence.

The prince raised one eyebrow. "Clumsiness."

"Some slip-up." This was rather more than a case for healing signs scratched on bits of wood.

"Aye." The tortured gaze suddenly slipped beyond him. "Do you know how they died?"

All the other hostages.

"Odin's double rite." Stabbing and— When the feverish head turned, he could see the imprint left by rope marks on the exposed neck. *Hanging.*

He realised Gainmar was talking.

"They did not mean to harm me," said the strained voice. "The noose was never fully used. Like the spear. The point was meant to glance past. But there was such confusion."

Aye. Well, there would have been. There was, even when I got there and—

"The blade cut too close."

Clumsiness, indeed. Too much damage, partly unintentional, like most of life's disasters. "But you are still alive and—"

"Why?"

That was it. The direct question, and the blood-shot eyes fixed on his. Princes were often made of steel. Occupational necessity. This was Gainmar.

"Thorkill is nervous that things will go badly for Guthrum. He plans to decamp on the proceeds of selling you to supplement the rest of his plunder." *Or if he decides against that and stays with Guthrum, he will let you die, which would be easy.* "So I am here to retrieve you."

"You could not even move me, and I cannot help you." The steel glinted in that unsparing assessment.

"Thorkill will take care of it all. He is going to sell you to us, to me, to be precise."

"No."

"What do you mean?"

"I knew when I came here what the odds were. Ransoming me would be throwing money away. We do not have money to throw away. I am dying."

No. Boda looked at the colourless face, the rope marks. It could not end in death. He could not accept that. It was time to rob the gallows tree of its spoils. It had to be the thief's turn.

"No," he said aloud. The word was flat. There was no place for argument. He did not know how good Olga's charms were, but they were unlikely to be that good.

"It is not over yet. The plans are made." He spoke to the man he had shared fighting with.

"There are others involved in the escape, not just you, two women who are captive, one of whom is helpless and also of your kin."

"What? Who?"

He recognised the fast calculation he had first seen in that spring skirmish two winters ago. He also saw the struggle behind the fevered eyes to assimilate all that he had said so rapidly.

"Ceolfrith's niece," he said carefully. "Ceolfrith gave her to the Vikings."

"Ceolfrith did what? His niece is here? It cannot be her. There were rumours she was simple—the one called Rosamund."

Chad's bones. Well, he had known, really. "Aye."

"I never knew she was here. That is something the earl did not say, not even to boast of."

So. And he had fallen into the trap of thinking the thrice-damned earl was predictable. Guthrum with his influence...

There did not seem much else to say, except a statement of fact. "The plan has to succeed."

"You are...determined on it."

"Aye." He forced his mind away from the yawning abyss and back onto details. "I am going to arrange the hand-over. Just work in with what they do. I—" He heard the noise outside. Gainmar, senses fever-blunted, had not. It was someone moving.

"I can hear Thorkill coming," he said. "I want him to catch me here."

"You are mad to go through with this. You must be able to find some other way for your Rosamund."

His Rosamund. There was a valuable moment in which he could not speak.

"Think," said Gainmar. "Thorkill is not going to want to take the risks involved in negotiating with Wessex under Guthrum's nose."

No. Thorkill would not. He had not wanted to burden a possibly dying prince with that particular explanation. The scuffling movement sounded again, closer, impatient. There was no time for more.

"It will work out. Lord," he added, because he had forgotten that, speaking to the fighter as though nothing else intervened.

"He will negotiate with me," he said more loudly and that was all he could say, simple words Thorkill could overhear, the only attempt at reassurance for all that courage. The heavy cover across the cart ripped back. He saw the leap of understanding in Gainmar's eyes, the realisation of who else would pay for his life and why. Same for princes as for slaves, there was always someone who wanted control of your fate.

For God's sake, he thought, *don't give up now.*

Thorkill's feet thudded into the cart.

CHAPTER ELEVEN

BODA STOOD islanded in bad torchlight. The chamber Thorkill had commandeered in the empty village stank of rancid tallow—and anger. The danger of it rolled off the crumbling walls, seeking its target. But it was the familiarity, the intimately ingrafted knowledge of what would come that raised sweat on his skin.

Thorkill paced, the fast violence frustrated, uncertain, yet, of the trail. But there were no secrets to Boda. Every step along the way was known to him and had been since he could think or remember. Feel.

He shut out the thoughts that were memories.

"Tell me," said Thorkill.

They were getting by in lamed English. He had no desire to betray that his knowledge of Danish was more than rudimentary.

"What else do you want to hear? I can get you the best price for what you hold, with the least…inconvenience to yourself." The Viking was in a tough spot. He let the glossed hesitation say it. The deep vein in Thorkill's forehead stood out.

"I want to hear the truth, not feeble boasting."

"I'll get it out of him." Unsheathed steel hissed out of the shadows—Arne, who had the obvious score to settle. Thorkill let him take a good three steps before he stopped him. Od, who had the more deeply hidden motives that Rosamund had shown him, did not move.

He could not allow his mind to touch on *Rosamund,* on the task she had set herself and would not give up.

Arne did not resheathe the *seax.* Od waited.

If he let his mind turn to Rosamund, he would not be able to control his thoughts. "Did you want to hear the deal?"

"You were trespassing," answered Thorkill.

In other words, *not yet.* Arne and Od were not the only ones with a score to settle. It was expected. He had to rely on the assumption that when it came down to self-interest, Thorkill was coldly practical at the core.

If not, this would go to the death.

He shrugged one shoulder and looked moody. "I was checking the goods. Not exactly in perfect condition."

Thorkill spun round. The rest would have been almost too fast to combat, even if he had tried. Thorkill body-drove him into the wall. The back of his skull cracked against the solid timber beam. The pain burst in his head. Too strong. If he lost consciousness, he was dead. Thorkill was mouthing at him.

"…I do not take complaints about the way I treat people. I do as I will. You…" The rest was invective. Boda tried to focus past the furious face, the sharp sickening pain.

"You will learn…" The knotted hand was fisted in his hair, dragging his head back. The movement nearly threw him into oblivion. Torchlight flared past him, heat. "Mercenary…" The hair-pulling was an insult, if you counted social niceties. "Peasant. No more worth than a slave…" The last word reached through. He felt it touch his own anger. *No.* He opened his eyes. There was one thing about peasants and thralls, they had thick skulls.

"Learn what?" asked Boda. "How to get into an impasse?"

There was an instant's jolt through the solidly-muscled arm.

"You will learn my power," yelled Thorkill.

There was the flash of steel. Thorkill's blade, not Arne's. He scarcely registered the fact that it was bloodstained. He had not felt the cut because of the greater pain. Because of the black lash of fury that had surged through him, strong enough to take control, the anger that built on too many dark things.

"I do as I will," said Thorkill. "That is my power."

Don't challenge it. He thought of Rosamund, alone. Gainmar. The rope mark on the chilled skin, the dead bodies hanging.

But all he could feel was the pent-up rage.

"You are nothing," yelled the distorted face inches from his.

The only warning was the change in grip, the imperative to keep clear of the knife. The straight-arm blow caught him across the ribs, landing precisely where Thorkill had kicked his chained target, the force of it enough to double up his body. He heard the blood-quickened yell of triumph and he knew what was wanted, the proof of successful power. The game always proceeded until that was achieved. He had set his own hand to this, so he let out a sound of pain. Thorkill was grinning.

"You see? You understand? I can show you…" His slackened weight slammed back against the wall. He avoided the knife but not the torch. His shoulder hit the iron bracket. The rancid tallow spat. Flame. Searing. He moved but Thorkill shoved him back. He cried out, the sound wordless, animal. The pressure holding him instantly released.

"Learn your place." It could have been now or the same words from the deeper blackness of his life. Thorkill's muscles flexed again.

"I will not countenance a thief." *A thief.* It brought his mind back into focus, but it also ripped the cover off the appalling anger. He could no longer react passively, yell on cue, play the part.

He could see too far back. There was nothing to shield him from the other hanged corpse, the thief on the gallows, his own flesh and blood. *Once a thief, always a thief in the black night.* Thorkill's face blurred under memories that held violence, the force so strong he could merge with it. A small step. He was capable of taking it. All of his life had taught him how.

Thorkill's hand slipped. Every muscle in his own body tensed, the reaction so fast, uncontrolled, primitive, greedy. The anger had blotted out the physical pain. It was only the smallest step. Payback for the pain. Not just the present pain, for all of it. The way to wipe it out. The thrall's revenge on its tormentor.

"...power..." yelled Thorkill.

His back was braced against the solid wall two inches from smoking flame. He did not know what stopped him levering his weight forward—the consciousness that the world had shifted, that something beyond the familiar, brutish blackness existed. Rosamund's world.

"Power changes." The words pushed their way out of the jagged dryness of his throat. "For everyone."

"You..."

He did not hear the rest. He forced himself to focus on the narrowed eyes, on Thorkill's face, Earl Guthrum's man who held Gainmar's fate and would hold Rosamund's if he could. All it would take was his own failure. His fault.

"Power changes for everyone." The words came. "For the earl." That was the point of weakness for

Thorkill—fear that the earl would fail and drag Thorkill into defeat with him. "For you."

"I—"

"I have the way out."

The narrow eyes blinked. He let Thorkill haul him away from the wall.

"Why should I believe you?" Thorkill's gaze was fixed, steady—the core of cold intelligence. It was there.

"Because it is easy." *Easy as killing.* "You want the payment. I have the buyer."

"King Ceolfrith of Mercia?"

"I am a Mercian." He was. Even slaves had roots. The truth held, even as his voice slid with practised ease into lies. "So are the rest of the men who will arrange to buy your prisoner. They are mercenaries, like me. We will go where the reward is, but we prefer our home, not Wessex. There will be no difficulties if you deal with us. A quiet transaction away from prying eyes. We have no interest beyond a fair payment. We will deliver the prisoner to Ceolfrith and Ceolfrith will take him."

He took a breath through the pain. The more bitter side of being Mercian came out, the truth inside the lies.

"The Mercian king would not want anyone else to lay hands on his kinsman."

He let the irony show in his face, convincing because it was real. Thorkill caught it. The ruthless intelligence had worked out the political implications of that statement. Ceolfrith would welcome his dangerous kinsman with open arms. He would also dispose of him. It would be a satisfactory end for a potential rival with inconveniently embarrassing connections to a West Saxon king, a man who was no longer on the same side. There was silence. He pushed it.

"Ceolfrith would not even object to…certain damage to the goods."

"Ceolfrith. That rat." Thorkill spat into the floor rushes.

"The rat will pay. Money is money, wherever it comes from. We take what we can."

"And what will you take, mercenary?" Od's voice cut the sharp focus between them. Thorkill turned his head. Arne was standing with his mouth hanging open, confused by the shifting action. It was Od who took a pace forward, slow and deliberate.

"I will receive Ceolfrith's reward. Just as you will take the ransom."

But the renewed suspicion had jumped in Thorkill's eyes.

Od kept moving, circling behind. Boda had given him the opportunity by letting Thorkill drag him back into the open space at the centre of the bower. But he had known what he was dealing with. Never expect that it would stop, that anything was changed. Od came to a halt at his back.

He would not see what was coming.

It was both the simplest trick and the one he hated.

"You surprise me," said Od's voice at his ear. "What was wrong with the rewards given out by Saxon Alfred?"

He shrugged. "Perhaps they were not enough. Besides, I am not suited to belief in grand ideas." It was simple enough to hold Thorkill's gaze with that statement, because it was no recognisable king's man but the peasant who was in this room. Thorkill saw it.

He could hear Od's fast breath. He concentrated on Thorkill, on the next point that might possibly tip the scales his way. "That kind of belief will stop the Saxon king from giving in. Guthrum should have worked that out. The way you did."

The hard-boned face tightened, because the disaster of the raiding party was fresh, the unexpected resistance, even the villages carefully emptied of anything usable for a desperate army like this one.

Think about it.

"Ceolfrith is a realist." His voice flowed, cajoling, beggar-skilled. Thorkill's eyes were sharp as the blade in his hand. "You understand that just as I do."

Behind him, Od shifted abruptly, and then as suddenly stilled—the unexpectedness he hated. He felt his breath lurch.

The whispered threat was in Danish, violent. "You have nothing—"

"It is the answer." His voice drowned Od's,

directed only at Thorkill. He knew how to do this. String the right words together. Give people what they want to hear—the shyster's trick. His trick. His throat felt raw, but his voice came out with the smoothness of rich mead.

"We both know how to get what we want, what is due. In the end, every man works for himself."

Tell them what they already think. He steadied his breath, his awareness on Thorkill, nothing to spare for Od, armed behind him. The walls of the Saxon bower seemed suddenly close, as though they would suffocate him and the blackness lapped at the ragged edges of his thoughts.

Always act as though things were possible.

He lifted one shoulder. "Is that not the only way?"

Od stirred at his back, as though he could feel the balance shift away from him. There was no other sound.

For God's sake, let him achieve this much. Rosamund's future and Merriwen's, Gainmar's life.

"The survivor's way," said Thorkill at last. "Tell me how much." He leaned back, let go. Boda's heartbeat slammed, as though it had stopped without his knowing. Things were possible....

"You cannot," screamed Od. "You cannot trust him." There was the thin hiss of metal behind him.

Chad's bones.

"What?" yelled Thorkill. "Will *you* tell me what I can and cannot do? I made you from nothing and

I can break you." He was shouting, but he still had not grasped the truth. If he saw Od's drawn knife, everything unravelled into bloodshed—the plan, Gainmar's safety, Rosamund. He launched himself backwards, twisting, unsure where the knife was. That it missed was mostly luck. They both slammed into the floor, his weight on top, but hampered by pain. Od sensed the weakness, fast as a cornered rat, striking out with hand and knee. But if Od was a dirty fighter, he was dirtier. He forced a stalemate. Od's hands grasped at his bleeding throat, but the right arm was so numbed it was unusable, even for retrieving the knife.

"You fool," spat Thorkill, seeing the blade. "Kill him now and you kill the money. Get up."

The word *now* hung by a thread. Od had drawn before the fight. The blade had been meant for Thorkill first. One word and everything fell apart. Od's hand was unsteady at his throat, like the shared breath of brutally violent exertion. The sweating face stared into his.

"Later," he said, so quietly that only the man straining to kill him could hear it. He was masked from Thorkill's line of sight. "Unless you are so poor a fighter you lose the next chance the way you lost this one."

"Get up." Thorkill's boot slammed against the knife, sending it spinning. At the same instant, Boda broke Od's grip.

He got up.

"Fool, indeed," He did not look at the other man. No need. They both understood, not just the promise in that challenge but the unspoken reason.

He haggled with Thorkill over money.

SHOCK HELD HIM for an instant in the blackness.

She had come looking for him.

It was Olga who held her back, not only with heated words, but with physical force.

Perhaps there were some remains of friendship there after all.

Boda pushed himself through the black shadows that were too close to Thorkill's bower. If either of the two women became aware of his movement, it was Olga. He stepped out into the weak moonlight on the other side of them.

Rosamund wrenched her arm free of Olga's. Her eyes burned. Olga gave him the kind of glance cast at demons, the sort that ought to be exorcised. She moved back into the shadows without a word.

"I thought you would not come back," said Rosamund. She had forced herself to wait until the faint trace of Olga's figure was far enough away. "I thought…I could not get rid of her and I had to find—" *You.*

The disbelief held him silent, the hot mess still locked inside him. *Not here.* Neither of them said it. He touched her because he could not help it. His hand closed over her arm. They turned and walked away from Thorkill, from the brutal violence. But he knew the taint of it still ran in his blood like a black stain. They reached tonight's bower in someone else's village. Silence. Rosamund shut the door. There was heat, the steaming water in the great cauldron like last night, flames in the hearth, a lamp. The light blinded him.

She touched him. One moment nothing, and then her warmth, the lithe curving shape of her in his arms, the soft, malleable heat of her mouth on his. The way she gave to every movement and every thought and every touch, to each breath. The way she invited him in.

The mess inside him was wound tight, like a disaster only she could release. There were no words, only the leap of feeling that confounded him whenever she was there. Only the imprint of her body on his, the rounded swell of her breasts, the dip of her waist, the fullness of her hips against his. He was rock-hard. So shot with desire, so tight that it could have been over in seconds.

She moved, the subtle press of her body against his hardened flesh almost enough to send him over the edge. All he had to do was bear that smooth flesh backwards and push inside her, and they would be together like last night. He would be lost in the same madness, the feel of her body round his, the scorching heat, the same insane blinding hunger. He did not know that he would even take the minimum care for her that he had taken last time.

It was as though something broke inside him. He

froze. And when he could breathe again, he was suddenly aware of the suppressed pain locked behind each movement, the bitter ache of abused muscle. Blood. He was aware of precisely what he was.

He could not touch her.

He pulled back and she made a small startled sound. Her hands at his shoulders tightened. She tried to hold him. She touched his neck underneath the loose mess of his hair, his head. He wrenched away, the movement not a matter of will this time, but animal reaction to blinding pain. Her fingers brushed against his throat.

Her breath choked.

For the first time since he had walked out of Thorkill's bower, she truly saw him.

"What happened?"

He looked at her fine clothes, her intricately twisted and ribboned hair, the delicate threads of silver at her ears, the smooth perfection of her face, and he could not say any of it. So he slammed the lock over the mess, over what was gone. *Think of the next step.*

"I have made an arrangement with Thorkill." He took a single breath. "This is what I have to tell you, what the plan is, what will happen." He ignored the physical pain, the still-volatile rush of desire. He concentrated everything on the barest and most profound fact that he would make an escape for her. "This is all that matters—"

"No."

He stayed motionless, the weight in his chest like lead. She still had hold of his arm.

"Do not tell me such things now. Not…" Her fingers moved again across his sleeve, the lethally tensed muscle beneath. His skin tightened, his breath. "Not yet." The tightness burned through him. She lowered her head. The lamplight slid like gold across her sleekly woven hair. Rosamund… But he had seen the sudden, abrupt fear in her eyes. There was the smallest copper trace on her pale fingers. His blood.

He stepped back, breaking the touch. He heard her sharp breath.

"Rosamund." It was not even her name. She answered to it. She raised her head. But she did not quite look at him.

"I have to tell you what is planned," he said again. "That is the only thing that matters."

"Yes. Of course it is." She took a step away.

"Thorkill will accept a ransom for Gainmar. He will deliver him to an agreed meeting place tomorrow." One step after another. He focussed on breathing. "All I had to do was make it simple for Thorkill. As far as he is concerned, he is selling Gainmar to a group of mercenaries. The mercenaries then sell Gainmar to King Ceolfrith. No dangerous West Saxon involvement, no chance of Earl Guthrum finding out until Thorkill is well away."

Her fingers twisted together. He thought of all

she felt about the earl, about Thorkill, the hidden thoughts in her head.

"Thorkill would believe that." She paused. "What about Od?"

"He will follow his commander."

"You are sure?"

"Yes."

Her fingers smoothed out. "I suppose they both know how kings like Ceolfrith work."

He could see that her hands were not quite steady. *Never get in the way of the powerful.* It was like an endless cycle. Except this time, it would stop.

"Macsen and the others will make the arrangements. Thorkill will be occupied collecting his ransom and while he is, Macsen's men will help you and Merriwen get away."

"What?" She whirled round, rich, crushed skirts flaring. She had expected naught from him. He understood that and so his face showed nothing. Her own expression was transparent. Then she blinked and glanced away.

"But I am a danger. Merriwen is a double danger, perhaps an impossible liability. Why would you risk such a thing?"

Because you are my dream when I did not think such things existed.

He could not say that. He did not know whether he would survive tomorrow. If something went amiss, he was the first target. Probably so, even if all went well.

Not good odds. And even survival changed nothing. He knew what he was—today had shown the mirror.

She looked at him.

He gave the right answer, the only one possible.

"I do not believe you can afford to stay here one day after I am gone. I am your prisoner." He watched the tense line of her shoulders, the long graceful sweep of her back. "I will disappear at the same time as Thorkill. People will want to know why. You and Merriwen cannot afford the slightest increase in vulnerability."

"The earl." She said it like a person chanting some precarious, long-held belief.

"Earl Guthrum is engaged in a massive risk." And the ruthless bastard was hardly likely to be in an indulgent mood this time. He tried to find the right words. He understood an unacceptable life view.

"The earl has to be feeling some uncertainty. Actions like Thorkill's just make it harder for him to convince his men he is on the right track. He is going to strike out after being betrayed and deserted by one of his captains. He will have to."

Guthrum's strength lay in doing what was necessary.

"He will not have time for subtle distinctions."

Her eyes narrowed. *You will not do anything to endanger me or those who are with me.* Almost her first words. She understood what was necessary for survival. He had simply made things worse for her.

She should have been in her fancy nunnery school with her books and her dreams, and that precious thane she was betrothed to should have kept his promise.

"The king's men will help you get to Cornwall, or if you want Wessex, they will make it possible."

She moved. It was startlingly abrupt, like someone driven. "No. I don't— My own plans will— I cannot—"

But the truth hit her. Some things were possible and some things were not. Not everyone could see the difference. Rosamund could. She stopped pacing.

"There isn't another way, is there?"

"No." He watched her accept the help from him that she would not have taken without the burden of responsibility for Merriwen. A king's retainer could not have done more, or been bound more narrowly.

"It will work out." He did not know where the absolute conviction in his voice came from. It had little enough to do with practicality. He only knew that this had to work out for her, if not for him. Otherwise there was nothing.

She touched him. He had not expected it and there was no time to draw back. She took hold of his arm. Her slender fingers settled slowly round his forearm, the deliberate touch of her hand halfway between the sexually loaded caress she had used earlier and the tight grip of a warrior—both the qualities she held.

She was all he wanted.

"Tomorrow is the end, then?"

"Yes."

"So there is tonight."

"Tonight is…" What? Meaningless. Perhaps seven hours before dawn. He had not intended staying with her, only being nearby. He could not stay.

Tonight was the compass of eternity.

"I cannot think of time," said Rosamund. "Of tomorrow. Not yet." He heard her take a small breath.

"Do you remember what Mercia was like?"

The abruptness of her question scored straight through him, taking a balance that was more than physical, that was far more precarious than he had thought.

"You see, I cannot." The steadiness in her voice was like ice over deep water, the kind of sorrow he did not know what to do with.

"It rained. There was an east wind that could freeze your b…ears off."

She made a small startled sound. "Ah. I can remember it now."

"Right. I do not know what it was like where your nunnery was, but along the river bank in the south if you did not see Mercia it was because of the fog."

"Well, perhaps that was not so very different." Her hand over his arm brushed bruising. He must reek of violence and black thoughts.

"I can remember the walled orchard," she said. "The pear trees in autumn with so much fruit, and the birds to be scared away before they ruined it." She shifted and his flesh reacted to the slightest movement. Her hand fisted in his tunic.

"There was always some fruit left in the grass and when it fermented the wasps would come. I used to like watching the wasps get too drunk to fly."

"Sympathetic wench, you were."

"So what do you remember? The River Thames?"

"Yes. That." He had not considered there was anything beyond that. The deep water, the hawthorn bushes grown to mark the corners of the estate, had been the boundaries of the known world.

His horizon had expanded at the crossroads. He flicked his mind away from that. "I remember the farm, the shadows of the oxen first thing in the morning, how cold it was, ploughing, the runes placed in each corner of the field."

"Runes? For magic?" she asked dubiously, the lost dreamer at odds with her convent education.

"To keep the weeds down," said the peasant and got an almost-laugh out of her. He could feel the way her tensed muscles started to relax, the way her warm weight drifted against him.

"Did that really stop weeds?" asked the thane's daughter.

"No." It was labour. He had done the lot, including scaring plagues of birds off ripening fruit.

"I can see it now," said his dreamer. "All the things I had thought were lost. It is as though I have them back when I am with you. Even the things I never really had, like the mist on the river."

It was madness. Their lives were nothing alike. He could not see a damned thing, only her. Her gold hair with its twisted ribbons and the white oval of her face, the shadows left by lost things he could not restore and probably did not even understand.

The desire for her choked him.

"You have to sleep before morning." He moved, breaking her grip. The pain across his ribs made him awkward, not nearly quick enough and she caught at him, the warmed and relaxed muscles of her body suddenly and tensely urgent.

"Do not go. Stay with me this last night, even if it is just being in the same room." Her hand was on his body. "You once slept with me."

He stopped, tightness in each muscle, the black bitter thoughts still in his head.

"You do not even know who—" *what* "—I am." It was all still there, the traces of blackness like the traces of blood dried into his skin.

"You have no idea what I have done, or what I may do tomorrow."

"It makes no difference. There are the hours

before dawn. This room." Her hand moved, the lightest touch across his fully-clothed body and he was lost, the reaction merciless, clear to her, because he heard the sudden change in her breath. He waited. It had to be her choice.

"This is what I want," she said, as though she were not afraid of him, or repulsed, and he had moved, the impulse unstoppable, his hands at her shoulders possessive. Her fingers slid up over his body and touched skin. The fire sprang between them. But her hand at his neck was too close to blood, the sudden harshness in his body too close to the mad edge that had taken him before.

He drew back carefully. She clung to him.

"Stay."

"I need the water."

She let go. There was a cut-off sound. She had touched the back of his shoulder. Her hand came away with small flakes of charred wool.

He moved away towards the water.

She would ask him.

Her eyes were wide, fixed on him. He turned away, waiting for her to speak, to ask him about Thorkill, the closed chamber.

If he could just get some of the marks off his skin, the scent of violence, the reek of greed and fear and frustration, the eagerness to inflict pain.

His own utterly unacceptable anger.

She had had the water already prepared beside the fire. There was silence. He began to take off his

clothes. The rustling sound behind him told him she
had followed. But she did not try to help him. She
did not speak. Perhaps she realised the things that
had driven him past the edge. That he was not
capable of replying.

Perhaps she was the one who understood, like a
gift he did not deserve.

The water was cooling, clean and untouched.
He worked quickly and she held back, out of the
pity she had for the maimed, out of horror because
of the marks. He did not know. Only that the awareness between them burned.

He knew she watched. He knew how close she
was, white flame in the dark. He stripped. He was
fully erect.

He poured water rapidly. He knew she saw not
only the fire but the fresh damage over the darkened
bruising across his ribs, the trail of dried blood at
his throat. For all he knew she saw where the sweat
had touched his skin and the bitter aftermath of the
unacceptable anger. He could do nothing about
that.

Water sluiced over his burning skin. It could
wash off only the surface marks, not the burn, the
black bruising…older scars that had been bedded
in long before the king's man existed. When he
had finished, he shoved a clean piece of linen
against the shallow cut at his throat to stop the last
of the bleeding. He heard her move. The air
between them burned, unbreathable. But he waited

before he turned, so that there would be nothing of the unacceptable disaster left. Because she had to have time to change her mind.

He saw her eyes, then the slender lines of her body against the pile of bedding beside the hearth. She still wore her fine dress, the warmly subtle curves beneath half shown, half guessed-at, enough to bring madness. Her gilded hair with its bright threads trailed out like the moonlight he had thought her made from in that first moment.

But it was her gaze that held him. He closed the gap between them. Seven hours before dawn. She held out her arms towards him. She had seen the truths that he could not alter, the things the insubstantiality of clear water would not eradicate, the shades of things he had done and things he would do. She still moved towards him and they touched. His mouth covered hers, but he held the fire back because every touch was farewell and it was the only language he had.

HER LOVER WAS FLAME. Bright pleasure. Rosamund melted into the spellbinding drug of his kiss. Her hands settled on his skin, densely rich over bunching muscle, intensely alive. Her fingers held the tremor of the sickening fear that had begun deep inside her the moment Merriwen had voiced Thorkill's name.

She let him touch her however he liked. Her warmed lips opened to his, to the fiery insistence of delight, the touch of his tongue, the smooth care, the complete, utterly predatory urgency that he hid. She wanted both, the care of her that was doubly precious because she was not used to it, and the hunter's need that would not let her go.

Her lips cleaved to the erotically firm masculine pressure of his mouth. Her tongue touched the soft underside of his lip, lingered until the sharp, fierce reaction was more than his tolerance and she was drawn into the predatory heat, the intense aliveness that was the defining quality of his being.

I thought you would be dead.

The sentence she had not dared to complete when she had seen him in the darkness played out its frantic beat in her head.

She kissed him and felt the tightness of his hands on her body through her dress and she wanted to hold him in return with all her strength, the fine skin and the powerful muscle, the solid weight. But she hardly dared to touch him, aware of the damage she had seen on his naked body.

Her hand flattened out, avoiding the distortion of a burn, moving over his shoulders, her palms against his warm flesh, the tremor of unsteadiness in her fingers now because of greed—and the fear that was still there.

He had made his arrangement with Thorkill. He had not told her precisely what had happened. He had shown her.

Her fingers dug tighter on living flesh. The kiss

prolonged until her senses drowned. Then it broke, his lips at her closed eyelids, her hair. She buried her face briefly against the uncut side of his neck. He moved, his hands at her breast, at the neckline of the exotic dress she had left on. For seduction. Or perhaps because some inner part of her was utterly vulnerable with him, the part that was trapped by the slightest change of expression in his eyes.

His fingers moved with slow care. It made her breath catch. Her skin was so tight that the brush of his hand as he untied the lacing of her tunic sent jolts of sensation through her and left her burning. She both wanted him to hurry and wanted the slowness that built fire, the touch of his hands that she would never have again. She watched the shadows on his face, the precisely incalculable arrangement that created beauty, the unsettling strength and the vicious marks of bruising. The light in the dark eyes focussed on her.

Her dress was open, the flimsy inadequate protection of her shift lost. She felt the brush of air on her skin. Enough to make her cry out. He bent his head. She felt the soft intimate whisper of his tangled hair, then warmth, the dark supple heat of his mouth. Her body twisted, alight with pleasure, every sense alive, attuned to him, to the feel of his mouth on her breast, teasing her nipple, to the repeated flick of his tongue, agonisingly light, more intense as her body craved it, as the sensation grew and sharpened. She writhed, the feeling so strong, spearing down through her body to flesh already moist and aching, and her senses dizzied, as though the release was so close, from this alone, from the way he concentrated on her pleasure.

She floated and the desire mixed with other and more deeply hidden things she thought had died with dreams, the ability to trust even a single instant of happiness to someone else.

She gasped, her body suddenly tight, seeking him. She felt his hand push her crushed skirts aside, touch her, the smooth glide of his fingers seeking her, finding her heated flesh, moistened and slick. She pushed against that touch, so lost that the first caress, the quick, light, intimate movement of his hand coupled with the pleasure-inducing tightness of his mouth against her breast, sent her into blindness and the dizzying fall of light.

Full consciousness came back only when he moved, raising his head. She was utterly aware of him, of the soft glide of his hair across her still-tingling flesh, of the whisper of his breath on her moistened skin, her tightly hardened nipple. Then the sense of cool air touching a body that still burned.

The coldness found its way into her heart in the same instant that the intense thread of physical contact broke, and heaven help her, her hands tightened on his flesh. The stab of fear was irrational, deep after three winters—the fear of being alone again the moment that heated touch was over.

She wanted to turn her head away, the survivor's instinct to hide hurt, but then her gaze caught his and she realised the spellbound closeness had only just begun. The hot desire fascinated her. It was focussed on her.

No man had ever tried to see her true self.

She wanted him to.

The tough, bruised face lowered to her skin. His mouth lingered for the briefest caress and it was her own need that made the excitement spill over when he pushed her back and peeled the dress from her desire-damp skin and his gaze touched her.

He leaned down, the strong bulk of his body over hers and her eyes took in each deliberate movement, the intent behind it, the bunch and slide of muscle. Marred beauty. Her sight dazzled on that, on the light reflected on gleaming skin. But what she saw most was the desire. She felt that in the touch of his hands and his supple mouth. He made her body ache anew for fulfilment. He saw her react and he understood the fever inside her. It was what he wanted.

She accepted all that he would give.

She let his hands move smoothly over every exposed curve of her body, every touch bringing her higher. And she trusted that. She trusted him. The desire kicked and there was nothing to hold back, no artifice, only herself, the nakedness of her skin beneath his lips, his hands framing her hips, the pure fire-tinged response of her body as his mouth moved lower. Lower still. She stopped breathing. There was an instant outside time, locked in the dream world, before he touched her. Then her body tightened, moved, the sound of her voice sharp in the silence.

He had already brought her so near, the moist flesh under his mouth aching, sensitised beyond her knowing.

Touch me, she thought, *as though we belonged.*

Her body arched into his hands, into the smoothly careful touch of his tongue and his fine lips, the hidden and wholly uncivilized edge of fire.

She did not let him go afterwards, but drew his body against hers, so close. Nothing existed outside the awareness of his harsh strength, his hand still between her thighs, the fierce exciting rapidness of his breath. Closeness.

But it had to work two ways.

She could give.

CHAPTER TWELVE

THERE WAS ONE CHANCE. Never another as long as she lived. All it took to use it was courage. Courage and belief.

Her head rested against the undamaged side of his neck.

Turn…turn your head. Suppose she did not have the right kind of courage?

She turned. Her mouth took hot skin, the fine curve of her lover's throat. She felt the tension, and all the bright virile power that had been held back. Her lips and her tongue traced the strong tendons of his neck, caressed the smooth hollow at the base. She possessed the skills to meet desire.

But she had to possess…other things. All the things she had lost.

The vulnerability appalled her. But there was also strength, the same strength that had drawn her straight to him in the seething mass of Guthrum's camp at Wareham like an arrow through the dark.

But her touch faltered and the tightness round her heart, its fast racing beat, were her own. They belonged to the person he had woken. They frightened her.

He moved, drawing her closer, his fingers locked in her braided hair. Her lips traced his skin. She avoided the cut, but her gaze lodged there for a moment that belonged to unguarded nightmares.

He made her look at his face.

"There is nothing you have to do." His eyes were ruthless.

"No." She turned her head just slightly against his hand, so that her ribboned hair spilled over his fingers, and her face, over-warm, flushed with the heat of sex, pressed into his palm. "Nothing I have to do."

She was the one who understood what the ruthlessness hid. Her own too-harshly beating heart told her. It was pain. She held his gaze, dark and hot and volatile. "There is only what I want to do."

He let her move and the hard-won courage, the vulnerability that finally showed truth, might be enough. She did not disguise what she felt. No defence. She chose to bend her head, so that her lips and her hands sought the hard lines of his face, the fierceness, the rough skin of his jaw, the exquisite curve at the corner of his eyelid.

He let her touch him, tough face and tougher body. She followed its contours, setting the soft heat of her lips to the fascinating tight ridges of muscle, the solidness, drawing her fingernails so lightly down the undamaged side of his torso,

flicking over one flat hard nipple and then taking
the fast catch of his breath with her mouth. Releas-
ing his lips to turn her own mouth back to his heated
skin, moving so that the long fall of her hair slid
across the brutally thick muscle, watching it tense,
feeling the pleasurable sweep of his own hands
across her slighter form. She was intensely aware
of the desire she had seen in his eyes. It was what
she wanted.

She was fiercely glad that she could give
pleasure.

Her touch firmed and lightened, avoiding the
damage with hands and lips and her gaze, skilfully,
so he would not sense either hesitation or the hard
knot of horror still at the back of her head, but only
the deep release of desire, only how much she
wanted him.

He pulled her against him and she could feel her
own flesh soften and warm under his touch, feel
herself falling into the spell. She cried out, biting
her lip, struggling for control, for the ability to give
all the care she wanted to show him.

She slid her hand along his inner thigh, her
action slow but utterly deliberate on that full
muscle, the heated skin, and she felt his arms
tighten sharply round her. She touched him, desire-
swollen weight, her fingers caressing lightly,
feeling him tighten in reaction. Her hand moved
over the living hardness, the super-smooth skin.

She sought his mouth before her hand closed

round him, so that she caught the sharp sound of his breath. She pushed against him, taking the fierce unsuppressed reaction of powerful muscle, the fast beat of his heart, all her senses alive.

Her fingers moved on him, slow and light, even though the dark, overwhelming potency burned through her straight from him. There was only now, the time to be experienced to every last breath because it would not be given again.

So she created the pleasure, sought and heightened and intensified it. Her touch brought all that harsh power to the brink, until he drew her closer, stopping the touching of her hand but bringing her tight into his heat, her hips against his, just as they lay, side by side, face to face. Her eyes suddenly locked on his.

She wanted to watch his face, to stay like this. He seemed to know, drawing her thigh high over his hip, positioning her body. He entered her slowly, so smoothly, the sensation of his flesh melding with hers at once dreamlike and intensely physical, every controlled inexorable push of his hard solid length intimately felt against heated flesh already sensitised by need, by his pleasuring. She thought the fast breath high in her throat would choke her, the fierce deep longing round her heart and she moved, taking him in, feeling the strong heightened thrust of his body, the fullness. The desire destroyed her control and she knew why she had chosen to watch his face. She could see all the deep, uncivilized truth that lay beneath.

Her own desire that must reflect in her eyes. His hand lighted on her face, her throat, her body, the careful, utterly capable fingers gliding down her burning, glistening flesh, touching her at the instant he thrust deep. Her response was true, deeply instinctive. Her body moved, taking the tight, sense-dizzying power of his, dreams and reality, the living strength and all the shadows that lived in his eyes.

"OF COURSE I will have the wench as well." Thorkill watched the somewhat bloodied head of his second-in-command turn on its scraggy neck.

"What do you mean?"

"Exactly what I say." He toyed with the unsheathed knife.

There was a point to be made, so Thorkill stabbed the *sax* deep into the scarred wood of the table.

It was Od's knife.

"What else have I ever meant?" Thorkill twisted the knife, his arm muscles rigid. He considered breaking the blade.

"Tell me," he continued, staring at the flushed face with its small trickle of blood, the over-bright eyes.

"Od?"

"You mean what you say." The hectic brightness died, like a fever extinguished.

"Good. I am prepared to overlook your half-witted attempt to kill the source of so much money, because you did not understand." Thorkill loosened his hand round the knife hilt. Od wanted the Mercian girl, among other things. It was making him foolish. He would have to learn to take his turn.

"I did not understand what?"

Power. Thorkill released the hilt. The blade vibrated.

"Lord?"

Perfect.

"I shall obtain the Mercian princess together with the Mercian money." He watched for the bitter light to rekindle in his second's greedy eyes. "I wonder whether she has worked it out yet? She might think she can shelter behind Jarl Guthrum's favour, but what is that to me, now? To any of us when we shall be well out of that devil's reach?"

Consider well, you fool.

"The mercenary has furnished me with the means to leave," said Thorkill. "And if I take something extra with me? We shall be quite comfortable, all of us together." He watched the half-hidden thoughts flick over Od's bloodied face and laughed inwardly. He was going to enjoy keeping this particular hold over Od.

He stood, suddenly impatient to get on. To make the arrangements with the rest of his men before morning. It all fitted together so well.

"You can fetch her to me." A little reward. Od would be so eager to comply. "But intact and not before tomorrow when the mercenary leaves to arrange the ransom."

"*Tomorrow*. What if he takes her with him? The mercenary?"

He swung round at the door. "You think the man is going to turn up at the Mercian court with his employer's unwanted niece as a public bed mate? And then expect Ceolfrith to thank him?" The man's brains were in his breeches.

"He would not need to show her. He—"

The lash of temper suddenly hit him, the violent, impatient rush that would take him and turn him into fortune's fool like Od. He had taken a step back towards Od, who abruptly shut his mouth.

He took a breath. He had won already. He always won. He had had the mercenary's blood on his own knife blade. Just a taste. He could have all the revenge he wanted. Things might turn ugly at the handing over of the ransom.

After he was sure of the money.

After he was sure of the Mercian *hor-kona*.

"Then you may watch him." Thorkill moved, fast as he always was. Faster than anyone. He slammed Od's hand away from the blade buried in the table with a force that smacked his second's fist back into the wall. Od's breath made a sharp choked sound of pain that was unstoppable.

"I said *watch*. You do one thing that endangers my plans and it will not be the mercenary's blood wetting steel." He jerked the blade out of the wood while Od still stared at him, motionless, breathing hard. He grinned. "We have shed blood together, fighting on the same side." He gave his second-in-command a few moments think about it. "Best to keep it that way, don't you think?"

He forced Od's gaze down. That was how it was done.

"Lord."

Only then did he turn. He was quite confident of leaving the blade for Od.

Od was wholly his.

IT WAS TIME to sever the connection.

Boda watched the shift in light, the winter slowness of it. The inevitability. Shadows crept across the makeshift bed, Rosamund's sleeping form.

The light changed until his aching eyes could distinguish details, the small rise and fall of her breathing, the supple lines he had touched in the firelit dark. It had been madness how much he had wanted her.

He wanted her more now.

He simply stayed. Because she was near. There was perhaps half an hour left, three quarters if he was lucky. He was adept at calculating the eternity of day and night into small defined increases. He would rather not have had that skill.

The naked skin of her shoulder touched him, the long pale skein of her hair, her hand.

Half an hour in which to break that.

Suppose he could not do it?

Suppose she, thane's daughter, alone in the world, was desperate enough, burdened enough to accept him?

The thane's daughter opened her eyes, in that precise moment, even though he had not moved and nothing physical could possibly have disturbed her. It was like fate.

"You are still there." Her hand curved round his.

He had the glib answer ready in his mind, the one that cajoled people into doing what he wanted.

"I can scarce believe you are really still here," she said into the silence and he caught the faint gleam that meant that she smiled. It was a tentative smile, because every time they had been together, he had left her to wake alone. Because of Thorkill. Because of some disaster and now she looked at him as though she wanted him to be there.

He knew what it was like to face disasters alone.

"What I wanted," said Rosamund. Her eyes held shadows, like someone caught between dreaming and waking. Her warm skin touched him. All he had to say was that this was what he wanted, too. All he had to do was hold her.

He turned his head. The waiting pain slammed through his skull, so violently complete that consciousness nearly broke. The abrupt sound of his voice was unintelligible, scarcely human. Like him.

He drew back, carefully because she was so fragile, because of the clumsiness of his body. Yesterday's payment in pain lanced down from the back of his skull through his neck, through stiffened muscles, shooting deep into his right arm, almost disabling.

Sufficient reminder of truths if he had needed it.

"I have to leave as soon as it is light."

"It is still night." She blinked, the dreamer awakening. It was as though he could see the dreams break. "You do not yet... I..."

He watched her bite her lip.

"You are not well. You do not have to go yet. Surely there is time?"

She made a good attempt at normal lightness. She felt sorry for him. Even for a brute beast, she could feel pity. She half sat up.

"You should not have to do all this." Her fine voice was suddenly passionate. "It is too much—Gainmar, Merriwen, me. You risk too much...."

He made some movement he could not control. But she kept speaking.

"It is true. No one has ever done so much for me." And she leaned towards him. The furs slid from the straightness of her shoulders, the pale, softly rounded flesh, the sleek, exotic fall of her hair. She was so close he could smell the scent of spice, the more subtle scent of her warm skin. All that he had touched.

"I do the king's task."

"Alfred. Aye. I know what you do, what you are—"

"*No.*"

She stopped speaking, just from that one word. Perhaps from the black force that clung to him.

He had to tell her.

"You do not know what I truly am."

"I know enough to understand you have a difficult background," she said with the kind of stiff defiance that would have become a princess. "I am not stupid. Sometimes you deliberately let me see it. What are you thinking? Am I supposed to be shocked that you have risen from, what, the life of a peasant to the life of a warrior?" She raised her head. "You would not be the first to do that, or the only one."

She looked at him with what he had always wanted—trust. She was smiling again. "I believe people can accept it. Especially in times of war."

It was what they all thought. Simple. The beaten thrall that still lurked in some dark corner of him wanted to say yes.

"I am not a blameless peasant. I am a marked criminal and the son of a criminal. I am a thief. I am a slave. I was born one. There has been no manumission, no granting of freedom. I am a runaway. For all I know, the man who owns me is still alive. I have no blood kindred left, or none who would acknowledge me. If I spoke the truth about myself openly, I am so far outside the law that I would be the next to be readied for stoning to death. Or for the gallows tree."

She had seen enough people hanged only days

ago. He saw the horror blossom over her face, over the fine features now discernable in the half dark, a familiar whiteness that stole blood and hope and life. If he could have been different. If he could have helped her. If he had been someone worthwhile.

"It is not a matter that can be changed."

"You have to tell me everything."

"My father stole things, all sorts of things."

She was sitting away from him, her eyes fixed on him, on whatever was visible in the half light. He made no attempt to hide the marks on his body. "He was a thief. He—"

"Sometimes people have to steal things to live, if they are poor, if there is a bad harvest." She had the defiant tilt to her head. She was doubtless thinking of the sad tale of the honest peasant faced with starvation, of *the poor who are always with us.* She had probably heard that at the nunnery. Read it for herself in one of Merriwen's books with gold pictures.

If that was part of his truth, it was not the whole truth. It was not what he remembered about living with his father. It was not likely.

"He stole. He got caught. He could not pay the fine. He got enslaved." He struggled to fit his world into something she could comprehend. He could not do it.

She stared at him with that look of horror and he could not take it away. He had moved before he knew, too fast, the bruising maiming him, the stab of rage so deep, black, the way he had felt in Thorkill's chamber. He wanted to hide that mindless rage from her, obliterate it. But he was supposed to show her. The worst. He sat back. He had no idea what kind of madness was in his eyes, but it did not matter. She was not looking at his face, but at the damage to his body.

"That is how things happen," he said carefully. "My father—" *What?* What in God's name did he say to someone like her who came from a good family? *He lied, so much that no one knew the truth. Each story more incredible than the last.*

"I do not know all that he stole. I do not know all the means that he used." *Say it.* "For all I know, he used violence. He was not only interested in survival. He was very interested in gain."

He framed the words he had heard all his life, the truth. "My father got what he deserved."

"Enslavement."

First step.

"Yes."

"As a punishment?"

"It is quite a good punishment if people want it to be. There are slaves who live out a blameless life on someone's estate and in some ways there is not much difference between them and the peasant who is free but pays rent by giving so much labour. Then there are…others."

"The chains," she said. "The day I won you as Thorkill's prisoner of war, when I kept the fetters on your wrists and you took the chain out of my hands and you… You already knew how to…"

Exactly. It had not been the first time.

"Someone else had kept you in chains."

"Now and then. Those who deserve it tend to attract trouble. Sometimes they cause it."

"Yes." She glanced at his face and then away again.

"You asked me what I remembered about Mercia. I said the shadows of the oxen in the early morning and the fields. That was all I knew. I would go out at this time every day. I was the boy with the hazel stick goad who drove the beasts forward, who shouted with a voice that would hardly work because of the cold." *Who steered the plough when his father was too drunk to do it.* "I did everything, pulled the weeds out of the ground, dealt with swine, threshed grain, built things, broke things, hammered metal for the smith." *Got into fights, constantly.* He took a breath and said, "Thieving."

She made a slight movement.

"My father could not leave that alone, even after he was enslaved. I believe there was a time of relative honesty while my mother was alive. But—"

"Did he…care for her, then? What was she like?"

He remembered Rosamund had had a proper family. He tried to imagine his father caring for something.

"She died."

"I am sorry. Perhaps…perhaps she cared for him."

Sorry. He could not remember what his mother had been like. There had been someone who milked cows and ground flour and brought food out to the fields and spun wool endlessly until she died. He had no idea what that person had thought. He had not known you could ask. It certainly would not have occurred to his father. She had simply given herself to the wrong man and then she had had a child. She had been trapped.

The worst sort of disaster.

"Whatever anyone thought, it made no difference. It changes nothing."

"No. I see."

Maybe she did. She was clever. Her gaze slid away. He blundered on, like some kind of *hell-thane* spawned into the wrong world.

"My father wanted more." Things had a tendency to turn to disaster if you wanted more. "A life from dawn to darkness ankle-deep in mud needed to be supplemented. So he took the things he wanted from those who already had them. And believe me, it is the easiest way." *Simple as hell.* "He explained it all, the grand necessity, the hopes of gain. He showed me how it is done and I did it."

He watched her averted head. He thought of her upbringing spent between a thane's hall and a nunnery. He did not say anything about regret. Regrets changed nothing. Guilt was guilt.

"He did not tell me what happened when you got caught."

"You are alive."

He stood, moving away, moving anywhere, just moving. He could not stop the violent power that drove him, even though the story was not finished. The pain of stiff muscles, abused flesh, the raging ache in his head slammed through him. The blinding, gut-churning force of purely physical pain was a relief. It stopped the useless thoughts, and the world temporarily narrowed to a small window, the single practical focus of staying on his feet, walking, finding his clothes.

He would tell her—

"You are still alive," said Rosamund, as though it meant something it simply did not. A brand snatched out of the burning.

"Yes."

She knew what the penalty for a thief had to be, for a slave who owned nothing and could not pay compensation, for a repeated offence. He found his tunic, trousers.

"It was not me they hanged. I was too young. Besides, the priest would not let them." He found the left shoe.

"How old were you?"

What did it matter? Was there any question he could answer? Anything that related to her world?

"I am not sure." Right shoe. He thought the rage would choke him, the lash of the pain through his ribs and his skull. Maybe it was just desperation. "Perhaps eleven or twelve winters." Who would have thought of counting?

"Eleven?" asked the thane's daughter.

"Maybe." Less than fourteen when childhood ended. That was what had saved him, that and a soft-hearted priest. But he had not been a child.

"You're twenty now?"

There were thanes of forty at Alfred's court who seemed younger than him. He did the fastening on the left shoe. The fingers on his right hand did not seem to work. Damn it, he had to get moving.

Say it. The leather lacing got stuck. "It was my father who climbed the gallows tree."

"He…"

"Hanged. Nothing else to be done." The words came out of him. "The right punishment." *I watched.* He nearly said that, too. Foolishness.

"Hanged?" He heard the fast rustle of the bedclothes behind his shoulder. *"Hanged."* Then she said, "Boda—" and he knew she was thinking of the corpses beside the river at Wareham and the fact that he had been there and—

His hands became still on the half-finished left shoe fastening. *Do not say it.* He had to get out of here still functioning. He had to deal with Thorkill and with Gainmar's escape and with hers and the daft wench Merriwen's.

Hers.

He fastened the shoe.

"The priest saved you," said Rosamund. "It was fate." Her voice had moved him smoothly on to the next step. He shoved his foot into the right shoe. The girl with the nunnery upbringing had given him his cue to spin some story of grateful redemption. The things she had chosen to say did not cover the truth. It had not been fate. He had not been grateful.

"The priest took me in. I stuck it for less than a year." No clean slate, only the hanged face in his mind every time he closed his eyes, the face of a dead thief. And he was still alive. "I walked out." *Before I did something worse and the priest ended up paying for it.* Even on the legal brink of manhood he must have understood that much. He fastened the shoe, the stiffness down his arm abating. His hand worked quite well.

Quite well would be enough to get a knife stuck though him by Thorkill. Or Od. Or to let a knife touch someone else. He stood up.

"After that?" asked Rosamund.

"I survived." There was little time left, but she would guess enough. "There was Viking raiding in Mercia by then and the Danes actually made it easier." The cloak would only hamper him. He discarded it. "There were a lot of placeless people and I was just one more. I could spin whatever tale I liked wherever I went."

"It must have been a terrible life."

It must have been a dangerous nunnery to teach charity over common sense.

"Boda?"

He could hear the quality that was her downfall in the tone of her voice, ready to thread its way through the horror. Pity. It took its shape in his own name while he stood still, one hand on the discarded cloak and the bitter force burning inside him.

The force still held greed.

"My life was what I made out of it. I could always do whatever it took."

"Whatever it took to survive," said Rosamund.

He let go of the cloak because he could not see it. The only thing in his scarcely functioning mind was her, her voice, her closeness in the rustling furs two paces behind him, the memory of the smooth glide of her skin. She had come to him even after what had happened with Thorkill, the marks of it still fresh on his body. And he had been weak enough to take whatever she would give. The daylight truth was that he had already made use of her pity.

"No one ever guessed what I was."

You still do not see. Blinded by kindness.

He knew the strength of her pity. He had seen it in the bond of steel that had held her to Merriwen through the past three winters. It would hold her until she choked under its weight. He could not let that happen. Her pity would hold her to anything it touched.

"Do you know why people would believe me? They always wanted to see something that was not there." *Know that. Understand it.*

Rosamund...

"And I always knew when I had to move on," he said.

He heard the rustle of furs.

She did not speak.

He picked up the second tunic that would keep out the cold, dragging it on over the first, forcing his arm to move as though nothing was wrong.

He picked up the belt.

"How did you find Alfred?" she asked, as though it were the last question possible between them. Indeed it was.

"I moved eastward along the Thames. After a long time, I ended up near Kingston. I met the goldsmith. She..."

"She?"

"Yes." His hand worked the belt buckle. *She.* The first unattainable woman. He had fancied at approximately sixteen that it had approached love. He had had no idea what that meant. He did not turn round because he could not.

"You stayed with her?"

"I made friends with her brother." But it was Gemma's presence that had started the change. Gemma who had first shown him what the courage of women meant—Gemma who had seen him as her brother's friend and married Ashbeorn.

She was like you in some ways. In that terrible courage. But nothing matches you.

"The man she married was sworn to Alfred."

"The man who—Sworn to the king like you?"

"Yes. I took a message for him into Wessex. I saw the king for the first time. I saw what he faced. I had already become friends with Ashbeorn."

"So you swore your oath."

"It was a suitable choice for me. I am a survivor. The odds for a thief's survival are not good."

"And the odds for a warrior in time of war are better?"

She would have made a fair swordsman herself. She had a keen eye for the weak points.

"Oh aye," he said. "Like the odds for today." That was what he had to set his mind to. They both did. For the first time, he turned round. He had the wry grin in place that had seen him through a survivor's life, the rock-hard confidence that persuaded. He would see this through. She had to know that much. He would get her and her daft companion out of this trap and they would have their lives back.

His eyes held hers and there was a moment outside time, outside the mutually exclusive worlds, hers and his.

He saw her courage.

"Alfred's man," she said.

He made the grin widen. "We never give in."

"No."

It was light enough to see her face. He had waited for that. One last look. The door slid open easily under his hand. "Fetch Merriwen."

CHAPTER THIRTEEN

THE PLAN WAS SIMPLE. All Rosamund had to do was get Merriwen down to the stream where there was so much rapid coming and going before the baggage train set off. Past the stream was a hazel coppice and the ground fell away unevenly. One of the West Saxons, Wihtred, would meet them.

It would be easy enough for her to slip away from there unnoticed with Merriwen. People were in a hurry, bleary-eyed and foul-tempered, utterly focussed on getting as fast as possible through deeply hostile land.

The very simplicity would make it work.

The West Saxon, muffled against the cold, utterly nondescript in the shadows of the trees scarcely registered. Not a single Viking bothered.

It was Merriwen who risked death.

"I'm cold."

"It is not as cold as yesterday and it will be warmer by the trees. We will go that way."

"I still do not see why."

"I explained. We have to go." *Now*. Rosamund seized an arm. "Come on."

"It is too cold for me."

It had been like this from the first moment, like last night's sudden tantrum, only redoubled. Every step, from getting out of bed to dressing, had been like this.

"Up to the trees. It is not far." *Just the road that would lead them out of here, the one and the best chance.*

"Why should I? You cannot make me." Merriwen, although considerably shorter, outweighed her. They came to an abrupt halt. Someone glanced up. The West Saxon beside the trees did not move. "I'm cold."

"Just this short way."

"I'm cold."

Yes. "Wrap your cloak tighter. No, do it like that." They managed a step, two. It was painfully slow.

"I don't want my cloak done like that."

She thought the man called Wihtred, lost in tree shadow, moved. It was his life at stake, too. All of their lives. No. *Do not come down and let them see you.* They stepped round someone who was sharpening a sword.

She forced half a dozen quicker paces. The West Saxon had melted back into shadow. They would do it. She would manage. She always managed. Somehow. But this time her heart beat so hard it hurt. She did not hurry. She did not dare. Every muscle in her body ached with the desire to run.

Five more steps.

"I said I did not want my cloak done like that."

"It is fine like that."

"I want to do it myself. You have to wait for me while I do it," said Merriwen.

It was as though she could sense hidden weakness by unspoken instinct, as though some demon drove her to say and do the most difficult thing at the worst possible moment. It was the way children cried at desperate mothers. And it was as though Merriwen had swept back to a more childish state than she had ever known. It was lethal.

"See how I do it?"

"Yes." Agreeing over small things was often the quickest way. The knowledge came from long experience. Merriwen lived in a separate existence. Rosamund had only fooled herself it was not so because the Mercian prisoner, the ex-slave, had made such a difference.

Boda.

"Is that right?" Merriwen was staring at her.

It was the desperation in herself that was the problem, desperation for a man she could not have, whose world she did not belong in. Fear for his life in a mad enterprise like this. Such fear. She could not hide it and Merriwen sensed it.

She forced calm.

"Perfect."

They made eight more steps.

"Which trees do we have to go to?"

She could see the man's cloak. The thicket of hazel and ash and thorn.

"Just over there." Someone brushed past her in the opposite direction. He looked at her. *Don't run.*

"Why?"

"We just…"

The Viking had hurried on. But there were fewer people here. She slowed her pace, aimless.

"Why?"

No one was watching, surely? She did not dare look round.

"Why do we have to?"

They were close, almost in the shadows.

"I told you. We are going to meet someone first."

"Is it Boda?"

Her foot stumbled on uneven ground. She did not care whether or not this was close enough. She glanced at the woods, at the cloaked figure King Alfred's man had sent. She saw him clearly, an unremarkable face, bearded like a Viking, ordinary… the slight negative movement of his head.

God's mercy. They, Merriwen's reluctance, the unceasing sound of her voice, had drawn attention.

"Look at the stream."

"What for?"

"Just look." Her voice scarcely registered above a whisper, but there was one thing about hidden desperation, the force of it could sometimes produce results.

Merriwen stared at the water, silent. Rosamund

reminded herself they had done nothing wrong, nothing exceptional. She bent down and took a drink. The water stung her throat. Merriwen looked at her, but did not move. She gave it two minutes. She aimed for three.

She could not last that long.

She looked round.

Wihtred's cloaked figure stepped back into the thicket. The shadows abruptly swallowed him.

"Come on."

The darkness was thick under the trees, but the West Saxon was still there, the prospect of escape after three years. There were crossed hazel branches on the ground in front of his feet like a sign that would ward away evil.

THE MAN WAS NOT Boda. Merriwen hung back, but Rosamund kept talking to the stranger, so that it was she, Merriwen herself, who had to point it out.

"That is not Boda."

Rosamund took no notice. She wanted them to go away with the stranger. Merriwen did not like strangers. Except Boda.

"You said we would go with Boda."

"We will find him," said Rosamund. But her voice did not sound sure.

Then she said, "Later."

Merriwen knew what *that* meant. It fobbed people off. Rosamund was going to make them go without Boda. She was going to leave him with the Vikings.

"I want Boda now."

But Rosamund got hold of her arm again and said they had to go. So did the stranger. They were going somewhere else and they would not come back. Rosamund had told her so.

"I cannot go without my parchments."

"I have them," said Rosamund and showed her some, rolled up inside leather under her cloak.

But she had not brought the casket with the angel carvings. She had left it behind like Boda. Suppose they put him in chains again and he had no one?

"I need my inks."

"We can get some more ink…"

And Merriwen waited for the fatal word *later.* But the stranger started talking to Rosamund. He was impatient. Rosamund had let go of her when she had shown her the parchments. The stranger and Rosamund wanted to leave. She took a step backwards. They did not notice.

She knew how to get all the way back to the cart. She had a head start even when they looked up. Rosamund wanted to come after her. The man seemed to hesitate for a fraction of a second, bending as if he would touch something on the ground but Rosamund pulled him on as though there were not a moment to lose.

Merriwen ran flat out. She was far enough ahead. She was a bit frightened, but it was easier than she had thought. They did not catch her before she was back. She saw Olga beside their cart. Relief flooded over her. She waved. But Olga shouted something at her and flapped her hands like someone shooing away chickens.

Then she saw Od.

He caught her and threw her into a room and shut the door.

She could not get out.

Rosamund did not come straightaway, even though Merriwen heard noises outside. And when she did come, she did not say anything, not even Merriwen's name. She had red splatters on her cloak. It was her best mantle.

"Are you angry?"

"Not with you."

But Merriwen did not believe her, not even when Rosamund sat down and put her arms round her. She knew she had done something wrong, but she had wanted the right things. Her own things. Boda.

She wanted to ask where the stranger was, but then Od came in with Olga and two men who stood at the door. Od had a worse red stain on his clothes, all across his left arm.

Rosamund got up and said, "You killed him."

"That bastard half killed me," said Od and started swearing.

Olga bound up the cut on his arm and Merriwen knew what had happened to the stranger.

She hated being near Od.

"Where is Boda?"

"Do you not know, little wench?"

She had asked Rosamund, but it was Od who answered, looking at her and making her heart jump. But then he turned away and stared at Rosamund. He liked Rosamund.

"The Mercian is where he should be at this moment, with Thorkill, exactly where I was supposed to be. But I knew better, because I am the one who understands, am I not, Rosamund?"

Rosamund said nothing and Merriwen realised she was frightened, the way she had been when they had first come to be with the Vikings. More so.

"It was me who worked out that devious mercenary scum would still want to take you with him. Thorkill did not believe he would take a Mercian misfit like you. Thorkill thought it was about politics.

"You and I know better." Od wrenched his arm out of Olga's grip and took a step forward. Rosamund stepped back.

"Do you not remember what we said?" asked Od and Olga stared at him with the bloodied linen in her hand and her face all white. "I told you Thorkill would win, whatever happened. You made the wrong choice."

Rosamund looked at him.

"And now you are going to find out," said Od. "There is no earl to frighten off your suitors now. Come." Od took hold of her elbow. Rosamund did not say anything. Od was whispering against her hair.

Merriwen heard him say, "The Mercian cannot help you now. He does not even know you are with us and he will not know until it is too late. You are ours, just as you should be. Everything will be put right. You will see."

"FOR PITY'S SAKE," said Olga. "Do what he wants."

Rosamund bunched her fist. Od's men shoved them through the door. But there was no help outside. Her eyes scanned the rapid activity. The front of the baggage train was already moving off.

There was no sign of Boda.

The utterly indifferent mass of a Viking army swirled past, thinned out. Od's men were armed. Nothing to be done. Od stopped beside a covered cart. He wanted them to get in. Merriwen clung to her.

"Do as he says," hissed Olga. "He is eager for death."

"Move." Death-keen. It was in his face.

She pushed Merriwen up into the cart, then followed, Olga still talking.

"Go on. There is only—"

There was a man. No. A *shinna,* a ghost beyond life's reach. She did not need to hear Olga say his name. She recognised the tenuous battered essence of all that had once been vivid and vital and commanding.

She had spent considerable effort avoiding him.

Chad's bones.

There was no way out. The cover of the wagon swung down, cutting off the light and the air. It was not Od who climbed into the confined space with them, but the silent one, Arne. That would make no difference in the end. It hardly mattered who told Thorkill that she had made a fool out of him for three winters by pretending to be someone she was not.

That should make him eager for vengeance.

She sat down in the stifling dimness beside Merriwen and waited for the only surviving hostage, Gainmar, prince and *Atheling* of Mercia, to open his eyes.

"Where are we going?" asked Merriwen.

Hell.

"We will have to wait and see."

Merriwen's solid body beside her was shaking. All this for a box of parchment inks. Rosamund took a breath. It was *not* Merriwen's fault. It was not. It was the fault of a violent invading army. Of Thorkill. Of King Ceolfrith the greedy dynastic squabbler of Mercia.

She waited for his kinsman to speak.

"It is an adventure," said Rosamund. She squeezed the princess's hand. The plump little fingers were frozen. "You have to wait and see what happens next."

She transferred her gaze from Arne's fighting knife to the ghost lying on the floor. Olga had gone immediately to kneel beside him, exactly as though that were an accustomed place. Rosamund caught the scent of feverfew. Olga was quite good with herbs, a reasonable healer, skilled hands. She reached out and touched him.

"Yes, but what will *happen?*" said Merriwen.

The ghost opened his bloodshot eyes. Olga's presence elicited no surprise, as though it were as familiar as Arne's. There was a moment during which she could not breathe and Gainmar assembled consciousness out of pain. Willpower.

There was nothing she could do. A cold hand tugged at hers. The poor helpless girl she had tried to protect would be torn down with her.

"Rosamund?"

The name seemed to echo round the confined space of the cart.

"Princess?"

Disaster in one word. Her most reckless gamble lost. Except, it was not Gainmar's shocked voice that echoed in her head. It was the memory of a different one, with a much rougher accent, the voice of someone who had to rely on their wits to survive.

You have spent three winters in the midst of an army and you cannot cheat…

"Hush, Merriwen," she said in the voice of authority. Then she turned her head, slowly, exactly as a rightful princess might have done it. "Yes? Gainmar?" He was watching her. *Cheat, Rosamund, cheat. You are a survivor.* "I do not believe we met in Mercia and our paths did not cross at

Wareham." Her voice rushed, a shade too fast. She controlled it. "Doubtless you have heard me mentioned." She could not speak Boda's name. It was just there in her mind like a shield. "I expect you know all about me and...my maid and companion who... I look after her." *I did not rob her of her place. It was the only way the two of us could survive.*

There was not the least hope a stranger prince out of his wits with illness was going to understand what she meant.

"Devoted," sneered Arne from the other side of the cart. Merriwen's strangeness repelled him. But he had given her the right word.

"Yes. People can be devoted, even in danger, especially..."

Arne rolled his eyes and toyed with the knife.

"Aye," the fine voice, hoarsened by illness, was uninflected, clear. "Princess." It was a moment before she could take in the word because of the way her heart beat.

"I have heard of you," said Gainmar. "And now that I see you, I understand. I see you are capable of giving devotion as well as inspiring it."

She could not speak, just sat there holding her royal mistress's hand like the deceiver she was. So many things had bound her to Merriwen, friendship and pity, the loyalty she had been trained to give since birth, all of those and a kind of appalling defiance, a rage against a world where the helpless

got crushed. She did not know whether that consti-
tuted devotion.

She only knew that people could become part of
life. That someone could become so deeply ingrained they became a part of thought and consciousness—that a man might achieve all that in a
matter of days. For good or ill.

Because that person touched deeply.

Because they were loved.

"Too much talking," said Olga to the patient.
"You have to drink." She fussed with a leather flask
smelling of poppy. Merriwen sighed. Arne fiddled
with his knife hilt.

She did not love. It was not possible in this
world.

Boda.

"Give me a hand with this," said Olga, the un-
stoppered flask in her hand. She eased forward,
helping Olga with the steel-eyed prince, her movements as competent as they could be, as full of
false assurance—the arch survivor. She was not the
sort to inspire something as profound and unreachable as devotion.

He was very ill. Heaven knew whether he would
live. After one half sip, he stopped drinking.

"Feed it to him," snarled Arne. "I want him unconscious, not causing trouble."

But they could not. Olga shrugged almost imper-
ceptibly and went through the motions. Rosamund
watched the prince's closed face that could have

been as unconscious as Arne desired, but was not. Her sight blurred.

One conclusion was inescapable. She would see Boda again. She and Merriwen were now indissolubly part of Thorkill's plan. His revenge. Exchanging the wounded hostage for silver was not going to be enough. She thought of Boda the king's man who had come to help her, his face. She bit her lip against making a sound.

"I am sorry," said Olga unexpectedly under cover of what they did. "I tried to tell you how things were."

She watched the movement of Olga's skilled hands. "Because you knew everything. You were involved with it all. Stop… You are going to spill that." She took the flask and the cup. "You were involved with Thorkill."

"Yes. You must have known."

"No." She put the cup down, the flask.

"It was nothing new. It is just you who would never have accepted it."

All this time and she had not realised. She had not understood what was in her only friend's mind because she would not have accepted it. They helped the prince lie back. She watched the eyes closed like death. Only then did she look at Olga's face.

"I tried to warn you not to cross Thorkill. You would not listen." Olga's kohl-rimmed eyes held hers. "You could not because of the hold that Mercian had over you."

The soft words would not be audible to Arne, lost in his sullen contemplation. Yet her hands went still on the fevered skin and she shivered as if the same deadly fever were in her.

"I did the next best thing," said Olga. "I explained it was a passing moment of indulgence, a fancy that meant nothing."

But it is not. Bedrock and dangerous truth. Unsaid. They were two women. They did not need words.

Arne shifted in his corner.

Madness. Love.

Devotion.

"We both understand, then." Friendship. "I am glad of that." She watched Olga's face, the naked truth in her eyes. Love and madness. "And I am sorry. It has all been dearly bought, has it not?"

"I was blind at first. Loneliness far from home." Olga's painted mouth twisted. "And then I saw…things like this. But I could not escape. I was useful. And so it went on."

Dead love.

Their hands rested on burning skin, but one step removed from that finality. Rosamund could see the consuming heat, the dull mark at the exposed neck made by a rope.

There were two kinds of death, to body and heart.

"You were right not to accept it," said Olga. "I have made a mistake."

There were a lot of mistakes in the world. They all demanded payment.

Their hands touched briefly, sprang apart as they worked. Together.

She heard movement outside, the sound of voices. Thorkill. *Boda.*

She turned her head.

"You had best keep quiet and still," said Arne. "The little maid and I will be sitting together, just to make sure. We don't want to spoil any surprises."

The atmosphere in the cart was dense with threat. She did not move. Outside, scarcely a pace away from her, she could hear Boda's low rough murmur, then laughter, clear in the open air.

Arne settled back in his corner with Merriwen. *He will not know until it is too late.*

The sound of his voice faded slowly, dissolving on the cold air until she could no longer hear it. Only silence and the harshness of Arne's breath.

EVERYTHING SPUN OUT according to plan. Raidwulf watched from the shelter of the trees above the slope. The last of the Viking baggage train was disappearing over the horizon.

The cart belonging to the *hersir* named Thorkill was firmly stuck, broken down. The well-dressed figure of what must be the Viking captain had summoned his men to fix the problem, with a view to catching up with the tail of an army that was not going to wait for any man, no matter how important.

He could see the man called Boda's solid bulk. Still alive.

Except that something always turned sour at ransom meetings. People got jittery about the strength of the truce arrangements, greedy for what they could get, suspicious they were being swindled out of something unknown, angry over imagined slights. Or stupid.

Wihtred and the two wenches should be here.

Sometimes you did everything right and chance came round and kicked you in the—

"Well?"

"Nowt." He remembered the man who had come up beside him was a southerner and translated. "Nothing. It all looks perfect. But no sign of the women." So where in Holy Cuthbert's name was Wihtred? How long did they wait for two wenches? He did not envy Macsen the prince from Devon having to make the decision.

Be alive, Wihtred, you soft southern idiot. Walk out of those trees and I'll let you beat me at dice.

"And the men you sent to check?"

"Not back ye— Over there." He saw the shadows move in the trees. Macsen was faster which showed how pressing the decision was. The shadows were not Wihtred and two wenches.

He listened to what the men had to say. It did not help. The sign had been there, a *tir* rune in branches near the stream, the sign that meant everything was going according to plan, escape successful.

There had been deeply scuffed footmarks round the branches. What the devil did that mean? Everything and nothing—Boda checking the first part of the plan was complete before the second began, stray Vikings. Raidwulf watched the terrible calculation through Macsen's face.

"We have a few minutes more. After that, we split. It is not that different from the original plan. I need to be out of sight with the reserve anyway in case someone recognises me for Alfred's man. We simply make the reserve larger. Raidwulf?"

Hell fire. "Fine."

"We have to cover the possibility that Thorkill has somehow taken the women. In which case he has seen Wihtred."

Which meant that brave Wihtred was dead. No chance to win silver off him at dice. He tried to stop himself from moving.

"The plan goes ahead," said Macsen. "Because whatever Thorkill thinks—" like feelings of eternal friendship towards Boda "—he is likely to go ahead with the deal. Too much is at stake for him to back out of that. And we can do nothing until Gainmar is handed over."

"Aye," said Raidwulf. That was his end of the job, because Macsen was too recognisable to be seen at the handover and because Raidwulf could manage midlands speech if he tried. "Makes no difference."

He would have a smaller force with which to

meet an irritated, murderously suspicious defector
who already had reason to feel aggrieved because
he had almost lost a nice piece of plunder compris-
ing two women. The organiser of this probably
failed misappropriation of goods was going to be
within the said Viking's reach until the last possible
moment. He hoped this Boda had eyes in the back
of his head.

"Are we set, then?"

BODA WATCHED Thorkill without seeming to. The
man was noticeably agitated. A certain amount of
volatility was to be expected in the face of a deal that
was going to change the course of Thorkill's plun-
dering career. But this was deeper, a dam about to
burst.

Od was back, heavily cloaked against the cold
and silent, brimming with something quite different. He knew what that was, the straightforward
desire to kill him, quite uncomplicated by the conflicting needs that pushed Thorkill. Od was trouble
with a blade ready to hand. But it would not happen
yet.

Too much at stake.

"Where are the Mercians?"

He shrugged, turning it off with some lewd jest
about where Thorkill might be feeling the cold
while he waited. "They will be here."

Thorkill's tight shoulders relaxed marginally.
Easily satisfied. But Boda was beginning to wonder

himself. Od fiddled with his sword hilt, making
sure his hand was visible. Subtle. Boda bit off a grin
that was likely to have been feral.

It would have been better if he could have seen
Gainmar, but they were not overly keen to let him
within twenty paces of the cart. Thorkill moved
from one foot to the other like a man on hot coals.
He reviewed everything in his mind for the hun-
dredth time. At least Rosamund and her little companion were no longer part of this. It was all he
could focus on. Rosamund.

She was safe.

She had to be.

He had seen the rune sign left by Wihtred with
his own eyes.

Stop thinking.

He spoke to Thorkill, the words flowing with no
hesitation, the easy patter of someone who talked
to survive. It distracted attention from the movement of his body. He could not stand still. The cold
was a good enough excuse for pacing round but the
truth was that he had to move stiffened muscles.
The pain dragged at him. He could not get rid of it.
Weakness.

He saw it—the movement of men and horses.
He did not react until Thorkill noticed. Then Od.

"Whoresons. About time."

He counted. Then he did it again.

The one called Raidwulf who came from somewhere in the north rode forward and dismounted.

So where were the rest? There was some movement against the treeline that hinted at greater numbers, but—

Raidwulf, of course, was unarmed. Chad's bones.

The wooden chest was placed carefully on the ground, clearly visible, nearer to the trees so that the Vikings would have to move forward.

He strode towards it with no hesitation before Thorkill got cold feet. Od made to follow. It seemed Od was the negotiator. He handed Thorkill his sword belt and the visible knife.

"The hostage?" asked Raidwulf politely, positioned in front of the oak chest. He sounded almost Mercian, Cheshire, perhaps. It was amazing.

Od stuck beside him and slightly behind. Boda stepped back so that he could keep Od in sight. The concealed knife hilt stuck out like dog's balls. At least Raidwulf must surely have noticed, although matters were rather too delicate to mention it.

"Open the lid," snapped Od in Norse-English.

No. Don't. He could not say anything without sending Od over the edge into violence. He need not have worried. Raidwulf was from the canny north.

"I need to see the key."

It took an instant for Od to work it out, at which point he thought they might get a look at the hidden knife. But instead Od signalled to those behind him, the gesture so abrupt that light stabbed off the silver at his wrist, a russet sleeve.

Raidwulf waited, an image of patience, no obvious threat. It might work. Then Raidwulf looked directly at him, face blank and he knew there was something else. What?

They carried Gainmar past on an open litter. Raidwulf opened the chest. Od watched, empty hand clenched as though missing a sword hilt, or the money.

Thorkill shouted at him to take the chest and get on with it.

Two of the litter bearers, Thorkill's men, stepped forward to take the chest. The lifeless figure on the litter moved, the gesture of one hand, forced like something unbearable, oddly and spine-chillingly urgent and at the same time slight, controlled. The iron will of a prince. Od, directing his men to refasten the chest, did not see. Thorkill would be too far away. You had to be close to notice, focussed.

Raidwulf had stepped instantly towards Gainmar. Some of the West Saxons moved forward, open handed. Only three. Still an even balance.

Nothing to disturb, except that urgent gesture from a wounded man. Raidwulf leaned over him, his body blocking Gainmar from sight.

The chest was fastened. Od signalled impatience.

The russet sleeve.

The first time Od had been visible, his tunic had been grey, at the moment before he had disappeared on some undisclosed errand. All those minutes un-accounted for, not explained.

Something disastrous had happened. Gainmar must know. He had tried to tell Raidwulf. What?

Raidwulf was occupied with the litter. Od's men had the chest.

Boda waited. Waited until the West Saxons had Gainmar safe.

Raidwulf stood up and turned his head, unable to say whatever Gainmar's message had been. Neither of them could speak. But Boda knew. He damned well knew by the bloom of horror that started from his heart.

It was as though he had always known, because right things were too rare, like something doomed. Nonexistent as a gambler's luck. Raidwulf's gaze flicked towards the cart.

What could the Saxon force do? Outnumbered, even if Macsen had reserves somewhere. Unable even to move for precious moments until Gainmar was far enough out of harm's way.

He took the fastest option, the one that would bring out the hidden disaster. Raidwulf's task was to secure Gainmar and it was Boda himself who was the sticking point. Unfinished business. He turned his back on Od to look at Thorkill.

CHAPTER FOURTEEN

IT TOOK OD one second to unsheathe the knife hidden under clothing. Half a second to aim, move. Boda counted. He threw himself right, because Od knew where his injuries were and would expect him to move left. The blade missed. He kicked on reflex, in the fractured instant before the pain hit him and robbed him of all power.

Landing on his damaged side might not have been such a clever idea after all. He had no breath left to shout out what was necessary. His body cramped with pain.

It did not matter. Thorkill had already reacted by bringing his other two captives out of the cart. Never miss a chance. Behind him Od started retching. He had lost the knife. Boda got as far as one knee. Then his feet.

Rosamund watched him.

He had to shorten the distance between them. Merriwen hung back. They both appeared unharmed. Thorkill had Rosamund by the arm. Her face was white, the green eyes unnaturally bright,

burning. She did not appear to be hurt. The thought
of Thorkill being able to hurt her kicked through
him with such violence he could hardly see. Or
hold himself back. Thorkill's free hand gripped a
seax. He brought Rosamund into plain sight, almost
in front of him.

Do not do anything dangerous. It was all that
filled his mind. He watched her burning eyes.
Don't. Because you cannot win from that position.
Merriwen appeared at her other side like a desperate shadow.

He forced himself to think, to take his own utterly unpalatable advice, his feet moving unsteadily,
staggering apparently at random like someone
dazed, but always pushing forward, closer, while
Raidwulf yelled at Thorkill over Od's treachery.
Thorkill bellowed back. The anger showed.

Od had bungled it. He had made his move too
soon and he had missed.

"The princess was my possession, not yours,"
yelled Thorkill, with the utter assurance that one
could own another person's will, that blind certainty that turned Boda insane with rage.

"That creature you sent would have stolen her
from me," said Thorkill.

Boda had covered considerable ground before
the attention snapped back onto him. Three more
steps before he reeled to a halt. Wihtred. Wihtred
was…

"The thief you sent to steal my goods is dead."

Raidwulf, now armed, had the effect of making Thorkill take an involuntary step back. Wihtred's dead spirit seemed to hover in the air between them.

"It is we who have been wronged," said Thorkill, too loudly, hectoring, as though the un-avenged dead had touched him. "We have a right to avenge an insult."

"Then try and take it. You or Od." His own inter-vention had a sharp effect. "Whichever feels man enough. I have no preference." He glanced at Od, who had hidden motives. And mistakes to make up for.

Od was on his feet, mottled with fury. He would crack, accept the challenge when he need not.

"I would—"

"No," shouted Rosamund at the same time.

The sudden violence of her voice caught him for one instant off balance. He stared at her white face, the deep fear and the criminal recklessness in her eyes.

"Don't—"

But her voice had already filled the fatal fraction of silence. "There is no necessity." The reckless gaze swept Thorkill, Od, not him.

"I will stay where I belong," said the trapped captive and it was too late. Unlike Od, Thorkill was not so far gone—a moment's reflection would save him. She had forced the instant required for thought from the relentless push of events. Even with the unsettling illusion of movement in the trees, Thorkill would gamble he had the superior force of numbers. And therefore he need do nothing.

"Just me," said Rosamund smoothly. "Give my maid back to the Mercians. They can have her. She is no use. You keep the princess. There will be no difficulties." Her gaze was fixed on Thorkill the butcher. Then on Od with his hidden greed. She was terrified. He could see straight through to that, to all that she hid. "I will stay where I *belong*."

The word unlocked the violence in him. He had already taken a step when he saw Merriwen like a blur.

"She is not the princess. I am."

Her small voice had the effect of stopping them all. She was pointing at Rosamund.

"You have to let her go," said Merriwen, "because I am the princess."

Thorkill would probably not have believed her, except for Rosamund's startled gasp and the indefinable quality of the silence that followed. Rosamund's mouth worked.

"Merriwen."

"I am Rosamund," corrected the small voice. "No one guessed in all this time. Even Earl Guthrum got it wrong when he took us from the nunnery and then—"

"You witless bitch—"

It was either a master stroke of Merriwen's, or it was death.

"Look out," yelled a voice from somewhere behind him.

He was moving without thought. He was unarmed, but he was close. Close enough. He had to be. Rosamund was in the danger spot, between Thorkill and Merriwen. He flung himself forward, hard, driving with his full weight, not knowing whether he was fast enough, the fear in the back of his head for Rosamund a black madness that pushed him. His weight connected with Thorkill's an instant before the blow aimed at Rosamund struck home and he was screaming at her.

"Get back."

He crashed into the ground with Thorkill. He was not aware of the impact, pain. Only of the way Rosamund moved, the fast streak of redness across her arm, high up, the tear in her sleeve.

He heard Raidwulf.

The rest belonged to the black abyss. He only knew he had to stop himself from instant killing or there would be annihilation.

He wrested the knife out of Thorkill's hand, nearly breaking bones; the competence was complete, the work of seconds. It was the first warrior's trick a king's man had taught him. The brutality behind it was something else. It came from a gutter brawler. Thorkill stopped moving. He forced an equal stillness. His weight crushed the other man, preventing access to the sword still sheathed at his hip. The intensity of the violence etched both their faces.

"You—" Thorkill's breath heaved. A stream of Norse-English abuse emerged.

"Then settle it," he said and glanced round. Raidwulf had Rosamund, Merriwen at her side. Rosamund's hand covered the cut. He knew it was not deadly. But only because he had reached Thorkill. Her eyes held shock, rage and underneath the hidden crippling edge of fear that belonged to someone trapped.

He wanted to do murder. The gutter brawler, the maddened slave, was capable of it.

It was not the right way out of the trap. He had only to make himself see it.

His gaze held hers for one split instant, as though he could convey across the distance of twenty paces some form of reassurance. He would not let go. There would be a way out. He and Raidwulf would find it.

He forced the pressure back slightly. Thorkill's breath hissed.

"You want vengeance?" said Boda. "You can settle it with me." *Not an unarmed woman, a girl with none of your strength. But twice the courage.* "Do you understand?"

"You? I have no business that concerns you. I have not the least need," screamed Thorkill who still had the advantage of greater numbers of Viking warriors. "I can—" Thorkill's voice stopped. The vicious gaze slid left.

It was worth seeing.

At that moment, with the unbreakable sense of flamboyance that belonged only to Celts, Macsen sent the rest of the king's force into view.

The balance of power shifted, suddenly unstable. Boda watched the fast reversal absorbed by that formidable will, saw the merciless eyes calculate. The advantage was still tipped to Thorkill but it was no longer so easy, neither was it quite sure.

"You scum."

"What is the matter? You wanted revenge. Perhaps you do not have the courage to take it." He could feel the thwarted fury in the coiled muscle beneath him. Thorkill had howled for vengeance. He had to take it or he was no longer a *hersir*. There was no place for those who lost pride.

It was personal.

And he had to keep it personal or there would be a bloodbath and Raidwulf's force might still lose. So he sat back. The solid sheet of muscle tightened instantly, seeing the advantage at last, ready to take it.

Offer the chance.

"Perhaps you think you cannot win," he said. "But then I understand you are not such a good gambler, are you?" He rolled aside before the sudden onslaught of raw strength. Fast. When Thorkill got to his feet, he found he had a small knife cut across his shoulder.

The course was set.

There were no preliminaries, just Thorkill's sword unsheathed, driving for him. He leaped back, the knife in his hand as good as useless against the sword's range in such an open area. There was yelling somewhere behind him. He could not see. He shouted the only thing that mattered.

"Leave him to me."

Raidwulf stopped whatever might have begun. He understood. This was the best choice. Take the Wessex king's service and you made the harsh decision. It was an unwritten code.

Boda risked one half glance across his shoulder, moving. The light caught Raidwulf's sword blade arcing towards him through the air. He turned. It should have been easy, but it was not. The twisting movement over previous damage made him stumble.

Thorkill would cut him off from the sword.

"Nithing." The deliberate female yell jarred through the tension. Rosamund. Thorkill the noble *hersir's* gaze flickered. It must be an international word of cowardice. Consummate timing. The unexpected lash of her voice gave him the half chance. He dived after the sword hilt, at the ultimate end of his reach, fingers scrabbling, sliding, gripping. Thorkill's blade missed severing his hand by a breath. Not even that. He could see the blood, but since his hand still worked, it was not serious. He gained his feet. Two of Raidwulf's men had Od under restraint.

Thorkill had stolen Od's moment.

"Whoreson—"

Probably only temporarily.

But he closed his thoughts against that, against everything except the few minutes that would come, focussing his mind on the balance of the unfamiliar sword in his hand, on Thorkill who had now stepped back.

What he could not shut out of his mind was everything that was at stake. Rosamund. Rosamund and her quick thoughts and her reckless courage. Her vulnerability. Merriwen's.

The number of lives that depended on this.

Thorkill circled right, carefully placed out of the range of his sword, a warrior's well-trained skill. The cold mind worked again, calculated, waited for the opening.

There was no denying the competence.

He matched, moving his feet in the same rhythm, but not pushing it. Thorkill knew every point of weakness on his body. He had inflicted it.

The self-absorbed confidence was complete. Thorkill grinned, circling, fluid. The forehand slash, when it came, was explosive. He blocked, angling the sword properly to take the force of the blow near the base of the blade. The steel clashed. Thorkill grunted. A split instant's surprise. But the follow-up backhand was quicker than expected, high, harder to parry, stretching the damaged muscles across his ribs, the combination of blows carefully calculated.

His reaction had the fatal seed of slowness.

"You are nothing. I showed you that yesterday," yelled Thorkill and then sprang back to avoid getting decapitated. The blow had been forced out of brute strength, out of the power of rage, almost enough to create the breach. But Thorkill was an expert. He backed, expression murderous, more cautious now, but balance perfect, controlled, waiting for the next opportunity.

He circled and then struck, the blows swift, repeated. Fast movement was the best defence. The strength of the sword blade had to be protected. If it broke or was seriously damaged, he was dead. There was no shield to absorb the force of his opponent's blow.

He sidestepped, pulling round still with relative ease. The assault did not slow. It was only brute strength that sustained him, strength that was already damaged. And the rage—the rage was purely dangerous, unstable. Far too deep.

He forced Thorkill back, but he was no swordsman fit to win the four treasures for style. In truth he was no swordsman at all. You had to start when you were seven. The brutal strength carried him.

He could see Raidwulf with Merriwen…Rosamund. He was supporting Rosamund.

Get them away from here.

"Do not think she is free."

The blow came out of nowhere, high, nearly slicing through his shoulder, forcing him to turn.

The twisting movement jarred pain through bruised muscle. He made an audible sound.

Thorkill's nostrils flared, a hound on the scent of blood. There was enough of it. The hand must be worse than he had thought. His grip on the silver-wired hilt had slipped.

"You are going to die," said Thorkill. "She will be next. She will know that. She will wish you had not deflected the knife blade. I—"

The violent yell came from Thorkill who was lucky still to have a foot attached to each leg. The bastard leaped, escaping the disabling blow by a hair's breadth. The return was viciously fast, aimed to sever Boda's neck, nearly connecting because the rage had made him reckless.

"Fool," yelled Thorkill. "A creature like you can never win. You are gone. I finished you yesterday when you came crawling to me. Now is just a joke."

The sword blade, the fine impenetrable skill, taunted him. Each forced movement brought pain, calculated, doubled by all that had happened.

"I have every right to kill you." There was nothing beyond that arrogant belief. The self-absorbed power that yesterday had smashed him into the wall. The look that had leaked from Thorkill's narrowed eyes when he had struck at Rosamund.

"It is over." The sword arced down, high. He blocked. But this time the pain choked his breath. He forced his arm higher, rolling his wrist to take the blow at right angles on his own blade, but his hand caved, the hilt slipped in blood. He leaped back, fatally unbalanced, and it ended abruptly. Thorkill drove at him, even as he fell, rolling and twisting like an eel to avoid death, the primitive instinct that of a brawler under the mead bench, not a warrior. The blade scored through his tunic. He had no idea whether it had cut. All he could feel was the pain through his side where he had fallen, through his head. That was the worst. He could not see. He tried to move, blindly, aching for breath.

"You are dead," yelled Thorkill from some vast distance above him. "So is she. So are they all. Do not think I will let them go."

Something moaned, twisting like a helpless cripple down on the ground, locked in the mire. He thought it was himself, crawling. Defeated.

"You have failed," said Thorkill. "A creature like you could not do anything else. *Failed.*"

It penetrated the morass of pain.

I have failed. His father's last words. His father's son.

Raidwulf's sword lay an inch from his hand, only the gleam of the hilt told him, a dragon warrior's sword. That was what he was. He was part of them or he had failed them.

He was with Rosamund, or dead.

He tried to move, the pain crippling. He could not do it—

Thorkill took a split instant to assert triumph before he struck, shouting. His fingers touched the glittering hilt, caught, held, just as Thorkill's blade slashed down. He saw the shadow, only that. He had moved inside the blow and the sword in his bleeding hand seemed to strike without him, giving the death blow that had been meant for him, because nothing else was possible. And then he was crawling forward over the slashed ground, yelling.

"Do not kill him," he shouted about Od. Because he knew what Od would do in that instant... Od was the key.

There was a howl of Norse. The tough, lean figure had wrenched itself free of restraint. One of his captors lunged. Boda was too far away, scrambling to his feet through clinging darkness, yelling.

Across the clearing, Od lurched forward, and it was Raidwulf who was closest, Raidwulf who had known to anticipate the next move. Raidwulf who had the clearest right to avenge.

Od's headlong rush stopped in the face of a twelve-inch rune blade.

"Leave him." The words had no justification in honour. Even Boda knew that. He hardly knew whether they had a basis in logic.

Raidwulf flicked him half a glance, the knife held steady. It was an apt instrument of vengeance. That must be how Od had killed Wihtred, Raidwulf's friend.

He fought for breath, the ability to speak through the crippling morass.

"Do not kill."

Od, angered, driven, still held the future. Raidwulf's eyes flickered. Light glanced off the copper inlaid blade. *Find the words.*

"There is a choice."

Raidwulf was Alfred's man. So was he. The same.

"You choose the end," he said to Od. "Leave." Od's harsh gaze raked him, then shifted away. "There is only death for you here. Nothing else."

"It should be your death. You owe—"

"Nothing. The payment is made." It was little enough for all those hanged men whose souls might haunt him. For Rosamund's life. But it was over. Done. There had to be a way out.

"Thorkill's death is not a matter that requires vengeance from you." He saw Od's mouth open but no sound came. There had been disputes with Thorkill. Loyalty cut two ways.

"Thorkill chose that fight. He took his chance. We all make choices."

Od's jaw clamped shut and their gazes clashed, caught, unexpected and incendiary as storm lightning. Od jerked his head away and the sudden contact broke. But it was too late. The truth was naked. It had been Od's voice that had yelled the warning when Thorkill had struck at Rosamund. Od had not cared that she was not a princess, or for honour. Just like him.

Od had his own will. Everyone did.

"A survivor's choice," snapped Od. "You can tell her that."

Rosamund. He did not look away. He could not. The instant of truth held him as surely as it held Od, the most dangerous weakness also the point of communication, the elusive glimpse of common ground that did not admit tribal boundaries. They were not that much different.

"Make the choice," said Raidwulf. "Take your men and leave this country. Leave England." The Viking force, close-packed, armed, ready, were Od's men now, if he could command their allegiance.

Boda waited, the sword in his probably useless grip, the wind cooling the sweat on his skin, the increase in pain through each abused muscle, through his head, relentless. He could not see Rosamund, but he knew she was there. She waited.

Od's mouth twisted. "I will hold what I have. The best place to do that is not here. Fate's will. I am going home."

At Od's gesture the massed weapons on the other side of the clearing relaxed, but only as far as wariness. The horses were brought forward. Od vanished. The rest followed. Easy enough to gain the border, the coast, a ship. Gone.

Boda wanted to say something to Raidwulf whose friend was dead. It was impossible to speak, to find words. There were none. He heard Rosamund's voice and then nothing.

ROSAMUND WATCHED his face, colourless, wreathed in firelight, the immobility and the remote silence impenetrable. Boda, the king's man. Across the chamber, scented applewood cracked in the hearth. Warmth flared.

She was in the same stranger's bower in the unknown village where she had spent the brief hours of the dark. With him. Hours filled with such longing and fierce despair. Such passion. The moments in which her life had changed.

The dangerous creator of all that change lay still, the big, deeply-shadowed bulk of his body stretched out on the heaped furs, lying on his side, nothing visible of the damage to his ribs, the back of his head, only the fading bruises on the tough face, the white blur of his hand efficiently strapped by Raidwulf. Nothing except the blank stillness.

She could not move away from him and Merriwen looked after her. It seemed to have been so from the moment she had declared her real self in order to save Rosamund from Thorkill. She kept bringing things, a cup of ale warmed by the fire. News.

"Olga has gone."

"What? Where?"

"No one knows. She just vanished."

Chad's bones. How would she live? No farewell, just vanished into a foreign, potentially hostile country. She waited for Merriwen to ask why. But the warm ale cup was pressed into her fingers.

"She did not go with Od. She left you this."

Something else touched her hand, smooth, cool. Glass. The scent came to her faintly through the stopper, sharper and sweeter than the steaming ale. She knew what it was.

"Olga said you deserved it."

It was a love potion.

Her mouth twisted. She thought of shared laughter amid the fear and the risk and the terrible calculation it took to survive. Her fingers slid round the rare and expensive glass. A fellow concubine's gift. And yet the few words they had shared in the cart under Arne's gaze had been those of true women, real. They had said everything there was to say and they had not needed a farewell. Yet Rosamund said it in her head: *wæs thu Olga hal.* Stay safe.

Olga had known her secrets. Her hand tightened on friendship's gift. She wanted to unstopper the small glass vial and swallow the dubious contents entire and whole. She had wanted *him* to swallow them. Fool.

She sipped her ale and watched the man who had moved so far beyond her, who was not hers. Her glance strayed to the rolled parchment lying on the wall bench that now made that doubly so.

"I will stoke up the fire," said Merriwen like a mother hen, like a different person, perhaps the person she was meant to be.

The familiar figure in its drab gown crossed the small room with a steady grace. Familiar and yet not so. The princess had been restored. Merriwen had ensured that by her own gesture of courage and everything was changed.

Her glance fell to the shuttered face. *You began that, just as you made all the changes.* Her eyes watched stillness. *You with your terrible courage and your clear decisions and your brutal ability to endure things.*

And kindness.

He looked at her.

It happened just like that. Merriwen, absorbed in mending the fire, did not notice and there was a moment which belonged only to them, in which the passion and the depthless longing which had filled the strangers' chamber seemed reborn and she could imagine things that did not belong to her, that were like dreams and at the same time, shockingly raw.

Then Merriwen's carefully stacked wood collapsed, crackling into a flare of light and a trail of sparks, and his dark gaze shifted. Merriwen turned her head.

"You are here." She was smiling. "I am glad." It seemed she had gone back into the Viking camp to find Boda.

The newly graceful little figure rose to its feet. "I was waiting for you."

"Were you, princess?" His voice sounded fathoms deep, rough. Merriwen showed dimples.

"Yes. So was Rosamund." It was prim. The blue

gaze that suddenly clashed with Rosamund's was anything but.

"I have to go and get some more wood for the fire," said the princess of Mercia. There was the flashing glimpse of the smile. Her white hand latched the door, then she was gone, like a sprite, a stranger. The brilliant beginnings of a woman.

The *princess.*

The newly-made fire hissed and threw light, fine warmth. She clenched her fist. Her nails dug into her palm, sharp with pain. She could not undo her fingers.

Tell him you understand the power of what he has done. Tell him who you are and then go and fetch Raidwulf-the-efficient to help him. Tell him he is free of you at last.

Begin. "Thank you." *The first two words.*

Her voice made an appalling choking sound. "I thought you would die." She took a breath but it scorched on tears she could not control. She was not going to cry. Crying solved nothing. Weak.

SHE CAME TO HERSELF wrapped in the furs, her shoulder under the warm curve of his elbow, his bandaged hand against her hair. She fought for steadiness, words. There was nothing. Nothing beyond the sense of his aliveness, the feel of his solid body against hers, the shallow rise of his breath that meant he would speak.

"I am sorry you had to see all that happened."

"Sorry?" Her voice found shape out of the rawness of her throat. "It is you who should never have had to endure all that. I thought you would—"

"No. Thick skull. Peasant. You should have known."

She forced herself to read beyond the sense-bespelling physical closeness, seeking the deeper closeness, the hidden things he would not put in words.

"Aye," she said blandly. "That gave you an unfair advantage." She felt the slight jolt in the solid body.

"Did you spill all the ale just before?" The question was equally bland. Turn anything with light words.

She moved her head under the heavy warmth of his arm. "I do not think so."

"Well then, ministering angel."

She moved, carefully because of the bandaged hand and the damage. There was ale left, still warmed. She helped him drink. Her hands were shaking.

"Better?"

"Aye. An improvement on the last time we did this and you fed me something drained straight from the midden."

"Straight—" She took a calming breath over a lifegiving spurt of indignation. "Those were rare herbs. You were lucky I had them."

"It was my luck, was it?"

"Yes." She took another breath. "It… Did it really taste that bad?"

"Aye. It is only that I was too polite to say so at the time. You know me."

"Polite?" She watched his eyes, the faint, welcome colour that had returned along the fiercely perfect line of his cheekbone after drinking the spiced ale, after sleeping so long. *Kind.*

"I was never a princess," she said abruptly. "I pretended. I lied."

"Aye."

"Of course you know. Merriwen, *Rosamund,* told Thorkill the truth."

"It was brave of her to choose that moment."

"Yes. It was brave, but it…"

"Also brought things to a head with Thorkill? I would have done that in any case. Merriwen found the most effective way, better than anything I could have done. But it speeded things up. Too fast. He hurt you."

His gaze fixed on hers for a moment that defied all constraints, that belonged to a different realm. Her heart missed its beat, then thudded, heavy, out of time and control.

"It should not have happened," he said. "I am sorry."

"It was, *is,* nothing, not even a cut worth stitches." Her arm ached, but it was irrelevant, *nothing* compared to what he had risked, what he had done.

"You saved my life and Merriwen's. You did such things. You should not have had to—"

"Do you think I regret it?" His rough voice cut hers.

"No." She tried to hold his gaze. "King's man," she said and saw clear truth. What she had to do was remove a burden he would not want.

"I have to tell you who I am."

What I have to tell you, is what I have done.

Rosamund let go of Boda's hand. "I have to tell you how I came to be with Merriwen."

Her gaze shifted to the flames in the hearth, the fire Merriwen had made so carefully, and the past was with her, the past no one could escape.

"My father was a thane, but not a particularly rich or powerful one, and when he and my mother died of the fever, my uncle had no time for me. And so saw his chance to send me to be a companion to a richer girl, to share her education at the nunnery. I hated being sent away from everything I knew, being suddenly powerless, frightened. I wanted to hate everyone and everything inside those stone walls. Then I saw Merriwen." She took a breath. How did she explain it?

"I was fifteen and at least I had the prospect of marriage in two years. Merriwen was not quite eleven. She would speak to no one." The hearth flames flickered in front of her eyes. "She talked to me. She had no parents. Neither did I. Her calculating uncle controlled her fate. So did mine. She felt alone. We made a bond."

"Two survivors."

"Yes. When my betrothal was broken, we just became closer. Two useless women against the world…and do not for all the saints' sake pity me."

Her voice cracked because he had made some movement as though he would touch her again and she could not bear that. The blocked desperation and the vicious longing inside her would break the last fragile bond of control and she would take that comfort.

She would take everything.

She forced the words out.

"It was my choice to go with Merriwen. She is my friend and also my princess. I owed her loyalty. You can understand that. You swore an oath to Alfred. Well, she was my lord." It was the same word, *hlaford,* male or female. It did not matter which.

"The loyalty mattered. The friendship mattered." She took a steadying breath of wood-smoked air, but in her mind, the warmth of the Mercian sun touched her frozen skin, the scent of ripe pears from the orchard filled her.

"What mattered," she said, "was that they shoved her outside the nunnery wall with all her worldly goods to wait alone."

He said a string of words even she had not heard connected. It was immensely steadying. She wanted so desperately to touch him, just for one moment.

Her mouth twisted at the frankness of his description. "I think they wanted to avoid that. It was a nunnery after all and it would not do to let a war band of Vikings through the gates. But the fact that everyone else abandoned the princess made it easy for me to assume her identity. All I had to do was walk through the gate."

"That was loyalty."

He said *manræden,* which had overtones of honour. She felt as though there were a huge crushing weight closing round her heart. She wanted him to think she was honourable, worth something. Worth his regard.

The honour was only a half truth.

"You make it sound heroic," she said. "And all those things do matter. Loyalty matters. But I was also angry, so wildly and bitterly enraged. It was as though every loss, every betrayal, every false, despicable moment of greed and self-interest had come together in that moment, every…every hurt."

Her hands twisted. She could not control them. She watched the knuckles go pure white.

"Have you ever been so angry? So utterly filled with anger that there is nothing else left, only the rage like a black beast which devours everything that exists inside you and still hungers for more? It is vile and you are pleased by its vileness because it gives you such strength and makes you immune from the pain—"

"And when you have that, you know you are going to survive."

It was not her voice that found the words, but one that was stronger. She looked at him and the understanding was complete, all the bitter knowledge there in his tough face with its bruising and its clear lines, in his deep eyes. She read the light and the darkness, good and bad, a harshly experienced world within a world.

"You know," she said. "You suffered more than I did. You fought it. You just know." She felt the harsh constriction round her heart split open, break. She could not see, or breathe, or speak. She was falling, but he held her. His arms closed round her. There was warmth, the soul-shattering, awareness of him, the physical wall of strength, the scent of his skin, the rough line of his jaw, his mouth against her hair, her skin. Closeness. The magic she had longed for, that had always been denied.

She did not know whether she cried. Only that if he let her go, she would die. Her senses filled with him, drowned.

Don't let me go.

Do not speak. Don't say the name that is not mine.

The fierce strength engulfed her. There were no words to break the spell. None possible because his mouth took hers. The desire was incendiary. Lightning.

Her voice made a sound that was harsh, uncivilized as all the grief-filled madness inside her. The uncivilized things did not stop him. There was only his warmth, power, the sound of her own sharp breathing, her hot skin, her fever-flushed face stained with dampness. The heat of passion. Tears. He did not stop even for that. He would not stop. He understood the demons. The relief flooded her and she could be herself.

Her hands clung to his shoulders, the smooth nakedness of skin, the shockingly thick muscle, the tenseness in it. Her uneven breath caught. The tight body moved against hers, the deep strength, his mouth on her skin, the touch of his fingers on her flesh beneath her clothes, moulding the hidden shape of her body, her heat, sending her senses spiralling.

She moved against him, her thigh sliding over his, over the dense, flaring muscle.

His damaged hand touched her face, the vulnerable line of her cheekbone, the damp trails on her skin. She pushed closer into the survivor's warmth. Their bodies locked. She could sense the way his heart beat, the sharp quickness of his breath, the scent of arousal on his skin.

He read the same signs in her, like a hunter, his beautiful weight already positioned over her, the next step inevitable.

He moved between her thighs.

Her hands were fastened on his arms, following the smooth slide of muscle under hot skin. The sound of her breath was uncontrolled, half-violent. He slid his undamaged hand between their bodies, touching the source of her heat. She jerked, the reaction uncontrolled, latent with all the force inside her. Her hands tightened on his arms.

She was urgent, her flesh hotly ready, soft under the relentless, pleasure-searing invasion of his fingers, then without warning the tight, steel-hard push of his body. She was so driven by the sheer physical intensity of her arousal, by the raw emotions in her head, she cried out, the sound as harsh as her tears.

There was a finitely breakable moment of highly charged stillness and then her breath shuddered and she said his name, only his name. He drove inwards, his heat filling her completely. Her hips rose instinctively to meet him. Her need stole sense. She was maddened with it. But most deep was her awareness of him, the living hotness and the moving power of his body, its driving urgency. The blinding knowledge in her mind of how much he wanted her.

It was the limitless depth of his desire that obliterated the dark, that brought the fierce release of unnamed demons. The light.

ROSAMUND LAY VERY STILL, unable to stir, like a creature newborn who does not yet know how to move its limbs. She kept her eyes shut.

But she felt Boda move, heard a faint sound. Pain. She was lying against him, her arm across his neck, her fingers twisted in the trailing ends of his hair. She had avoided bruises, the burnt skin, but she shifted her weight away.

"Stay there."

That was it. Just two words in that rough voice and she was lying in the shadowed curve of his body, locked in warmth, the hot scent of his skin, muskiness and sex. Closeness. As though it could always be like this.

She opened her eyes on the flickering glow of the hearth and filtered sunlight.

"I have done such things."

"Aye."

He did not move. If there had been tears left, she would have wept them. She watched the glitter of daylight.

"I mean…unacceptable things."

"Which things are you thinking of?" he asked. "Saving that poor wench when no one else would? Or lying with Ingolf?" Only being an ex-peasant he did not exactly say *lying with*. Always call a spade a shovel.

"That," she said. "Lying with Ingolf. I shared a bed with him and—" She frowned at the dancing light. Her eyes ached. "Sometimes with the earl." *The ambitious, treacherous, mood-proud, utterly brilliant bastard who started all this—the reason you risk your life and Wihtred got killed.*

She heard the sound of his inward breath. "Does he wear that gold arm-ring that is supposed to weigh two pounds in bed, or does it get in the way?"

"The—"

"It's a fair question. He could brain someone with it."

The fruits of ruthless pillage. She choked.

"I can see you are not going to tell."

It does not matter. You can still lie here in this circle of magic. I can look past it.

She bit her lip.

No. Not even you.

Especially not you.

"You do not understand. It was part of my plan. It was I who did everything to make sure it happened. I wanted the earl in my bed."

"You mean you planned all that while you were reading books and playing knucklebones at the nunnery? Or you planned it when you found yourself in the middle of a hostile army?"

"With the army." *Do not take kindness. It is not fair.* "All the things I have done since I found myself in the middle of a hostile army are part of me. As much a part of me as living at the nunnery. That is how it is."

"Yes."

"Oh, God. You already know that." She had not meant to look at his eyes, not with so many things unsaid and the sense of that impossible newness still shimmering through her body.

"I went straight for him," she said. "I told you it was Ingolf, but he was secondary. He was part of my plan, but not the whole. I decided that if I really wanted to survive, the earl was the one who could provide the key. I was going to take it."

She made herself concentrate on the light, explain the next bit.

"I did not expect to bc the one and only mistress and bed companion of a Viking earl. What I wanted and sought and schemed to get was something else—his goodwill, his…friendship." That word had so many meanings, from the plain and simple to the transactions between men and women, and the subtle complexities of fealty to a lord—loyalty and honour. The last would be what truly damned her.

"Handy."

"Yes. It worked. I was interesting because he thought I was a princess. It was a high status triumph having me. He is a man for quick decisions. He played fair—in my case."

Not with the hostages, all those dead men. Hanged. Why in God's name did she have to say such things?

"He let me choose. I chose Ingolf." The light made her eyes ache. She tried to focus on that, not on him, on kindness. "The earl was happy enough for his kinsman to have my keeping. I had Ingolf to keep the wolves away and behind him, stood the earl. Everyone knew that. So no one else dared approach me, or the insignificant little girl in her drab clothes who did duty as my maid. And so I achieved it. I made sure Merriwen was safe, even though they threw her outside the nunnery walls and the Vikings claimed her like so much plundered loot. I was proud of that. The pride went well with the anger. And there was not just her need. Looking after Merriwen, having to focus my thoughts on her and not just myself, was what saved me."

She steadied her breath. "And as for me…"

"You survived." His rough voice said it for her, the basic truth they both understood. What she had not understood was the cost, the unacknowledged bitterness, the things that had been changed.

"I owed Ingolf a great deal. He was pleased to have a princess in his bed and I was pleased to be part of his household. It made the perfect transaction. What more could I have asked?"

"You do not see things in such terms. Transactions. Did you like Ingolf?"

No. To anyone else, she would have said it and lied.

No one else would have asked, not in this way, out of that appalling, unbreachable kindness.

She had just made love with him. She was still touching him. She tried to pick her words.

"I liked some things about him. You see, I…I did not expect to be lonely. I did not understand what the isolation would be like. I do not know why I did not count on that. Three years. Not only because I was among foreign invaders, but because I was no longer even myself, always acting a part. It is hard to sustain. So stupid." What was the point of hiding? She had no pride left to salvage. She had let him see everything.

"Sometimes I felt desperate. I felt…lost. Ingolf was there, a constant. He would have taken me with him back to Denmark when he left—I thought about going with him."

She waited for the reaction. Even the ex-slave under her hand, the man who knew how to cheat at dice and gutter-fight, would react.

"I remember you liked the idea of Hedeby."

Speak. Just keep speaking. Her body was trembling, locked against the unmoving solidity of his. "I nearly got to see it. When I used to lie awake in the dark and I could no longer remember what Mercia looked like, only what Ceolfrith had done, I thought about going to Hedeby with Ingolf."

"But you did not."

"It was not a heroic decision. I think it was probably Merriwen who saved me from it. She changed. She was so much younger than me, always the child, and then suddenly she was not. There was *the bosom fit for a drink-house jezebel.*"

"Chad's bones. I have a way with words do I not?"

"Yes. It was so true and although Ingolf had never touched her, I just knew one day that he had noticed, drab clothes or not, and I was afraid. That was when I decided on escaping and making for Cornwall as soon as the army halted its western march. Neither of us could go back to Mercia."

She watched the way the firelight and the sun-light brought red fire out of his hair wound between her fingers. "It is not possible to go back."

She waited for his agreement, the relentless ac-knowledgement of truth.

"You could stay in Wessex," he said. "It is a far easier prospect than Cornwall."

"Wessex? Oh, I would be very welcome. Three winters spent with the Vikings, a woman who took the name of her helpless mistress, an embarrassing reject from King Ceolfrith's court. No. Perhaps for Merriwen, that is, for Rosamund. She might stay here if that is what she wants. If your brilliant king would take pity on her."

"He would give her a place, and not out of pity. Just as he would for you. You are a thane's daughter. Think. You stayed with your mistress through dan-ger. You proved the highest loyalty. You showed all those thanely virtues. *Manræeden*."

She could not look at him, at the living gold of his skin, the red-streaked brilliance of his hair under her hand.

"I cannot."

"You could. You have to say no more than you wish about what happened in the last three years. No one is going to question you, because you would have the king's support. That is what matters. And perhaps more important for you, you would have the queen's. She is Mercian and no supporter of what Ceolfrith has done. Gainmar is her kinsman. You helped him."

"I did nothing that mattered."

"What matters about a future in Wessex is that you have the courage and the strength. You can still make your own life."

Her own life. It was what she had wanted, sustained by anger and bitterness. But the anger was no longer there. There seemed nothing left to sustain her, only emptiness.

"Do not throw the chance away. You have the right qualities." There was a pause. "And you have good birth. I would give much for that. Even to be born into freedom."

Her gaze moved from the dazzling light and shadow to his eyes and she knew she was selfish to feel so lost, to ache with longing for things she could not have.

"You are right. I was born with so much and I took it for granted, like a right that was mine without thinking. You had nothing, less than that. You should have had freedom, a better life, not such bitter regrets."

She was so close she felt the savage movement of his body.

"The thief in the dark weather?" The movement was cut off by that terrible strength, the light answer turned her words aside. He would—

"What I regret is that I cannot be worth someone like you."

The abruptness confounded her, so that she could not for an instant take in what he had said.

"You do not mean it." Her heart thudded against her ribs. No one had ever wanted her except in the way they had just shared, even when she had been a thane's daughter living in a nunnery. No one talked about being *worthy*.

"You know what I am," said Boda who was stronger and more generous than herself. "A slave."

"Yes, and you are one of King Alfred's men, oath sworn. It was the first thing you ever told me about yourself. You cannot deny how much it means."

"No."

"I am enough of a thane's daughter to know that loyalty works two ways. You are one of those who are chosen, one of the brotherhood of the golden dragon."

"With a good sword to win fame and riches? I am not a thane. I will never be one. That is not what I am."

"Yes, it is." She had the parchment from Gainmar to give him. *Tell him.*

She unclenched her hand from the very edge of his disordered hair. Her fingers had been so long in that position, so tight on that tenuous last connection, that they ached.

"No," he said.

She moved her arm from his warm, warm skin.

"It is the truth." She slid across the heaped furs, leaving him. He lay still, the dark eyes watching her, unreadable. She found the rolled parchment on the wall bench. Her stiff fingers curled round it.

"Gainmar had this made for you."

"A book?"

"Yes."

She held out the charter. He did not touch it.

"It would take me half a day to work that out."

Ex-slave. *If you were still that, I would throw everything else aside and run away with you.*

She unfurled the parchment. Her hands were shaking.

"It is a grant of land. Eight hides. A witnessed gift. It is yours."

"It is *what?*"

"A reward. You said something about a good sword. You saved his life."

"That was…"

"The sworn duty of a king's man? This is a royal reward."

"Duty and… It was something that I had to do. Because of the dead hostages. I had to do it because…"

She was still sitting near him. The careful scribe's writing describing a thane's estate blurred under her eyes. You were close to someone or you were not. Her hand fastened on his.

"Because they were hanged."

"Aye. I am not the best witness to that." The solid fingers suddenly convulsed. "You know why."

"Because of your father. I am sorry."

"It was justice. But to me, he was the only thing I had."

She looked down at their joined hands.

"He was your father."

"Aye." Just that short word. But she was touching him and she felt the reaction. He did not speak, and then he said, "Slave's son. Gainmar cannot give me land."

"It is land in Wessex. It is a fitting reward. Wessex owes you. You gave the first warning that Guthrum was breaking out of Wareham."

"You worked that out straightaway, didn't you?"

"Yes. You and the hostages and the beacon fires. It was too much of a coincidence."

"That dice game. You were mad to do that."

"Thorkill said you were Mercian. I did not want that to mean anything to me, but it did."

"Love of home?"

"Yes. I had lost it, but you gave that back to me."

"By talking about rain and fog?"

"Aye." *Precisely by that. By words full of jest that mean something else, something more, something as deep as your thoughts and as strong as your heart.*

She did not know what he wanted. There had only been that single, abrupt, discordant sentence.

What I regret is that I cannot be worth someone like you.

She watched their joined hands. What was she, if not a reckless gambler?

"The other reason, the other love, was purely for you."

"No."

The jolt shot through her, through the small point of contact between their hands. Her mouth went dry. She registered the hard movement of his body. Away from her. The fast glimpse of his eyes. Fire.

He had said she had courage. He believed that of her. *Be worth it.*

"Why not?"

"Because I am what I am. Do you think a piece of parchment that I can hardly read has the power to change that? I cannot even accept it."

"It is a gift made in honour."

"Honour—"

"Yes. It is for an honourable deed. You cannot refuse it without dishonouring the giver. You told me you have already refused Gainmar once. I believe you regret that."

"I do not recall the law allowing slaves to own land."

"Here in Wessex, you are a king's man."

"No—"

"You can—"

"Can what? Take the land and pretend to you that I am something I am not?"

She saw his eyes.

"You said that the last three winters of your life were part of you and could not be changed. I could say that for the first sixteen years of my life. That is who I am. The rest, the four years at the king's court are just a covering over a foundation that was already there and always will be there. You have to understand how things are."

He watched her from the rumpled mess of the bed where he had slept, wounded, and they had lain together in that fierce outpouring of…what? Passion beyond measure. Despair.

Love.

She could no longer say that. She could only watch him and know that whatever he thought had to be said.

"I will never be a thane even if I take eight hides of land from someone like Gainmar. I do not think the right way. I cannot. Sometimes I do not even see the difference until it is too late. All I can do is put on the trappings. I can walk round the court with the rest of the king's men and talk and manage table manners and pass round the ale cup when I am supposed to. I had a good enough teacher."

"Tell me." She pushed the words out of her dry throat and she watched him, the vivid face, the tough, hard body with its bruising, the complex, impossibly riveting beauty where there should be none.

"I learned from Ashbeorn." The blood brother. There was so much she did not know. "He spent his own time with a Viking army."

"What?"

"It was not his choice. He escaped from them at much the same age I was when I joined the king's men. So he knew what it was like to have to acquire an acceptable face to present to the world. He understood, even though he had been born a thane. And so he helped me do it, to put on the trappings to survive in this world. I cannot say I always thanked him at the time, although I do now. It was hard work."

"Bitter." She thought about what it was like presenting such a face to the world, like a coat of armour, woven steel.

"But if it had not been such hard work I would have turned into a barbarian. I have a lot of strength." *Understatement.* The dark gaze slid away, masked by the thick dark brown lashes. "I had already learned a lot of the things that go into the creation of a wolf's head, an outlaw. I would have made a spectacularly successful one. For a while. And then in the end it would have been me dancing from the gallows tree."

Rosamund watched the tough profile already roughened with stubble, the hard bones.

"Yes. You might have made a perfect wolf's head. It was the first thing I saw about you, all that strength. But you are not an outlaw. You are a king's man. Because you chose it. That is something to rely on."

"You were afraid of me." Nothing changed in his face—impassive. But she knew that was not how he felt. The knowledge was simply there in her head. Not her head, her heart. She could see through because of all the things that had happened to her. The legacy of them no longer made her blind with pain. It made her see.

She did not like what she had to say, but it was the truth and he already knew it. Brutal coin.

"I was a little afraid. But only at first. And it was mostly because I knew I had done something wrong with those chains. No one should suffer that."

"You did not have many options."

He made a slight movement of one powerful shoulder—bitterness, impatience. Acceptance? There was no blame. That was the worst thing and she knew that what she had said had not been enough.

She felt a wholly different kind of fear. But it was not possible to give in. If she did, he would be alone. They would both be alone.

"But there was something else, even though I was afraid, even though I did not then know you." She sought the knowledge inside her, the clearness out of pain that might provide the way out. "It was inexplicable, like a lightning flash of recognition. I looked at all that deep rage and I understood. Not what you had been through, or what the chains meant, but what it is like to be that angry. So…so enraged and bitter with it."

She wanted to touch his solid, tensed flesh and she did not know how. "I have felt just something of the same kind of anger. I told you that and you did not turn away from me." Her hand lighted on his shoulder.

"You did not turn away."

Time seemed to hang suspended. Her fingers touched solid flesh. It did not move.

"No. I did not turn away from you. I cannot."

Her heart thudded against her ribs. She touched his flesh, hard, stone-muscled. He turned his head.

"I am a slave. I was born one," he said and his eyes met hers, naked, the gesture almost brutally forced. "You have seen what I am." It was all there, all the conflicting emotions laid out for her to read, things that she recognised, things that were new. Or perhaps they had always been there, but he had not let her see. Or she had been too blind, too damaged.

Too afraid. She could feel that fear now at the back of her head, like a killing frost. But there had to be some good in the world. There *had* to be.

"Nothing will change what I am," he said, while her voice stayed suspended, far beyond her reach.

Gambler.

"Nothing can—"

"Good." She had the words, the right ones with the power. *Please let it be so.* "You cannot change. That is the person I saw, the chained *hell-thane,* the devious mercenary, the brawler, the one who would be able to cheat at dice if I needed it, who understands what people will do if they are pushed into a corner. That is the person I fell in love with. That is the person I need, that I cannot live without. The person without whom I would be alone. What I do not know is whether the king's man will accept someone without honour—"

His mouth came down on hers. It was so fast, so close to violent, she did not even see it. She heard the harsh sound of his breath, sensed the fleeting moment of power and then the kiss turned molten and she was lost, drowned in overwhelming sensation. In joy.

She opened her eyes with her head resting against his throat and his arms holding her. She tried not to lie on bruises. "That is the thing I like most about you. You have no idea what honour is." Her hand rested on warm supple flesh, aliveness. "Can I live in your keeping?"

"Live in my— Certainly not." He sounded like the most outraged prude. She shut her eyes against tears, the impossible, still half-frightening joy.

"Only, I thought as you have an estate now and since I brought some of my Viking loot stashed away in my clothing—"

"We are getting properly wed. You can have Gainmar's land as your morning gift."

"*No.*" It was genuine. "That is too much. It was meant for you."

"My just reward?"

"Yes."

"Then I can do what I like with it. You are a thane's daughter. You can have it. Besides—" his voice cut off hers "—I want you to have something like that, something that is indisputably yours to replace what you lost, so that you will know you always have a choice. I want you to know that you are safe."

It was too great a gift, but he had made it because a slave understood what a thane would not. All her nightmares wiped out. Never to be at anyone else's mercy again.

"You are my choice. I do not need such a gift. Not now."

"I want to give it."

"An honour gift."

"Because it is for you. That is what matters to me." He paused and then said, "It was something that mattered to Od in the end. Did you see? He did not care for insulted honour. He tried to warn even me, if that meant saving your life from Thorkill."

"Yes. He did do that. And then he left without fighting. You stopped them from killing him."

"Aye. Raidwulf was generous. More than I expected. And I thought…I half understood Od. And I wanted to find the way out." The deep gaze fixed on hers. "That is all I have ever wanted, to find the way out. I could not find it for myself. Taking the king's service showed me the path, but there were still things inside me that I could not get rid of. I thought those things would cut me off from you. I did not think loving you would be enough."

"You. It was all that I wanted. But I was afraid of it."

"Afraid? I just wanted it the way a drowning man wants air. When I opened my eyes and saw you, that was it. But I knew that a woman like you did not belong to someone who would have given much just to be called a peasant. I knew I had things to hide, things even I would not look at. Thorkill brought me face to face with them. There was no pretence left and I had to tell you what I was. You had to know. Everything. That I could not give a future. Or give you back your dreams."

"But you have. You gave me back the view of Mercia I had lost. You did give me dreams because what I want is entirely bound up in you. But the best was that you gave me what I truly wanted, something that is real." Her hand settled over the warmth of his skin. "You give more than you know."

She did not say any more and he did not want to speak. She lay in the unlooked-for boon of closeness and let the words rest. *Believe them.*

"We can look after the little wench." *The princess becoming a woman.* "Or she may want to stay with the queen's women, being Mercian royalty. Either way, you can keep an eye on her, Rosamund. Or is the little princess called Rosamund, now, and I am marrying some other wench?"

You give more than you know. "She made me a present of the name. She says she feels like Merriwen, now. Or she is flirting with Paullina in honour of Saint Paul in case she enters some Wessex nunnery and draws manuscripts forever. But she has not decided yet. It will be interesting to see. So who am *I* marrying?"

"What?"

"I never knew whether it was your real name. Boda. I was always afraid of losing you, so I did not dare ask."

"It is real. It is… Who else would have a fine peasant's name like that?"

Boda. Messenger. "I like it." The one who brought me out of disaster. She held on to him hard.

"Everything was real with you."

"It is real now. It will have to be. You are going to have to play five-stones with Merriwen." She got the shade of that cutthroat, thatch-gallows grin and her heart swelled.

"Chad's bones. I cannot keep either of you two wenches from gambling. I am going to be wed to Rosamund. I suppose I will have to make do." His hand was stroking her hair, so slow and careful.

"Make do?" She arched one eyebrow, as though she were the princess. Or the concubine. She felt like both with him. More than that, she was herself. She produced her best smile and watched the fire. "Is that what you think?"

The loosened skeins of her hair slid through his fingers. "I think I was always like the thief lusting after gold."

"I would suit a thief."

"You are going to suit a respectable king's man."

"Not too respectable, I hope." Her mouth hovered just above his skin.

EPILOGUE

Western Mercia, A.D. 881

HE SWUNG HIMSELF DOWN from the saddle. The stallion arched its neck and sunlight glittered off silvered harness fittings, a suitable sign of wealth, respectability. He was twenty-five. Probably. It was the age at which one traditionally settled down. He was married, parent of a girl and a boy.

He could see ghosts. They waited for him on the open ground in front of the small wooden church. One of them was himself, twelve winters old and furious. Lost.

He handed the reins to a nervous groom.

His wife did not follow, but stayed back, one smooth hand soothing her own fidgeting mount. He knew she would keep the others away. When it came to the sticking point, they shared thoughts. The respectable life had not been won simply, for either of them. But she had courage. He crossed the empty space alone and she waited for him. His *wife*. It was the thing that mattered above all else.

He walked behind the church and the small bower with its crumbling thatch. The priest looked up from where he knelt on the ground. The thin face, a little older and more lined, showed no surprise, so Boda asked.

"Why should I be surprised when I knew you would come back?"

There was not an answer to that. Boda knelt down beside the priest. It was not so much a case of blessing as of weeding. He extracted a young hogweed plant. The priest's hands were full of them. Twitch grass and hogweed and vetch. The same plants. The past moved into the present as though there had never been a break.

"You should get a mattock."

"That is what you said last time. You were concerned for me."

He did not remember that. The hogweed came out and splattered Mercian soil over his sleeve, over the heavy silver arm-ring. He took the ring off. No point in damaging the gift. He held it out. The priest took it.

"What do you want?"

"A manumission." *Freedom.* Strands of vetch slid through his fingers.

"With this?"

It was a large amount of silver and pure. Gemma the goldsmith had made it for him. She had come with Rosamund and Merriwen to bear them company. Her husband Ashbeorn and her brother Edgefrith had come for him. They all waited.

"I probably took some things with me when I went. Maybe that would cover both." He extracted another three handfuls of twitch grass to the priest's one. The man had no technique.

"You did not take them with you."

No. He did remember that. He had left everything behind after the hanging because he could not stand the sight of it. Just as he had not been able to stand the sight of a blameless and kindhearted priest. The stolen things he had been ashamed of, he had buried in the earth behind the cabbage patch. Because he had not known what else to do.

"You and your benighted gardening." Perhaps his companion did have some technique after all. "I hope the cabbages grew."

"They did," said the priest after letting him sweat over an entire row of late carrots, and deservedly so. "You are too late."

"Too late?" The weed-free carrots seemed to disintegrate before his eyes. The bitter ghost of the twelve-winters-old runaway wolf's head watched him. Perhaps some things were too late and there wasn't a way out. "I am sorry."

"Come inside." The priest held out the arm-ring.

"Keep it. You can use it for church business. And get the roof rethatched. I can finish the garden after." He could do that much. A lot of things needed repairing. He had remembered an abundance of wealth, fat cattle and tended fields and corn.

"I will not say such wealth is not welcome, even though this is Lord Athelred's land now. Regained from the Vikings into Mercian hands only this year. The old lord never came back. The new lord has much to do."

"Aye." They all did. He stood up when the priest did.

"No," said the priest when he turned. "You should come in. I have something to show you. I keep it with the Bible in the church. Come."

He owed that much for bad behaviour.

Whatever it was, was locked in a casket. A rolled parchment. There was not a lot of light in the cool, dim interior of the church. The priest lit a lamp. Boda knew enough by now not to totally disgrace himself over reading if he took his time.

It was a manumission, a grant of freedom. It was his. He looked at the date several times. Then he looked at the name again.

"I had it from your former master when your father was taken to justice." *Hanged.* "And I took you. That was the condition, that you were to be free. But I did not believe you were ready to hear it and when I would have told you, you had gone. It is on my conscience that I should have told you sooner."

His hand crushed the glossy edges. *Yes.*

And what would that have achieved when he

had been a hell-raiser of scarcely thirteen winters? The last restraint would have gone.

"It worked out." He tried to get the creases out of the charter.

"But I did know," said the man of God, "that all I had to do was keep the parchment and you would return. You were never one to leave things unfinished."

"Like giving you my thanks."

"Not to me. This is God's house. Wait. I will fetch your companions."

He wanted to sit down before the ground came up and hit him. But it would hardly have been respectful. So he stood with his shoulder against the carved post and attempted praying.

They left him just enough time to master all the things that were left, which was as well. Then he heard Rosamund's voice and her light step, just that and it was enough.

Merriwen followed, then Ashbeorn with Gemma and Gemma's brother Edgefrith who was taller than her now. The priest came with them. There were no ghosts. They must have gone to rest.

He could not speak, but it was all right. His happy, clever, educated wife scanned the contents of the parchment in seconds and then passed it round. She folded her small hand into his and she understood. That was truly all that mattered.

HISTORICAL NOTE

The Vikings who invaded Britain were no fools. The Norse earls brought their armies to a land containing a patchwork of separate Anglo-Saxon kingdoms. Disputes between these kingdoms had always been common. Disputes between royal contenders for the throne inside each kingdom were even more common—and more damaging.

The Vikings knew how to take advantage of these dynastic quarrels and by 876, a devastating combination of force and politics had given them power over all of the Saxon kingdoms except Wessex under its brilliant King Alfred.

In Mercia, across the northern border from Wessex, two rival Saxon royal dynasties had long struggled for supremacy. The Vikings made use of this. They managed to depose the existing Mercian king and replace him with a puppet ruler from the rival dynasty—King Ceolfrith. The unhappy King Ceolfrith was forever damned by the West Saxon Anglo Saxon Chronicle as "foolish."

The coup took place at Repton where the church

contained the bones of Saint Wigstan, the martyr of a previous dynastic dispute. Saint Wigstan had been on Ceolfrith's side.

The price paid by Ceolfrith for his limited power at the Vikings' hands is not known. "Ceolfrith's niece" in my story is an invention.